the Truth About Otis Battersby

the Truth About Otis Battersby

SUSAN C. TURNER

The Truth About Otis Battersby
A Novel
by Susan C. Turner

2022 Harry Douglas Press Paperback Edition

Published in the United States of America by Harry Douglas Press

Harry Douglas Press
704 West Swann Avenue
Tampa, FL 33606
USA

ISBNs:
978-0-9847232-5-6 (softcover)
978-0-9847232-6-3 (eBook)

Printed in the United States of America

Cover and Interior design: 1106 Design

To John
The Best of Men

Later, much later, she realized that none of it would have come to pass—not the attempts on her life, not the others' deaths—if she had not fled London that day, if the two of them had not both somehow found their way to that singular compartment on the train. She might never have faced the truth about her husband, might never have discovered what kind of man Otis Battersby was, nor the web of intrigue he inhabited. Be that as it was, she might have preferred that he remain her beloved husband. She might have clung to her old life, her old state of mind. Not now, though. Not now that she knew what he had done.

Chapter One

12 May 1949, London. Eve squinted up at the St. Pancras departure board and tried to make sense of the numbers, jumbled as they were. Overhead, the speaker squawked, an explosion of fits and starts, "Edinburgh, points north, final boarding, Platform Four." She hurried along the platform, weaving her way through the thick tide of morning commuters, peering at the carriage windows, a glaze of morning mist hindering her search. The thin shoe strap bit into her ankle, and she cursed herself for choosing so unsuitable a pair for traveling.

Halfway down the second carriage, an empty compartment came into view, and she pushed through a path to the nearest entry. The dark corridor momentarily blinded her, but she managed to make her way, the overnight bag clutched tight against her chest. Out of breath and perspiring, she reached the compartment and stumbled inside. The satisfying click of closure told her the door was secure. With a heavy thud, the overnight bag found the floor.

A broad bench fitted snug against one wall of the compartment, and she leaned across it, tugging at the tightly braided window cord. The shade unfurled, and the outside world—sunlight and crowds—grew dim. The slight trembling in her legs subsided. One by one, she kicked off the red lacquered heels, thankful to be rid of them for a time, once again wondering what possessed her to wear them today, of all days. Certain she was very much alone, she shrugged out of her trench coat, weighed down with the bundles of cash hidden within, and sank onto the bench, legs askew, an anxious tension finally fading from her shoulders. She brought gloved hands together and sat utterly still, eyes closed, engulfed in almost-perfect isolation.

Find a carriage and disappear, a stranger among strangers. A precious few hours of anonymity.

In the distance, she heard the muffled shouts of the conductor, and a moment later, the train lurched, wobbling out of the station, picking up speed as it cleared the complex web of tracks. Secure in its cradle-like rocking, Eve nearly allowed herself to relax. Before settling in for the eight-hour trip, she required one last assurance, and so she rose, cracked the door—risking that a stranger stood just on the other side—and located the bright red exit signs fore and aft. In a rare flash of self-awareness, she understood she had spent her life looking for exit signs, the fastest and easiest ways out. Indeed true to form, here she was, exiting once more. Though this time, she knew exactly why she was leaving London. She meant to address her lurking suspicions, to seek the truth of Otis's death. Traveling to Edinburgh was a risk, an uncertain road, perhaps a pointless one. She had few clues and fewer answers. It was possibly a road to nowhere. How would she know unless she tried? She owed him that. And more, much more.

She closed the door and turned to face the double seats, grateful for the notable luxury of the first-class compartment, the pillowed benches of rich maroon brocade, the walls of inlaid walnut, the window shades of tawny silk, the crystal-covered reading lamps precisely within arm's reach. Yes, the subtly contrived glamour pleased her no end.

Hat unpinned, she lifted the finely tatted black veil, and set it on the rack above the bench, then bent for her coat, intending to hang it on the line of pegs near the door. But the rich turquoise of her gloves—the smooth buttery leather—distracted her intent. She recalled the joy on Otis's face when, on their last day in Madrid, he presented them to her. Five finely tailored buttons lined the cuff. She traced the delicate stitching along the base of the thumb, the glove straining against her fingers, flattening the back of her hand. Images slipped through her mind. She, lying in his arms, hands trembling across his skin, his eyes on hers. For countless hours, she had replayed these small details, reliving the memories minute by minute, wanting nothing more than to remain forever within them.

Deep into her dream, she failed to register the click of the compartment door.

"May I?" he asked and sat down before she had actually responded.

"If you must," she said, a quick flash of irritation evident in her tone.

He stared openly at her naked feet, raised his eyebrows, and shifted his gaze to the three-inch heels that lay on the floor between them.

"They belong to me," she said, unconsciously exercising her toes.

"No doubt," he replied.

Something in his manner, the singularity of his voice—*A trace of accent?*—aroused her curiosity.

"Harry, Harry Douglas." He stood, bent forward, extended his hand.

She sniffed the faint scent of tobacco.

He raised his hat, held it for an instant, and replaced it at a jaunty angle, reminiscent of that roguish gangster in the gritty black-and-white noir she had enjoyed at the Odeon.

She recognized the hat as the latest Dobbs, the newest style out of New York. Before meeting Otis, she never observed such things. Within a few months, he had taught her one thing and another about men's fashion. Now, she paid attention.

"I'm Eve." She touched the white ruffle on her blouse, then a wayward strand of hair, loosened when she had removed the hat. It occurred to her she had an almost infinite choice of surnames from which to select. "Eve Battersby," she settled on.

She offered her hand, the last button of her glove tangling itself on the sleeve of his jacket. The glove, her hand within it, dangled for an instant, slender threads binding her to him. He smiled broadly, looked directly into her emerald eyes, and gently disengaged the glove.

"Beautiful color," he said, almost to himself. She was not sure if he referred to her glove or her eyes.

A confident man. Later, she reflected on this first impression of Harry Douglas. It was, in her memory, both perceptive and prophetic.

Her shoes, coat, and overnight bag, strewn on the floor between them, conjured up the props to a French farce she and Otis had seen on opening night at the Aldwych Theatre. She stooped to retrieve the coat.

"Let me help with that," he offered.

"Don't bother. I'll manage." She chose not to create some fabrication about the coat's unusual weight.

"No bother at all," he insisted.

"I'll hang the coat," she said hastily. "If you must, you may place my bag there." She pointed to the shelf above her seat.

Without comment, he lifted the bag and secured it on the rack, careful to avoid the lace of her hat. When he turned to face her, she became aware that he had not so much as an overcoat with him.

Good grief. What's the man going to do for eight hours?

In Eve's mind, the anonymity of train travel was its most positive virtue. A nod of acknowledgment passed for polite conversation. One could hide behind a newspaper or book, under no obligation to chat up one's neighbor or compartment mate. Aside from some serious thinking—never her strong suit—she planned an uneventful ride north and was not about to entertain this man with pointless chatter. No matter how handsome he happened to be.

She removed her gloves, shoved her shoes into a corner, sat down, and opened the *Times*, noisily straightening the crease. She meant the message to be quite clear. Her eyes rested on the dark headline. BERLIN BLOCKADE LIFTED: WEST GERMANY OFFICIAL

"Mind if I have a look?" He sat on the edge of the seat, elbows on knees, invading the small space between them. He scanned the page, concentrated on the article beneath the headline.

She gritted her teeth. "I'll finish in a moment."

"Fair enough." Harry turned his body to the side, stretched out his legs, lowered his head, pulled the brim of the hat over his eyes and folded his hands in his lap. "Ever been to Berlin?"

"No, but I suppose you have." She emphasized the next to the last word. Unaccustomed to talking to a faceless hat, she kept her eyes glued to the newspaper.

With one finger, he pushed up the hat's brim and looked over the paper at her. "I worked there a couple of years after the war." He paused. "I was more than sorry to have missed the Tiergarten before we obliterated it." He twiddled his thumbs and hummed a nameless tune.

She felt him staring at some part of her and shifted slightly in response. Without looking up from the page, she remarked, "It won't help."

"What's that?"

"What you're doing. Humming and twiddling. It won't make me read any faster," she said.

"No reason why it should." His hat now covered one eye; his thumbs continued twiddling, and he began to hum a new tune. Eve recognized Perry Como's latest hit, "A, You're Adorable." She suppressed a smile.

With him thus situated, she was uncertain where to look. He disturbed her thoughts, the ones she had sworn to examine on the ride to Scotland. Rarely did she go in for introspection, never a particular talent. This lengthy train ride, she resolved, was her long overdue opportunity.

Absently, she patted her hair into place, smoothed her skirt, and stole a glance in his direction. It was not as if she minded Harry Douglas watching her. Accustomed to men's appreciative glances, Eve did not need anyone to tell her she was beautiful. All the same, she repositioned the newspaper and gripped it firmly in front of her so he could not see her face. She supposed she should be thankful her unwelcome compartment companion was not slurping tea or telling off-color jokes. She despised such things.

Minutes later, having managed to read not the first article, let alone the news about Berlin, she lowered the paper an inch and peeked cautiously over its top. His eyes closed, breathing soft and regular, eyelids fluttering as if he were dreaming. Since Otis's death, Eve had not been drawn to any man, any person for that matter, and she surprised herself by thinking Harry Douglas quite attractive.

An inch over six feet. Thinnish, but seemingly solid. Not much hair under that hat. Good-looking, except for the small, some would say tiny, wart at the end of his left nostril. The angles of his face were not as sharp—nor as exquisite—as Otis's were. Still, an expressive face that drew one's attention. A slight dimple, an indentation at least, on the chin. An old scar on the cheek. The suit up-to-date, stylish. Brown was not a color she would have chosen, but given the shade of his skin and hair and brows, it suited him. The expensive ecru shirt included a monogrammed cuff. The tie, an odd pattern of racehorses on a deep-blue background, was unquestionably out of fashion and not in keeping with the rest. She wondered about its origin. Could his age be thirty-five? Older? The well-manicured hands bore no wedding band.

Before she could complete her appraisal, the tea trolley's wheels squeaked to a stop outside the compartment door, and the attendant announced, at full volume, its presence. Harry blinked awake, raised his arms above his head and yawned, his hat now crooked atop his head.

"Can I get you something?" he inquired, thumb pointed toward the door.

His eyes, she noted, were a light shade of gray.

"Only if that cart stocks Campari and cigarettes," she answered curtly. She wondered when it had become his responsibility to see to her dietary needs.

"Campari? I figured you for whiskey," he said, a slight flicker of amusement in his eyes. "Or gin."

"How did you guess?" She mocked him. "Not at this hour, thank you," she added, "but if you must." She gestured toward the door.

"I believe I might." Harry shrugged a little, adjusted his ancient tie, and rose. He stepped into the corridor and closed the door, leaving her refreshingly alone.

For weeks, she had eaten nothing of substance, existing mostly on air and water.

She recalled dimly the thin package of saltines she nibbled last night before she crawled into bed, unable to sleep. It had ceased to matter to her what she ate since she no longer mattered to anyone. Still, the thinness of her arm alarmed her. There was a constant buzzing in her head. A cigarette would help, but she had given them up. Along with every other pleasure in life. After a life of ease, her body longed for discomfort. Odd, since she had always guarded against difficult things, painful things. Strangest of all, she had begun to think about the scattered flimsiness of her life, to view herself from a distance, as if she were a specimen under a study glass. Eve Palmer, seeker of ease and comfort, lover of all things attractive and symmetrical, drenched in self-doubt. Depleted. Transformed beyond recognition. Could she possibly be so vacuous?

Those first months, Eve grieved for Otis. The emptiness gripped her. With stunning clarity, she knew she had finally, irrevocably, loved him. She could not be certain when she first began to doubt the circumstances of his death.

⁞⁞⁞⁞⁞

On a raw day in mid-December, unexpected and uninvited, Otis Battersby turned up out of nowhere and dropped into Eve's life. One week he did not exist; the following week, she could not get rid of him. They first bumped, literally, into each other on the fifth floor of Fortnum & Mason, he in a desperate hurry to purchase a dozen gold-plated collar stays, she perusing the perfectly coordinated necktie trays for her brother's Christmas gift. They collided, her packages flying, in front of a stack of ostrich-bound appointment books on which a miniature brass plate signaled the upcoming new year, 1948.

After the customary English "So sorry," Otis, with a slight bow, stuffed a business card into her hand and dashed for the waiting elevator, gesturing in the direction of the floor clerk as he fled. When her head cleared and Eve turned, the clerk gently placed a new, unwrinkled shopping bag on her arm and said, "So sorry, madam, Mr. Battersby was in a bit of a rush. His client was waiting—impatiently, I might assume—some distance away."

"What sort of client?" she inquired as she adjusted the heel of her shoe, still feeling slightly manhandled.

The clerk helped her stand upright, cupped her hand in his, smoothed out the business card crushed within it, and explained, "Yes, madam, Mr. Battersby owns the Lansdowne Clothiers at Number 32 Savile Row."

"A clothing shop?"

"Lansdowne. London's oldest establishment of its kind. Custom English tailoring. Quite admired. In addition, Mr. Battersby designs many of our ties, one of which you purchased. On the unusual occasion he runs out of collar stays, we are his most convenient and ready source. I assure you he regrets this calamity and would welcome the opportunity to further apologize, should you consider it."

Eve nodded and had indeed already considered the idea of meeting Mr. Battersby again. Jostling aside, he exhibited a certain degree of fine manners, not to mention other equally appealing attributes. Tall, lean, eyes as blue as a Texas sky, and remarkably warm hands. Seemingly, he was employed in a civilized profession with a ready and regular source of income, unlike many of the men she met on her frequent evenings at the Savoy Bar. Since moving to London, she had spent many a night roaming the Strand and sipping dry martinis throughout the theatre district.

Abruptly, one morning last June, she had packed up and left the United States. Ostensibly, to get away from the Texas heat and humidity for a month or two in London. On a whim, truth be told. She ended up staying an extra week, then another, until six months passed, and she felt very much at home, as if she finally had found a place that matched her spirit.

By the time Eve joined the bustle of holiday tourists outside Fortnum & Mason's front door and headed toward Piccadilly Circus, she had forgotten about Otis Battersby and his business card. It was two days later when she thought of it again.

She had recently learned of mystery writer Dorothy Hughes and found her way to the Charing Cross bookshop owned by the flamboyant Christina Foyle where Hughes' latest volume was the subject of the afternoon literary lecture. Such an event did not happen often, and Eve arrived early to a full-blown mob assembled outside the ground floor. A sign read "*Lecture delayed. Patrons are invited to wait in Room 6.*"

The sharp December air abated as Eve entered. The shop's narrow aisles were clogged four-deep, people good-naturedly jostling one another to reach a coveted Arthur Conan Doyle or a Dorothy Sayers' first edition. Anticipating a virtual heat wave, Eve removed her cape and plunged forward in the direction of the tiny back room where the lecture crowd was gathering for instructions. Head down, she elbowed a path through an interior doorway, only to find herself wedged between a large-bodied, square-faced woman wearing a serape smelling of alpaca, and a dark-skinned man of considerable height. Eve's left cheek rested against the buttons of the man's sweater vest. She was not altogether thrilled at its scent. Neither of her captors showed signs of allowing her to pass.

She moved her head just enough to spot a familiar-looking face.

The memorable Mr. Battersby. How fortunate. Perhaps in this instance he can be of assistance.

Rather loudly, she cleared her throat, straining in his direction. "Mr. Battersby, is it?" She nearly fell as the alpaca serape squeezed past her.

He squinted at her until a spark of recognition ignited. "Ah, Miss Fortnum & Mason. I do hope you've not lost your parcels again. In this mob, you'll have a devil of a time recovering them."

"As I recall, correctly so, you were the cause of my lost packages, Mr. Battersby, and then had the poor manners to flee the scene, leaving the clerk to mop up your error." Eve was not about to let him blame his victim. She managed to breathe as the sweater vest and its odor disappeared from under her nose.

"Right you are. Allow me to set things right. I have every intention of doing so." He swept his arm to let her pass into the next room and gave that abbreviated bow she had seen two days before. "Shall we begin anew?"

Room 6 proved a bit less crowded. Miles more oxygen, and Eve chanced to inhale a deeper breath. "Before the lecture begins, you can help me find the newest Hughes mystery. I think it's called . . ."

Otis Battersby's brow furrowed slightly, giving his face a more serious look. "*In a Lonely Place* is the most recent publication, or do you mean *Ride the Pink Horse* out a good year ago? Which do you prefer?"

"You know more about this than I. My daughter is a recent fan. The book is a gift. How about the newer one? And tell me more about Dorothy."

"To date, Mrs. Hughes has written at least a dozen novels and a book of poetry, as I recall. She is, of course, an American treasure, though we English would love to claim her. You and your daughter are in good company with, I daresay, millions of her fans." Otis reached up and pulled a book from the top shelf. "Perhaps she'll sign it for you," he said and handed the book to Eve.

Even his half smile is endlessly charming, she thought. "You are a fount of information and assistance, Mr. Battersby." She liked the sound of his name. "I'm grateful for the literature lesson. Annie, my daughter, will be impressed." She lowered her head slightly and looked up at him, careful not to flirt too blatantly.

A thunderous crash erupted behind them as an entire shelf tumbled to the floor, scattering people and books, pages fluttering in all directions. A small man holding an oversized clipboard appeared, delicately framed glasses balanced on the tip of his nose. "Dear. Dear. Please, everyone clear the room. We will have this up and good as new in a quick jiffy. Do not despair. The books will be fine, but I fear the next news is unwelcome. Our lecturer has been delayed and must be rescheduled for another day."

Following a collective groan and a smatter of grumbles, the room's occupants, including Eve and Otis, shuffled into the adjoining chamber. Another crush of humanity engulfed them, squeezing Eve's ribs as she hugged the book and her cape to her chest. Disoriented, she could not decide which way to go or how to pay for the book she held. Foyles' purchasing system was notoriously confusing and inefficient. She followed the flow into a larger room to her left and joined what appeared to be the cashier's queue, Otis Battersby nowhere in sight.

Twenty minutes and three conversations later, the book was hers, and she stood on the street juggling her cape and her parcel. Since her entry, the outside temperature had dropped a considerable ten degrees, the wind having picked up as well. She walked quickly to the tube station.

London is a social place, she thought. I may see Mr. Battersby again. Of course, I do have his card.

Once again, Eve's attention focused on other matters. Two days later, on December 20, Annie—a solid sophomore at NYU—arrived for the Christmas holidays. It was her first trip abroad, and Eve was determined to impress her with London's sights. After the traditional Big Bus Tour (Annie happily braved the 40-degree chill in the open top), Annie was sufficiently enthralled with the city and Eve's elegant two-bedroom flat at 34 Swan Court in Chelsea. In truth, Annie was most eager to meet Agatha Christie and her husband who resided in Number 48, two floors below. Eve resolved to arrange an accidental encounter before Annie departed.

The following morning, mother and daughter set out for a day of gallery hopping in Mayfair, Eve targeting the Albemarle Gallery to begin her quest for a Dali or Magritte sketch. Two weeks before, she had attended a lecture at the Tate on the subject of surrealism of the 1920s and '30s, and she vowed to find a work within her budget. At ten o'clock when the Albemarle opened, they strolled among the visitors checking out the featured artists. When Eve inquired, the gallery director announced—with a sniff—that surrealism works "are *never* displayed" at the Albemarle. He suggested the Medici Gallery on Cork.

Dodging raindrops and fighting fierce gusts of wind, the two continued to Cork Street, a collection of local specialty galleries presently awash in holiday shoppers and tourists. A blast of wind lifted Eve's scarf across her face, blinding her as she struggled up the three steps toward the Medici's entry. Eve held the door for Annie who was now shivering with cold.

"We'll find you a warmer coat," Eve said. "I don't want you catching cold and dying in London. Your father would never forget."

"You mean forgive, Mom, he'd never forgive you," said Annie.

"Forgive, forget." Eve had said exactly what she meant to say. "You know your father." She thought fleetingly of Rip Dexter, athlete extraordinaire, Annie's father and Eve's first husband. The first man she loved. The first man she stopped loving.

"Mother, I do not need another coat. There are at least three hanging in my dorm closet. Dad delivered them before the fall term started. He's never forgotten that time I fell in the lake."

What did I tell you? Eve thought. Indeed, the word was forget, not forgive. To Eve's mind, Annie possessed too many of her father's qualities. *How long have we been having these conversations?* Nineteen years. Half of Eve's life.

That sobering fact nearly ruined Eve's morning. Her hand searched the floor of her purse for the hard edge of the Dunhill package. She pulled out a limp cigarette and looked around for a light. She must have looked ridiculous—wet hair plastered around her face, scarf askew, runny mascara on damp eyelashes, a soggy white stick between her fingers.

"You're looking lovely as ever, Miss Fortnum & Mason. Each time we meet, I fall further in love." Otis Battersby said. "This must surely be Annie."

!!!!!

Five months later on May 1, 1948, standing amidst pale shafts of sunlight that dappled the reconstructed walls of Chelsea Old Church, Eve stunned herself and a dozen of Otis's friends by adding Battersby to the long list of surnames she had acquired over the past twenty years.

Eve Palmer Dexter Kicklighter Pierce Battersby. One more to remember. Their order increasingly blurred.

Surrounded by hundreds of brilliant yellow daffodils and orange lilies, Eve was undeniably the most dazzling flower on display. Her gown's light hue matched her peach complexion. Her long auburn hair piled high on her head, an errant twist escaped casually down her back. She carried a simple bouquet of roses—apricot and white.

Otis Battersby must have thought her the most gorgeous, and outrageous, creature on the Earth. Much to her delight, he announced to the assembled audience that each time he looked at her, she took his breath away. After the ceremony, a black limousine, a gigantic orange bow sprawled across its highly polished bonnet, swept them off to Heathrow and a private plane waiting on the tarmac.

They spent two lighthearted weeks at the Palace Hotel in Madrid and stopped briefly in San Sebastian, where Otis delivered a package of newly created tie designs, and conferred with a new business partner. In June, they moved into a four-level townhouse with roof terrace on Chelsea's Bramerton Street, a short walk off the Thames.

The world was theirs, and she let Otis love her. In her mind, she was quite . . . What were the right words for the feeling? Mad with desire? Definitely. Content? Richly so. But in love? She wanted desperately to return Otis's love. Over the last dozen years, she had built a wall, a guardedness about matters of the heart.

Chapter Two

The compartment door opened. Eve, calling herself back from memory, noted two steaming cups of tea in Harry Douglas's hands, a sausage roll under one elbow.

"Thought you could use something hot to drink. Especially since you've lost your shoes and stockings." He handed her a cup and sat down with his own.

"Don't be ridiculous, Mr. Douglas. My shoes are in plain view," she teased. "And the location of my stockings is not subject for discussion. Why ever would you assume they are lost?"

"A leap in the dark."

"You are presumptuous." Eve started to thank him for the tea when a knock on the compartment door startled her into silence. She froze, her heart suddenly pounding. She glanced first at her coat hanging on the peg, then up at the bag over her head. A second knock, louder and firmer, followed the first. She shrank lower into her seat.

The door handle clicked as if someone meant to open it, and Harry moved smoothly to place his hand upon the handle, sliding open the door a few inches, situating himself so that no one could enter or see into the compartment.

"Can I be of assistance?" Eve heard him ask. When the intruder murmured a lengthy response, Harry raised his voice and replied, "You must be mistaken. I've encountered no one of that name or description."

He eased the door closed, latched it, and turned to face her. "Care to talk about it?"

Eve opened her mouth, closed it again. Finally, she whispered, shifting the emphasis away from herself, "Who was that?"

"No one I recognize. Average-looking fellow, wiry build, pinched round glasses, needle nose, pale hair, light topcoat. Bit of an accent. Polite sort. A bit nervous. Turned his hat round and round in his hand. Inquired about a Mrs. Pierce."

Eve's breath caught in her throat. Now certain that she had not imagined any of it, she had a vivid recollection of a hat turning round in a man's hand. *What can he want?*

"That name struck a nerve. Mind telling me who Mrs. Pierce is?"

Eve rolled the teacup between her palms and wondered how much she should say to Harry Douglas. After all, she knew nothing about him, except, for some unknown reason, she rather liked him. Before deciding how much to reveal, she needed a clearer head.

"My name was once Pierce," she volunteered. She thought that admission safe enough.

"So your name is not Eve Battersby?" He made it a question.

"Yes, it is. Battersby, I mean. Pierce, too, if you must know. It's a bit difficult, I'm afraid. Not in the least sordid. Just difficult." Exhausted at the thought of explaining it, she said, "I must have a nap. Then, perhaps we can talk. No promises, mind you." She pressed her lips together and stared at him, hoping he did not press her further.

He removed the now-tepid cup of tea from her hands. "At last, I'll get a chance to read that newspaper."

Relieved, Eve swung her feet up onto the seat, lay her head down, and closed her eyes. She wrapped her arms tightly around herself, and, in less than a minute, found herself drifting away.

iiiii

Like the wind, he was gone. One Saturday afternoon in late September, her life changed course. Chasing a drop shot at full speed, Otis Battersby stumbled face forward across the net of court number seven at the Chelsea Athletic Club. Thomas Jasper, his barrister, doubles partner and friend, rushed to his aid. To no reward. Twenty minutes later, Otis Battersby—successful, highly respected, forty-two-year-old Savile Row clothier, in outwardly fine physical condition—was pronounced dead on arrival at the Chelsea and Westminster Hospital, reportedly a victim of the then-rare phenomenon known as sudden cardiac arrest.

An hour later, Thomas Jasper broke the unthinkable news to Eve. That same afternoon, Myrna Stewart, Jasper's legal assistant, volunteered to make the arrangements for Otis's funeral and burial. In a fog, Eve agreed.

Thrice-divorced, once-widowed Eve secluded herself on the second floor of her Bramerton residence. By day, she chain-smoked Gauloises and downed double shots of whiskey that the local spirits shop delivered to her doorstep. By night, she inspected each page of Otis's collection of European cookbooks, seeking his thumbprint on a favorite recipe, a sign he had lived, until she discovered an elaborate stew or exotic sauce. At four in the morning, or whenever her body tired enough to sleep without waking, she placed her latest gastronomic attempt in a broad-mouthed pot in the middle of the graveled path in her rear garden, a plentiful breakfast for Chelsea's stray cats. Later in the day when she retrieved it, the pot might be whistle-clean or remain filled to the brim. In such matters, she trusted the cats' judgments more than her own.

Why she chose cooking vast amounts of foreign meats and gravies to satisfy her hunger for peace of mind, Eve could not say. Oftentimes, she wandered through the night among Chelsea's streets and alleyways, but she could find no way to communicate with the dead, to say goodbye to Otis, to experience his death. At odd moments, she remembered a look, a touch, the sound of his voice. She felt as if she were falling into some dark well, vanishing bit by bit. She knew feeding a collection of feral cats hardly served as fitting psychoanalysis, but she chose not to hear the sound of her own voice, or other people's voices. She was neither one to sit and brood nor share herself with others. Intricate recipes, the more difficult and obscure the better, saw her through the endless nights and eased her loneliness. The rich scents of simmering spices soothed her body. She considered them her own unique form of aromatherapy.

This strange grieving process continued for several months until the Christmas holidays came and went. When she had exhausted the cookbooks and tired of the taste of whiskey and the smell of Turkish tobacco, Eve, like an objective reporter, examined her present existence, wondering what lasts and what slips away. She came to realize she was very much alone, that her longing would not bring Otis home, that she could no longer pretend she would awaken one morning to find him once again beside her. Whether by her own volition or the course of time, her memory of him blurred. His presence, then his absence.

Though she could not change the endings in her life, she resolved to make a wild effort at another beginning. One morning, she tossed out two unopened cartons of cigarettes, returned a case of whiskey to the corner spirits store, arranged with a neighbor to feed the now dependent and somewhat beloved cats, assembled several trunks with her belongings, and relocated to a Victorian townhouse on the edge of Holland Park.

It was several weeks later that she began to notice the misplaced or misshapen objects. Nothing large or expensive, an envelope from the table, a crushed flower in the garden. But these irregularities occurred frequently. At one point, she thought someone had searched through a stack of papers on the kitchen counter. She considered that things might have gone missing for months, so, too, from the Bramerton address, but in her dazed state, she had not detected them.

She called the estate agent from whom she purchased the Holland Park house to inquire whether a previous owner might still possess a key to the premises. She changed the locks, secured the windows, and asked her neighbors if they had observed suspicious persons on the block. She thought about hiring an auditing firm to inventory the contents of the house. When Eve sensed she was being followed one day, she altered her walking route, took a bus, and then the tube to the crowded and very public stop at Leicester Square in hopes of losing her feelings of unease.

She was not frightened, merely puzzled.

What could I have that someone would want? As far as she knew, only inconsequential things had been misplaced.

Increasingly, however, as the days wore on, she felt a gnawing sense of disquiet. When Thomas Jasper's calling card appeared once again in her mailbox she decided, at last, to meet with him.

iiiii

Jasper kept an office on The Strand just west of Somerset House. Shortly after Otis's death, he contacted Eve for the purpose of settling Otis's estate. The barrister preserved his patience as Eve repeatedly put him off, advising him she was not ready to discuss either the circumstances or the outcome of her husband's death.

She did not want to know anything. She did not want to decide anything. Leave me alone, she had said.

Eve tried to explain her feelings to Jasper, but he insisted on some ritual form of closure. In her saner moments, she worried Otis's clothing company would be affected by her reluctance to confer with Thomas. Remembering Otis's contacts in Madrid, she was bothered that business-related decisions required attention. Still, she could not bring herself to make the appointment. She feared it would involve some deeper commitment. One she was not prepared to make. It was six months since Otis died, a lifetime ago or as fresh as yesterday.

As a compromise to what she considered the dreadful formality of an office visit, Eve agreed to meet Thomas Jasper for lunch. She reasoned that if she were compelled to listen to an hour of legal jargon, she could at least push a Cornish crab cake around her plate, sip a decent martini, and wear a stunning pair of shoes.

She arrived at Simpson's at noon, passed her coat and scarf through the cloak window, and entered the long dining room. Halfway down the left aisle, she saw Thomas Jasper rise from his chair.

Early in their honeymoon, Otis explained that he and Thomas had been friends for almost thirty years. Their fathers, like other men of their age and class, insisted their young sons become proficient in German. Thus, Otis and Thomas were shipped off to Bavaria for three months of summer leadership camp. There, they developed a friendship that continued during their studies at Cambridge. Upon graduation, each returned to London to his father's business, Otis to the upscale clothier trade, Thomas to the practice of law. Over two decades, Thomas Jasper had become Otis Battersby's barrister, financial advisor, confidant, and weekly doubles partner. During the war, they served as officers together. "Captains, First Cavalry, Tenth Armoured Division," Otis liked to say, punctuating each word in that inflection only the British could manage.

In addition, Thomas prepared and kept Otis's will and acted as executor for his estate.

"Eve." He pulled out her chair. "What can I get you to drink?"

"There's a question I can answer. I'll have a martini, American-style, two olives please," her voice forcibly calm.

His hand rested on her arm as he helped her into the chair. The warmth of it took her by surprise. For months, she had not felt another human being's touch. Granted, she had not the slightest interest in Thomas Jasper. In truth, something about his manner put her off. Unlike Otis, who possessed a casual charm with no trace of upper-class British snobbery, Thomas Jasper's style was quite the opposite. Graceful and sophisticated, he struck Eve as a smooth manipulator, more taken with himself than anyone else in the room. Still, in her more generous moments, Eve acknowledged she might have misjudged him. Indeed, both Thomas and his assistant Myrna had been exceptionally responsible and more than kind during the period following Otis's death. Myrna, in particular, took special care to call on Eve, to review Otis's records, to invite her out in the evenings, though Eve always declined such invitations.

The arrival of her martini and his gin and tonic signaled the start of their conversation. While not entirely in control of her emotions, Eve tried to sound self-assured. "All right, Thomas. For whatever reasons, none of which I can explain sufficiently to you or to anyone else, I've been avoiding you for . . . how many months?"

"Six and counting." Thomas Jasper removed his valise from beneath the table. "There are several items to address. None of it will get any easier, I'm afraid. Let's clear everything up and be done with it."

"Be done with it? You mean Otis's death? Be done with Otis's death?" her voice shot up at the end. As she feared, she was losing control.

A deep breath. *Slowly, calmly,* she thought. *A polite expression will do.*

"What is it you want from me?" She willed the tremble from her hands as she picked up the delicately etched glass. The conical bowl curved in her hands, and she took a long, slow swallow as a lovely coolness stole through her body. She stared down at the olives lying on the bottom. Her voice softened. "Shall we order lunch and then discuss this business?"

"Whatever makes you comfortable. We simply need to take care of this today. Unfortunately, there are timelines written into Otis's instructions and deadlines that must be met. If you will allow me." Thomas Jasper removed four pieces of paper and a pen from his case and placed them on the table.

"Go ahead if you must. I'm not hungry." Suddenly tired, Eve set the glass on the table, settled back in her chair and waited.

"This will not be a burden to you. Otis was careful in planning for your future. Of course, at the time, he supposed the two of you would be together for the foreseeable days ahead. I doubt you discussed, in any detail, Otis's financial status. His investments were complicated by his deceased father's holdings, as well as the two businesses maintained principally in Otis's name. His partner in the Lansdowne shop preferred to purchase Otis's fifty-one percent investment outright. That part of the estate is already settled. It was one of the conditions written into their business agreement. A sort of prenuptial clause, if you will. Of course, you were present last May when the manufacturer in Madrid assumed partial ownership for Otis's tie company."

Thomas cleared his throat and leafed to the second page of the paper stack, his manner conveying long familiarity with the task. "I, of course, can be of some assistance in securing, tracking, and maintaining these holdings, if you so desire."

"The only holding I'm aware of is the Bramerton house. I've placed it with an agent as I have no further need for it, nor do I wish to live there any longer."

Eve was not easily bewildered by financial discussions. She kept a reasonable amount of cash, minus the price of the Holland Park townhome she had just purchased, from the Nolan Pierce divorce settlement. Luckily, the Texas judge had released Nolan's bank accounts in the amount of her owed payment before Nolan's creditors came calling, and he packed off to prison.

Thomas was right in that she and Otis never got around to discussing Otis's financial holdings. As far as she determined, he had not been secretive about them. Amidst their social events and months of frantic desire, they simply found no time for such conversations.

Thomas drummed his pen on the table. “There are substantially more assets in addition to the Bramerton house. We can begin to liquidate them as soon as you are informed. Of course, there are taxes to consider, and I advise you to consult an estate solicitor so you know the extent of those obligations. I do not deal in those taxes, but I can put you in touch with a highly regarded colleague. This issue is one of time restrictions. We must consider them.”

“I'm trying to follow you, Thomas. Give it to me plainly, if you please. For the record, I think it dreadfully unfair to expect me to pay the taxes on Otis's business investments.” She polished off her martini and signaled for another. “Make it a double,” she smiled at the waiter.

“I assure you, Eve,” he emphasized her name as if to get her full attention, “you'll have more than enough to cover your payment to the Chancellor of the Exchequer. You simply don't want to overpay him by making an untimely exchange.”

Thomas thumbed to the last page in the stack and read silently. He lifted his head and looked around at the adjacent diners before he spoke, then lowered his voice. “The total amount of Otis's estate, immediately prior to today's luncheon, lies in excess of twelve million pounds. Loosely converted at current rates, you are due to receive more than forty-four million American dollars.”

Eve gripped the edge of the table. “Jesus Christ. You can't be serious. Forty-four million dollars.”

Chapter Three

Eve awoke to find her coat draped over her legs, the glow of sunlight through the window, and the smell of tobacco in the air.

"That was quite some nap," Harry said from behind the newspaper. "You've slept nigh on two hours."

"Meanwhile, you've taken the opportunity to rearrange the entire cabin." She stood, jerked the shade cords down and tucked the edges tight against the window frames.

He folded the paper deliberately, taking time to mark his place, and set it on the seat beside him while she hung up her coat. He picked up the briar pipe from the table near the window ledge and took a puff. "What's going on with you?" He paused. "If you don't mind my asking."

She swiveled around to face him. "Whatever do you mean by that question?"

"Let me rephrase it for you." Harry studied her. "You're a mighty attractive, and very tense, woman with several last names, traveling alone with a coat full of cash and one heavy suitcase.

You're either allergic to sunlight, or you don't want anyone seeing you through these windows. You're scared breathless when someone knocks on the compartment door. You look like you haven't eaten in months. Did I forget to mention that no woman in her right mind could walk a block in those shoes?"

"You're an observant man, Harry Douglas."

"Comes in handy in my line of work," he said.

"Which is?"

"I'm a gambler." He hesitated. "At the moment."

"Sounds temporary," she said, and then added, "I thought you said you worked in Berlin. What does Berlin have to do with gambling?"

Harry gave a small chuckle. "My work in Berlin had little to do with gambling, but that's a whole other story. I said I used to work in Berlin. These days, I sit in on a few poker games and catch a horse race or two. Mostly on the Continent, but here in the U.K. on occasion. I'm headed to Edinburgh for a key game. Invitation only. Small table. Big stakes."

"Invitation only," she repeated. "You're a lucky man to receive such an invitation."

"Luck has little to do with it," he said. "Now, before you changed the subject, you were telling me about yourself."

"Was I?" She collapsed onto the seat. "Oh dear." She needed to tell someone, to get another take on her suspicions, to know if they were at least sane, and decide what to do if they were. *What harm can it do?* She hardly knew the man. *In a way, that might be better,* she thought. A stranger on a train. How very dramatic. After the next five hours, she would never see him again.

"Let's make a deal," she said. "I'll tell you about my situation after you tell me about how you found yourself in Berlin." She would decide what to tell him after she heard his story.

"What do you want to know?" he asked.

"Everything, of course."

"A recap of the last fifteen years of my life is a bit of a bore," said Harry, somewhat ironically.

"I'll take a chance," she said, interested already.

Harry was careful to stick to the professional aspects of his life. At age twenty-three, having completed a graduate degree in political science at McGill University in Montreal, Harry joined the King's Service. Intelligence. "Schooled in the fine arts of spying," he said.

"And those are?" she inquired.

"Handling weapons, monitoring radio transmissions, deciphering clandestine documents," he said.

"I suspect you omitted a few," said Eve.

Harry ignored the remark, continued. Fluent in French, Italian and German, Harry spent five years in Milan prior to the start of the war. He and a team of other Canadian and British agents monitored certain activities of Mussolini's fascist government. In no time at all, they found they had their work cut out for them. Within four years, they observed and recorded the invasion and annexation of Ethiopia, the Italian friendship pact with Germany, and the Italian attack on Albania.

"So you were in Italy during the war," said Eve.

Harry shook his head. "In June 1940, when the French surrendered and Italy invaded France, my partner and I left Milan in a hurry. For the duration, we traveled in and out of London, assigned to locations of interest to the Prime Minister. When the Third Reich surrendered in spring 1945, I moved into Germany and set up shop in the former Berlin opera house. From there, I tracked gold and currency reserves and works of art the Nazis confiscated from the countries they had conquered." Harry said he developed a knack for spotting significant documents.

"You said you moved into Germany. What happened to your partner?"

"He went home, married his sweetheart."

"I've never been to Berlin. What was it like after the war?" she asked.

Harry's expression grew grim. "When I think back, my first images are icy, gray dawns, streets jammed with bombed-out buildings, rubble, naked trees, armed soldiers in the streets, people standing in line for a piece of meat. Not a side of meat, mind you, just a piece. That was late '45 and most of '46. Then, the airlift. A bleak existence. Bleaker for those involved."

Eve knew little about the airlift, but was not about to admit as much. "What on earth kept you in Berlin?" she asked.

"When they found the slave-labor and death camps, the Allied intelligence services were interested in two things: seeking justice for the Nazis responsible, and shipping west as many rocket scientists as they could find. Before the Russians got them." Harry studied a bit of tobacco residue on his thumb. "I was involved with the justice part of that plan. The Nuremberg trials began in November '45 and continued for a year, until October '46."

"That's an awfully long time. Surely, there weren't that many to find." Eve folded her hands and leaned forward, their knees almost touching. She felt awkward, asking such questions, but she was interested in knowing.

"That's where you're wrong. There are hundreds—no thousands—of them. Hitler's high command. SS extermination squads. Camp commanders, guards, executioners. Mass murderers. Nasty murderous bastards. Preying on others who couldn't fight back. Some of the most brutal among them have yet to be found."

In the course of his narrative, Harry's pipe had gone out. With one finger, he tamped the tobacco in the bowl. He struck a match and held it over the chamber, sucking on the stem until a puff of smoke floated into the air. A sweet scent hung in the compartment.

"Even when we weren't in Berlin, we were all prisoners of those trials in one way or another, hearing the testimony, riveted by the extent—and brutality—of the crimes."

Eve confessed to knowing little of the shadowy world of postwar European politics. "How do you even begin to find such people?"

"Some surrendered to the Americans or Brits, thinking they had a better chance than waiting for the Russians to find them and shoot them on sight. Others we found through bank records, newspaper clippings, neighbors. The Americans and the Brits impounded plenty of documents with names, SS numbers, hometowns, dates of birth, assignments, even photographs. A lot of detective work and a bit of luck led us to a location. Then, an arrest. Sometimes, it was a dead end. By the time the war finally came to an end, many of the senior-ranking Nazi officers had already fled. They knew the end was near and hightailed it out of Germany."

"But where could they go? Who would help such people?" she asked.

"Some went into hiding or went home. They were easy to find. Others headed to Egypt or friendly fascist countries like Spain or Argentina. With enough cash and connections, they bought new identities—birth certificates, passports, travel documents.

Those are the hardest to track. As for who helps them, you'd be surprised at the number of people willing to do anything for a shilling. Enough gold can buy you half a dozen new names and birthdates." Harry sat back and stared at nothing.

Eve was silent. She thought of Nolan Pierce, who knew about doing things for money. The price he paid for it. Finally, she spoke. "I imagine you got tired of it. Tracking these war criminals." She looked sideways at Harry and waited.

"Something like that," he said.

"Something like what? C'mon, Harry. What aren't you saying? If you didn't catch them all, why are you here? Surely, you don't just walk away from a job like that. To become a gambler."

"It's my business, isn't it?"

"Suit yourself. But we had a deal, and you're not holding up your end," she said.

"Apparently, you've got your own problems. Why hear about mine?" A certain edge appeared in his voice, his mouth a thin line.

She paused. "Because I'm trying to decide if I can trust you. If I so decide, how much to share with you. That's why." She looked quickly at him, then tilted back her head and closed her eyes.

She had come this far without relying on anyone. More than once, she tried to confirm that her house was under scrutiny and that someone was following her. Twice in the past weeks, since their meeting about Otis's estate, she approached Thomas Jasper about hiring a private investigator. At least to put her mind at ease. Thomas listened well enough to her notions and asked questions regarding what she thought someone might want from her. He proved of no assistance. Using his polished barrister's manner, he insisted she was imagining her stalkers and burglars, grief playing tricks on her mind, remembering things not as they were, but as a lonely widow might fear them to be. A hysterical response to the shocks she had endured. Further, he recommended she take Otis's money and move back to the States where, in his words, she should purchase a reasonably sized estate and some servants, and live comfortably for the rest of her life.

For no discernible reason she could identify, she had neglected to tell Thomas, or anyone, what she had found in the basement of the Bramerton townhouse at three o'clock one morning. In the throes of a cooking spree, she descended the basement stairs in search of a large stew pot, one with a sturdy lid to contain a dense, rosy chicken paprikash. In a dark corner on the bottom shelf of Otis's baking pantry, she discovered what she was looking for and carried it upstairs into the kitchen. When she lifted the lid, it contained, curiously, a bundle of portrait photographs, a dozen blank passports in a language she recognized as Spanish, and other travel documents she later identified as visas and medical cards.

She held the photographs at arm's length to get a better view. The men in the pictures looked familiar, but she could not place them in her memory. Confused, she set the bundle on a side table, promising herself, once the cats were fed, to examine them more closely. Days later, she discovered, in the same line of pantry shelving, a thick trove of neatly stacked Swiss bonds, sealed in waxed paper and covered with a heavy black cast-iron baking sheet. She had no idea of their worth, but both they and the bundle of documents now lay in the overnight bag above her head.

When Thomas proved less than helpful, Eve talked Myrna Stewart, Thomas's assistant, into hiring a private police officer to keep an eye on the Holland Park residence. Indeed, a friend of

Myrna's spent several days shadowing Eve. After his surveillance, he brought her a full report showing no activity of the type Eve suspected. She received the report and the information he provided and paid him for his time. Still, she felt something was amiss.

Not about to run away in terror, she decided to take matters into her own hands. One night, as the sun went down, she sat in the dark, waiting in the shadows alongside the curtains of her front window, her own form of covert surveillance. After more than an hour, she spotted a thin man in a trench coat strolling to and fro on the far side of the street. He kept it up for three to four turns, moving past under the streetlamps. He started to cross the street toward her. Almost at once, a couple appeared, two yapping Springer Spaniels on leash. They hushed the dogs, apologized to the trench-coated man who removed his hat and turned it round and round in his hand. She saw him shake his head, replace the hat, then over his shoulder, take one last look at her home and head off in the direction of High Street.

For two weeks after that night, she collected cash, storing it in various lockers and rental mailboxes in Kensington, Holland Park, and Bayswater, careful to record each deposit and the bank from which she withdrew significant amounts of Otis's money. Retracing her steps the last few days, she pretended to mail a parcel or change her clothes at a health club until she retrieved as much money as the lining in her trench coat could convey. To save space, she requested large bills from her bank withdrawals. But then, she reasoned people would remember the woman who paid with the thousand-pound note. From then on, she collected a number of smaller bills to use without attracting undue notice. She rubber-banded additional wads of notes and hid them in her purse. She did not know the exact total of her accumulation, but she determined she had collected more than enough cash to outlast several months or more.

She thought about going to Rome, she spoke a little Italian, or to Istanbul, both cities that swallowed their inhabitants. But that meant using her passport. With a large amount of cash, she dared not leave the U.K. She settled on Edinburgh.

With no experience in planning for or operating on the run, Eve wavered between bouts of manic energy and extreme exhaustion. Hence, her present nervous state and her need to confide in someone.

She had almost decided to tell Harry Douglas at least part of her story when he spoke again.

"I gave up too easily," he said. Harry propped one ankle on the opposite knee and looked at her expectantly.

Eve detected none of the amusement of their earlier conversations and was careful to proceed.

"You mean before they were all captured," she said.

"No, that's not what I mean." Harry shifted in his seat. "The Service gave me a job to do, and I botched it."

Clearly, the memory was painful. "Botched it how?" She wrinkled her brow, tried to appreciate how an intelligence mission could get "botched."

"I was assigned to work on this one fellow, a Dutch SS man sentenced to death in absentia by a Belgian court. For almost two years, I tracked his money trail. The German and Swiss authorities declined to help, but through blind luck and stubbornness, I got a line on his documents. At first, I had a good idea he was bound for Argentina. But, then, he threw me a curve. Under a new alias and a Red Cross passport he bought a ticket to Dublin."

"Dublin? Why would he go to Dublin?"

"I figured he guessed he was made and needed somewhere to hide. I figured he would lay low in Dublin for a couple of months until he decided we were focused on someone else or lost his trail. We learned enough about these fugitives to know they usually made their way to Argentina by ocean liner from Genoa or a lesser ship off the northern coast of Spain. But this fellow headed way north of there. I thought I could keep an eye on his whereabouts, wait until he settled down, and then go get him. But I was wrong."

"How did you know?" Eve asked.

"Because two days after he arrived in Dublin, he escaped with eight sacks of gold coins and jewelry. Left with his family and two other war criminals. Later, we discovered two British officers greased his way to board a schooner headed for South America. He probably paid them off with a ninth sack of whatever he was carrying. The two Brits were scheduled for court-martial for their part. I was accused of collusion and dismissed from the Service. Nothing criminal, but the Service charged me with neglect of duty. I never got a chance to set things straight. End of story."

"When did this happen?" she asked.

"September 1948," he answered.

"I don't understand what you mean when you say you gave up too easily," she said.

"I made the wrong decision about the fellow. Cocksure, I was. Thought I knew all there was to know. What I *should* have known was a Nazi with a death sentence is not going to chance hiding out. I *should* have stuck with him every minute, found out his family's plans. Located him immediately and had him captured before he could leave the Continent."

"Well, it looks to me as if you're doing all right for yourself now. Why not leave all that behind and go on with your life?" As soon as the words slipped from her mouth, she could see she had touched some kind of nerve in him.

"That remark tells me you've never been accused of something you didn't do."

Harry neglected to add the whole business had turned his life upside down. Changed his view of himself, for a time. Colleagues thinking he could do something so despicable as collusion. Fourteen years of solid work. He'd like to have it back, that decision. Spying was a brutal business. He knew that going in.

A weariness showed on Harry's face as he took up his pipe, relit the tobacco, and settled into place. They rolled on in silence, Eve contemplating what trusting Harry Douglas would cost her. A wordless understanding passed between them. Eve was torn between wanting to trust him and wishing he would go quietly away. She fingered the buttons on her blouse, reluctant to begin.

"My husband, Otis Battersby, died," she said.

She unwound the story haltingly, alternately crossing her arms and rubbing her hands, as if the story chilled her through. She recounted meeting and marrying Otis, his sudden death, her resultant isolation and loneliness, the slow onset of her insecurities, her frustrations with Thomas Jasper and the hired private investigator. After a while, she got up and paced the compartment, talking as much to herself as to Harry.

He did not interrupt, said nothing, but kept his eyes upon her. Finally, she stopped and rested her back against the wall. She clasped her hands, knuckles white, in front of her, waiting for his comment.

When Harry did not speak, she asked, "Am I imagining things? Am I mad?" she added.

Harry waited for her to finish. "Mind if I ask a few questions?"

"If you must, but at least give me a few thoughts about what I've said."

"It's quite a story. I'm not sure what to think. You may be right that someone is entering your property and watching you. I'm not clear why anyone would want to do either."

Annoyed, she said, "Why won't anyone believe me?"

"Did I say I don't believe you? That's not what I meant. Not by a long shot. But you've left out a few things." Harry lowered his voice. "Over the years, in my line of work—both lines of work—I've learned to trust my gut. Our bodies tell us things our brains can't. People think they pay attention, but they don't. You think you miss nothing, but you do. I have some questions. First, tell me why you find your husband's death suspicious."

"Because Otis was perfectly healthy. There was no reason for him to have a heart attack. He would have told me if he were ill. That morning, we had gone for a brisk walk. Two days before his death, he returned from Madrid. To celebrate, we had cocktails and dined with Otis's friends at the Claridge. He was perfectly fine." Her voice edged higher.

"OK," he acknowledged. "Most people don't keel over without a few warning signs. There must have been something more that made you think twice about his death."

"It's these damn coincidences. What the attending physician said. He asked if Otis had been exposed to industrial solvents recently, or if I had noticed him disoriented or clumsy. He said Otis's skin was unusually pink. At first, I thought little of his questions. Later, I began to wonder about them. So, I made an appointment to see the man. He told me he served in Italy and France during the Great War and saw young soldiers die of smoke inhalation, from burning rubber and other chemicals. He called it some sort of poisoning. He said Otis's body looked much like those young men's bodies. It mystified him. This notion of a heart attack."

"What did you do with that information?" Harry asked.

"There was nothing to do. Two days after his death, Otis was cremated, his ashes taken to Bavaria to be strewn in this lake Thomas said he loved."

"Besides the doctor, who knew about this conversation?"

"No one comes to mind."

"When did you get the impression that someone was following you or watching you?"

"I'm not sure. I do recall a few days after I moved from Chelsea, I decided to take a short walk around Holland Park. It started to drizzle, so I went back to the house and peeked inside the front door where the umbrellas hang. A shadow startled me. I shut the door quickly and ran around to the garden gate, thinking a burglar might be inside. I waited there in the light rain for the longest time, but no one appeared. I convinced myself that what I saw had been a cloud moving across the mirror at the very instant I opened the door.

"That may have been the first time I felt the uneasiness. After that, I was more aware. I caught glimpses of the same olive drab coat standing on the street, in the grocery, always turning away before I got a good look. Twice, when I returned home from an outing, a stack of mail—once on the entry table, once in the kitchen—looked out of alignment, as if shuffled through and restacked. And I caught a lingering scent, as if a person or an animal had been there when I wasn't." Eve wrinkled her nose.

"What kind of scent? Perfume?"

"No, nothing like that. More like damp leather. Like when a pair of shoes or gloves gets soaked and is trying to dry out."

"Anything missing?"

"Not that I could tell."

"And you say the private investigator found nothing?"

"I have his report in my bag," she said, moving in the direction of the overhead rack. She stopped. "No, I'm mistaken. I didn't bring it," she lied. She was not ready to share the photographs and passports with Harry. She had yet to figure out what they could mean and how Otis came to have them and the other documents in his possession. Until she did, she would keep the information to herself.

"The man who came to the door," Harry gestured with his head to the compartment door, "looking for Mrs. Pierce. How does that fit?"

"I was once married to Nolan Pierce."

Harry raised his eyebrows and waited. "And?"

"And I'm not anymore." Eve sat down slowly, pulling her feet up, arranging her skirt over them. She was hesitant to speak further. In truth, she was embarrassed about her impulsive liaison with the likes of Nolan Pierce. "Our younger selves commit foolish acts."

"Could he be the one following you? Ex-husbands can be a jealous lot."

"Not likely. Nolan's in a Texas jail for the next ten years, at least. Caught with his hand in the till of his utility company. He's not going anywhere, and I doubt anyone would care to help him. Not much reason to."

"Why, then, would someone identify you by that name? Who knows that's your name, or once was?"

"Not many people in London would know. After I married Otis, my passport was legally changed. A few of Otis's friends might remember me as Eve Pierce. Or the proprietor of the flat I first rented in Chelsea may have known."

"That narrows it. The man who came to the door this morning distinctly asked for Mrs. Pierce. He had to have gotten that information from one of the people you mentioned. He either knows you or has been hired to keep a close eye on you."

"How do I know you're not the one hired to do just that?"

"You don't now, do you?" answered Harry.

Chapter Four

The train slowed.

"Why are we stopping?" she asked, sliding away from the window.

"Must be the Newcastle station. Usually, the train stops here for eight, ten minutes to unload and take on passengers," he explained.

He picked up his pipe and opened the compartment door. "Gives everyone a chance for some fresh air and a bit of a stretch. Are you coming?"

"I might be along in a minute. You go ahead." She ached to get out and exercise her legs, but she was not keen to leave the compartment. When Harry departed, she put on her shoes, draped her coat over her shoulders, and glanced into the passageway. She spotted the WC three doors down and headed in that direction.

On her return a few moments later, the corridor was empty. She first walked past her compartment door. She knew she had drawn the door closed when she left. Seeing it ajar, she assumed she had miscounted the number of doorways and kept moving. When she realized her mistake and turned around, she supposed Harry had already returned and left the door open for her.

Her overnight bag lay open on the seat, a lean man standing over it, his hat perched low on his forehead. A jolt ran through her body, and she gave a sharp gasp. The man looked up from his task. She sensed him calculating his escape, the distance between her and his exit. It was then she noticed the large brown envelope in his hand.

"Give that to me. It's mine," she said, reaching for it.

He gave her a cold stare, said nothing, gripped the envelope with both hands, and made for the door, shoving her aside as he charged. In an instant, he was out the door, running down the corridor.

She recovered her balance and yelled after him, "Thief, come back! Stop him! Thief!" She ran, as best her heels allowed, but she lost ground with every step.

She saw Harry emerge through the platform door, the last passenger coming up the steps. She grabbed his sleeve and pulled him with her as she ran.

"He stole it from my bag. Stop him!"

The man turned his head briefly. Eve could see the hat slipping from his head as he grappled with the entry door to the next car. She heard a swift whoosh as the door slammed shut, and the man disappeared from view.

In an instant, Harry took after him. Eve stood in the connecting passageway as the train rumbled beneath them and lurched away from the platform. She lost her balance and staggered backward, pressing herself on the uneven wall, fearful she would slip and fall between the cars to the rails below.

Through the dim glass portal that separated her from the next car, she saw two silhouettes struggling against the door, their weight causing it alternately to open and close. Abruptly, the door burst open, the sharp sound of metal against glass. In a tangle, the two men crashed through it, a pile of thrashing arms and legs.

Harry slammed the man against the open door, then back into the wall. The other man dropped to one knee, then came up fast, eyes wide, fists out. With his open right hand, Harry blocked a blow.

The man lunged again, but not fast enough. Harry's punch hit an upturned jaw. Spitting blood, the man broke toward Eve.

Unsure in which direction to escape, she inched aside, turned her back to him, and teetered between the open exit door and the metal jamb that supported it. To keep from falling, she gripped the handrail.

The train picked up speed, the blast of its acceleration in her ears. In quick bursts of green and gray, the countryside passed before her.

From her position, Eve saw Harry close in, but the man ducked beneath him.

Harry slipped, stuck out his left hand to break his fall, and his shoulder bore the brunt of it.

Crouching, the man clawed his way along the floor, the envelope still in one hand. When Harry reached for it and held on, the man's face turned to stone. Without warning, he heaved himself sideways through the open door, his body dissolving away as the train separated from him, the envelope's contents spilling after him, a flash of dark objects floating in midair.

In Harry's hand, the ragged edge of the empty envelope.

Eve hollered, her legs caving beneath her. Harry scooped her to him and propelled her into the dim corridor that led to their compartment. She made an effort to speak, but he shushed her with a finger to her lips.

Before they reached the compartment entry, she recovered her step and tried to stand on her own. She bent forward, her forehead against the door, but could not summon the strength to turn the handle. Harry positioned his hand gently at her waist and steered her into the compartment. She crumpled onto the seat, trembling, until her eyes lit on the open overnight bag. Eve tried to struggle to her feet, determined to discover what was missing.

Harry placed both hands on her shoulders, holding her in place.

"Stay where you are." He left the compartment, only to reappear seconds later, a hat in hand. Two hats, actually, and a pair of rimless glasses. He still held the ragged corner of the empty envelope.

"That chap, whoever he is, left a thing or two behind on his way out the door." Eve watched him hang his own hat on the peg and turn over the other to inspect the band inside. "German made. The glasses, too, by the looks of them." Harry sat down on the edge of the seat and rolled the lenses back and forth with his fingertips. He held them up and peered through them. "If he survived that jump, he's going to need these."

Harry tucked the glasses into his coat pocket and adjusted his upturned collar. The broken skin over his knuckles stung when he wiggled his fingers. With his handkerchief, he wiped a spot of blood from his chin.

Eve stared at him in disbelief. "How can you be so calm? We were nearly killed."

"I thought you wanted to find out what killed your husband." He stood, pulled her up from the seat and steadied her. "I wasn't even close to being killed. Were you nearly killed? I must have missed that part," he said, holding her hand longer than necessary.

"Yes, I was nearly killed." She nodded vigorously, adding, "You must pay better attention."

She began to sort through the overnight bag, looking to account for each item she had packed, no longer concerned that Harry could see its contents.

"There aren't many clothes in that bag. What are those? They look like bank bonds."

She snapped shut the bag and waited for Harry to replace it on the shelf above her head. "As I mentioned before, you are very observant." She settled into her seat and struggled to regain her composure.

"Was that the man who came to the door earlier?" she asked.

"The same. Any idea what he wanted in that envelope?"

"I'm not sure. It held a few dozen Spanish passports, nothing more. I can't say what else he was after. I may have interrupted him before he got everything he wanted from the case."

"Spanish passports," he repeated. "Where did you get them?"

Her hand lingered over the envelope. She could tell a simple lie. She wondered what harm it would do. Everyone tells those, don't they?

He said, "It could be important to know. Regarding your husband's death, I mean."

Finally, she said, "They weren't anyone's. They were blank. I found them in an empty stew pot in my basement pantry. I don't know how they got there."

"But someone knew you had them and came looking for them. I suspect he's your constant burglar." Harry stared at his red knuckles. "They were blank," he said to himself. Then, to Eve, "He, or someone who hired him, wanted them badly enough to follow you here and chance getting caught in the process."

"But why risk a life for something that can easily be replaced?" Eve asked. She had no clue as to their importance. "And what would they have to do with Otis?"

"Troublesome questions," he answered. "What else do you have in that case?"

"Photographs of our honeymoon. A daily journal I keep. A book of Otis's writings." Eve felt a wave of protectiveness for Otis. She omitted the mention of several pertinent items, and was not ready to say more. "At the very least, I know he's real. I'm not having delusions. There is someone. I was right to leave."

"How long do you plan to stay in Edinburgh?" Harry asked.

"Until I sort things through. Recollect our time together. Loosen my memory. Little things may be important. I want to know more about the doctor's questions. I thought I'd visit the library and newspaper archives. I'm not really sure what I'm looking for."

A sudden shiver ran up her spine. "Do you suppose he's alive?"

"After that fall? Could go either way. He's a strong fellow. If he landed in a soft spot, he'll be all right. Aside from a bruise or two. If not . . ." Harry shrugged and chanced raising the window shades, revealing a view of the blue-gray sea and the green pasture land that ran to the edge of it.

Harry slid open the glass pane and inhaled the salted air.

"You're taking this all rather coolly," she remarked, the fresh breeze lifting the ruffle on her blouse. They sat close against each other.

"It's not me he was after now, is it?"

iiiii

When they arrived at the Edinburgh railway station, a crisp light shone through the open window. The sun would not set until after eight o'clock. That left Eve plenty of time to make her obligatory stop and then locate an inn away from the center city.

While Eve collected her hat and coat, strapped on her shoes, and drew on her gloves, Harry passed her bag through the open window to the porter working the platform. The three of them climbed the steps up to Princes Street where Harry relieved the porter of Eve's bag. A line of taxis waited at the curb.

"Where's it going?" He lifted the bag, then looked at her expectantly.

"I have a few stops to make," she said.

"So this is goodbye, Mrs. Battersby?" He touched the brim of his hat.

"I hope your poker table brings you luck," she said. She stepped into the back seat of the taxi, holding her hat in place. Harry closed the door after her, his bare hand resting on the open window ledge.

"I don't think you're dressed warmly enough for this weather," she said.

She placed her glove upon the window ledge and cleared her throat. "I'm grateful for your help, Harry." She held out her hand, and he took it. "Those aren't the precise words."

"Whatever you're doing, be careful." He squeezed her glove and signaled the driver.

Through the rear window, she watched him cross the street, hat on the back of his head, hands in his pockets, and stared after him until he disappeared into the crowd. Cars sped by. The taxi driver, a pink-skinned man with deep jowls, gauged the traffic flow and pulled away from the curb. Eve sat back and said, "St. Mary's Cathedral, please, east entrance."

Chapter Five

"Well, look at us. Sinners be praised. It's Harry Douglas, is it, under that hat? It's been an age or three." Mick MacLeod, his big thumb on the tap handle, watched Harry hang his hat on the rack and lower himself onto a stool. Mick slid a glass of thick, dark ale along the counter three stools down. With his elbow, he wiped the spot where Harry sat and reached out his hand for a shake. Harry grabbed it firmly and pulled Mick MacLeod to him.

"A pie and a pint for you, Harry? Or have the years changed your appetite?"

"Sounds right. Your memory hasn't failed you." Harry spied the large selection of ales on the shelf over the bar, shifted forward to check the board for the daily specials. "You and the Kenilworth still holding up your end of the Rose?"

"Safe to say the likes of us will be here till the doomsday comes." Mick raised a bottle in Harry's direction, a query on his face.

"That'll do for a start," said Harry.

Mick poured two fingers of whiskey into a glass and placed it and a glass of pale ale on the counter. "What brings you this way, chap? What's it been? Three years now? Kate has missed your ugly mug. She'll be thankful such a man as Harry Douglas still walks the earth."

"Where is the lovely Kate MacLeod?"

"Gone to the shops with her mum. And for a walk among the gardens, I'll wager, to see the flowers blooming. It was a hard winter, it was. Hold on a wee minute." Mick topped off three glasses, carried them to the far end of the bar, and returned a moment later with a heaping platter. "You've not told me why you're here, where you're staying, how long you'll be."

Harry sniffed the beef and mushroom pie and healthy portion of chips Mick shoved under his nose. He held up a fork and squinted at it in the light. "If the Mussel Inn still lets a few rooms, I'll be there a night or two. Maybe the week. Have a seat at a game. Tomorrow night. The Caledonian. As long as the cards last, as far as they take me, I'll be here."

Mick rubbed his chin. "Heard you left the Service. We made a good team, the two of us."

"That we did. Good days, partner, good days." Harry downed the whiskey in one gulp. "Like to have some of them back. Not all, mind you. The good ones."

"I didn't love it like you did, Harry. End of the war. That was it for me. The Kenil was here, waiting. I didn't need the action. Sorry about that business, old chum. Drink up. I'll pour you another."

"Save it," said Harry. His plate now clean, he wiped his mouth. "Delicious pie. Tell Kate I'll be back tomorrow for a hug."

"She'll track you down if you don't show," said Mick. "Be mindful of yourself."

Harry laughed. As partners, it was the phrase they used before every mission.

Harry plucked his hat from the rack and grabbed the door pull. Before he started into the street, he turned toward Mick. "In the old days, you and me, what would we be thinking if we came across an envelope filled with a dozen Spanish passports, blank?"

"Too easy, pal," said Mick. "Too easy."

iiiii

It was after nine o'clock when Harry checked himself into the Mussel Inn, got his key, paid cash for a drafty cell of a room. When he raised his arms above his head, his hands lay flat against the cracked ceiling. The north wind blew hard against the shutters, sending a faint constant whistle through the air.

The sunset and the light rain took with them the last of the natural light, the single bedside lamp a sad glow against the gloom of the gray room. Since he could neither read nor make out the faded prints hanging on the walls, he placed his jacket over the back of the chair, removed his tie, and lay down upon the bed, hoping to doze a little before he headed out to the game he had arranged minutes before. No denying it, the bed smelled of sour drunkenness and dried sweat. He'd lain in worse places. Eyes closed, he listened to the rain fall from the eave and run into the gutters outside the window.

Her hair smelled of roses. And a bit of lilac.

Customers came and went downstairs, a clatter of stools, the rise and fall of pub chatter, the occasional holler heralding a new arrival or shocking bit of news.

When Harry left Mick at the Kenilworth, he ran headlong into Andy Blake, and Andy, as usual, was hot for a game. Knew just how and where to arrange it. The game started at ten. Harry figured he needed the practice and could think of no better group than the five assembled this evening. Ruthless cutthroats and bloodthirsty bluffers, an unpredictable lot. He knew their type. Their fast play could demolish him in a matter of hours. Or he could control the tempo, slow it down, keep the other players in to build the pot, play as if the money meant nothing to him.

After a few seconds, he could read people. It was a skill he had built over time. In the early days, as a neophyte in London and later in Berlin, Harry frequented the underground card rooms. He cringed when he thought of those dumps, the risks he had taken, the money needlessly lost, always a whisker away from winning. Once he knew something of what he was doing, he stayed out of cheap gambling dens and away from bad players. He frequented the low-stakes tournaments, honing his instincts and awareness. Until he built his bankroll. Until his hands did not shake when he scooped the pot and stacked his profits. Until he lost that careless foolishness that urged him toward the big win. Until he became the shark instead of the mark.

Harry needed to test himself tonight, to polish his routine, read his opponents, and keep his cockiness in check. In tomorrow's stakes game, overconfidence alone could ruin him. Two months ago, it had done just that. He would not easily forget, and now counted that failure as a great asset. For the rest of his career, he told himself, he would be reminded of that night, how it could all go wrong.

⁞⁞⁞⁞⁞

When he arrived in Gibraltar, Harry was riding a hot streak, coming off two big scores in Venice and Madrid. He only needed a deck of cards, a few chips, and a seat at the table. In record time, he found what he considered a tame little game at a fashionable private residence. A few hours later, his method of play had proved successful. In three days, he made more than enough money to move to the Rock Hotel. From the balcony of his room, he had spectacular views of the Straits and Morocco's Atlas Mountains in the distance.

Word got around that Harry Douglas, ace player with a sizeable bankroll, was in town. Within the week, he got his first taste of a serious game—high stakes and polished, if not sane, opponents. The other players included two identical mustachioed brothers from Egypt; a gravelly voiced Moroccan; a wiry, wild-eyed Scandinavian; and a young, soft-spoken Irishman. Until the wee hours of the morning, they chain-smoked Spanish cigarettes and played no-limit five-card stud.

Harry's foremost rule was not to dig himself a hole when he first sat down, so he started slow and observed the others around the table. After a couple of hands, he got a read on his opponents. Once he knew their subtle tics and more obvious signals, he settled in and picked up the pace. When they made a mistake, he took advantage. He convinced himself he was above them. Four times, he doubled his stack. That first night, Harry sat on a tidy profit. The next night, one of the Egyptians decided to vary the game.

When the game changed, so did Harry's edge. As the rounds wore on, he felt the room begin to narrow, and he made his first missteps. He let the Irish kid push him off a winning hand. He lost his concentration and his aggression. Harry's stack got short. To make it up, he stayed in when he should have folded, foolishly played to an inside straight. He figured to bluff his way back.

Harry, who prided himself on never ruffling, let ego override judgment; fear of failure overpowered his discipline. No more complicated than that. By the seventh hand of play, Harry was deep in a hole. His unflappable genius had failed him.

Ever since that game, Harry had found himself stuck on a cold streak. Returning to London made no difference. Even the glow of the lavish gaming salons did not change the direction of his luck. It all ran bad. He knew better, however, than to complain about bad luck.

Desperate to repair his bankroll and create some breathing room, Harry switched his allegiance. He knew horse racing. During his wartime assignment in London, he and Mick learned how to study a racing form. Moreover, they made a game of teaching each other about track surfaces, trainers, jockeys and odds makers. Which ones deserved a second look. Who to put money on. Over their years together, Mick—one of the sharpest analysts around—developed a keen sense of the ponies, as he called them. Harry remembered one race at the Windsor Racecourse where Mick put down six months' pay on a long shot. It paid out at 84 to one. Mick's stake in the Kenilworth belonged to that horse.

Harry needed a big win. In late April, the horses were running at Sandown Park. Harry knew its turf and race lengths, and could catch the train from Victoria for the 1:35 race. On spring days, the Park ran race after race until six in the evening.

His luck had not completely dried up. From his seat opposite the winning post, he watched the odds and gauged his chances on each race. By the end of the week, clever betting and careful observation restored much of his bankroll, enough to finance the trip to Edinburgh for an opening seat in the richest poker game he had ever imagined.

A cold wind swept Harry past the closed doors of the shops, deserted at this hour. "I don't think you're dressed warmly enough," she'd said. That smooth texture in her voice.

When he turned the corner, he saw the alley entrance and sniffed the stench of stale garbage. He turned up his collar against it. Halfway down the steep narrow steps, the recessed door stood ajar, a dusty reddish glow illuminating the threshold. He hurried inside, took the stairs two at a time, and knocked on the first door off the landing. A smoky haze greeted him.

"Where the hell you been, Harry?" A fat hand slapped him on the shoulder. "Always the last to arrive. Sure, we should have started without your sorry ass." Andy Blake, the undisputed king of northern Scotland's poker scene, loosened his collar. "You're here." He pointed to the chair on his left. "Mark the shortest distance from your chips to mine." With exaggerated emphasis, Andy puffed on the soggy end of his stogie and grinned.

"Gentlemen." Harry acknowledged the men in turn. Wordlessly, he hung his jacket on the back of his assigned chair, rolled up his sleeves, and sat down. Not many years ago, he had shared tables with each man. He remembered their habits—their tells. Doyle Hardy, red-faced and overweight, squinted and gnawed on a corner of his lower lip when he faced a bad hand. Gordie Graves, the card counter, blinked his artificial eye and moved his hands away from his stack before he folded. Will Macfarlane, the cranky kid who smelled of mold and mildew, raised his chin when his cards were good. He would be the one to make risky bluffs, even when there was no need. Andy Blake, thickset, a black-haired scoundrel accustomed to winning, played too fast at the beginning and too slow at the end. Known to be a whiner, Andy liked to intimidate. For that, he was a tough read. But Harry knew his jaw tightened when the cards did not go his way. When Andy was ahead, he leaned back, put his big hands behind his head, and spread his legs out under the table, undisturbed, pleased with the world.

"Seven-card stud," Gordie announced. "Two down, four up, last card down." He shuffled the cards.

From the start, no matter the cards dealt, those around the table favored aggressive betting. As predicted, Doyle and Will bluffed relentlessly. Harry let them. They all needled each other. Harry joined in the provocation just to keep them all loose. As the night wore on and the drinks took their toll, the room became a blur of cards and acrid smoke. Chips exchanged hands with increasing speed. By three o'clock, the mood was dark and testy. As always, Andy held the edge.

Doyle, nursing the shortest stack, inhaled the limp cigarette in his lips, exhaled a circle of smoke, squinted through the haze, and shuffled the cards. He dealt each player two cards, face down. "Shut your traps and play the hand, lads."

In the hole, Harry held a queen of spades and a three of diamonds.

They were all in—even Doyle—on the first round of betting.

In turn, Harry's next four cards emerged on the table—two aces, three of clubs, seven of hearts. He was looking at two pair, aces high. A solid hand, possibilities for another ace, another three for the river card. Whoever beat him would need at least three of a kind.

Of course, Andy's hole cards were a mystery, but four spades lay on the table in front of him: seven, eight, nine, ten. Straight flush. A six or a jack of spades would win it. Purely possible. Nothing like it on the table. Andy's luck was running good, his jaw unclenched the better part of the night.

By the fifth round, nearly six hundred pounds lay in the pot, a veritable fortune. Only Andy and Harry remained. The others watched as Doyle dealt the last card—the river card—down. First Andy, then Harry. Before Harry picked it up, he adjusted his hat low on his forehead and planted his feet flat. He did not want any part of his body to reveal the strength or weakness of his hand. Harry lifted his card—ace of diamonds—full house, aces over threes. Only a few hands could beat it, including a straight flush. What were the odds?

Harry cupped his hands together in front of his face, covering his mouth and nose. His eyes stared straight ahead. Andy's bet.

"I'm all in," Andy said too quickly. In his upturned palm, he held the chips loosely. A hair over fifty-five pounds hovered the pot. Once more, Andy stared at Harry, the cigar butt tucked into the corner of his mouth. He did not blink.

A duel only one of them would win. Harry detected no telltale clench in Andy's jaw. His impulse was to fold. A foolish move?

You're holding a full house, for Christ's sake.

Harry had noted neither Andy's coveted six nor jack on the table. Was there a better-than-average chance they lay among Andy's cards? Harry told himself he should quit before he lost more of the reserve he needed for the more lucrative Caledonian game.

But, he reminded himself, money was not the reason he was here tonight.

The other men, pretending indifference, watched Harry as he took a long look at Andy Blake.

"What are you looking at? C'mon, you sissy fascist, time to fold your cards and go home," Andy said.

Harry could not say exactly what it was. Something about Andy's posture interested him. The man's left hand extended a bit too far, held the chips a beat too long. Andy lowered his chin, stared as the chips clattered into the pot. He withdrew his hand quickly and sat stiffly, as if holding his breath. Harry could feel Andy's impatience. Not eagerness, mind you. More like annoyance. Or fear.

Nameless instincts. Learn to trust them. Harry fixed his gaze on a discolored bit of wood on the edge of the table, then on the thick layer of dust on the grille beneath the window. He did not look at Andy's face, kept his voice low.

"Call," said Harry, matching Andy's chip count.

A blast of sheer, quick anger startled the dead air. Andy Blake's body heaved up, his chair slamming backward onto the floor. Onto the table, he flung his smoldering cigar and his cards. Like a stricken bull, he bellowed, "God damn you to hell, Douglas. You rotten son of a bitch."

Harry's luck had turned. He was ready for the Caledonian.

Chapter Six

A fine rain fell on the windshield, blurring Eve's view of the shops and restaurants that lined the street near the cathedral. Once the taxi turned off Princes Street and made its way down Palmerston Place, she saw the silent spires rise against the gray sky. She stepped from the taxi and hurried up the walk, the Japanese lilacs sweet in the air. Inside the entrance door, her eyes adjusted to the dim interior. In the marked recess, she deposited the overnight bag and took off her coat, carrying it with her down the center aisle. The twilight evensong, scheduled for half-past five, had already begun. She chose a seat in the next to the last row, and lowered herself onto the kneeling pad. She bowed her head as a hundred choir voices floated above.

Her eyes followed the long gray lines of the gothic pillars to the distant ceiling, and took in the polished mahogany and stained glass that surrounded her. Scents of incense and burning wax reminded her of why she had come. Praying to God was not something Eve did regularly, so it did not come naturally. Still, she offered thanks for the months she and Otis had spent together. She imagined him as a young soldier in uniform, eager and handsome. The sudden jolt of his death, the solemn service, the crowd of black and gray visitors who, in a blur, came and went. He who had survived the hazards of war, perished on a common tennis court.

She prayed for Annie whom she had not seen in over a year. Annie, who had cared deeply for Otis, who had begged to attend the memorial service, and afterwards to stay in London and comfort Eve. Eve dissuaded her. There was no reason for Annie to sit and watch her mother grieve. Once this business was behind her—when Eve learned what she needed to know about Otis's death—she would send for Annie. Love her. Listen to her. Not now, not before this search for answers was finished. Not before she knew.

For a moment, she merely sat, alone in the pew, straining to see someone who might signal her obligations—when to stand or kneel, the ups and downs of a ritual she knew little of. In a rack over the kneeling pad, she reached for the aged hymnal and turned the first brittle pages, seeking a clue as to the length of the service. It had been years since she attended a church ceremony, save her own nuptials. Surprising herself, she whispered the names of Rip Dexter and Herbie Kicklighter, praying for those she had once loved, bestowing what few blessings she had earned upon these husbands. The marriage failures had not been theirs.

iiiii

The day she married Rip Dexter, nineteen and newly pregnant, she had genuinely loved him, as intensely as any nineteen-year-old can love another. Through the next eight years—Annie's birth, Rip's graduate school, one brief job after another—she continued to love him, not as intensely, perhaps, but love him she did. She could not pinpoint the exact moment at which love left her. She did not know exactly which one-sided compromise, which finger-pointing argument, which ego-crushing disappointment had done it, but one day she found her love for him had vanished. Their intimate connection no longer existed. For Annie's sake, they stayed together for another year, even though Eve knew, in the end, it was a useless act.

Herbie Kicklighter was a different story, entirely. Ten years after her first marriage, at the seemingly more mature age of twenty-nine, Eve moved to Chicago to take an administrative office position. When Annie was away, she would pass Saturday nights sitting in dark corners of cellar jazz clubs, nursing watery Manhattans, captivated by sublime music. On one such evening, in the middle of the band's second set, Eve fell head over heels for the loose, spontaneous saxophonist. Two weeks later, in a red-hot fever, she and Herbie Kicklighter married. Almost as quickly, the music that had brought them together took him from her. Herbie arrived home one morning to announce he had been invited to join Count Basie's band and was off to Kansas City the next day. The marriage lasted little more than a year. The fever a little longer.

iiiii

Walking the length of the aisle toward her, Eve recognized the Reverend Canon Will Gordon and rose to meet him, stepping sideways from the end of the pew. She had forgotten how large a man he was—almost bearish around the middle, a big head, a thickness to his ears and jaw. In the month after she and Otis married, immediately after they returned from Madrid, Gordon visited them in London. One starry June night, after a catered dinner on the terrace, he and Otis took a walk along the Thames while Eve prepared a tray of warm cognac and Spanish almonds for their return. As they came through the door, she heard Otis promise Gordon to make a sizeable donation to the cathedral. Later, when she asked him about it, Otis explained that the cathedral's bells had been damaged. Bombed repeatedly during the war, he had said. He intended to send funds to the Reverend Gordon, sufficient for their repair, so that the city of Edinburgh would once again hear the peal of St. Mary's beloved bells every morning.

Will Gordon was broad shouldered and solid, hair steel-gray, a stiff white collar at his neck. Eve's hands vanished in his as he squeezed them gently. "Our sad condolences on Mr. Battersby's passing. He was a great friend to our cathedral and our diocese. I wish I had known him better."

"I understand his affection for your cathedral," she said. "Here is a respite from the world."

She followed him along the edge of the sanctuary into an office furnished in dark polished woods, deep-blue velvets, and richly patterned rugs. The strong scent of camphor overpowered her, and she covered her nose and mouth with her glove. Once again, the light was dim, and Eve stood at the doorway until her eyes and nose adjusted.

"I was more than surprised to receive your letter," the Reverend Gordon began. "Sit down and tell me why you've come." Two low chairs sat in front of the finely tooled desk. He led her to them and stood behind the one on the right, away from the door, holding the sides until she settled within it, her coat arranged on her lap. He moved the adjacent chair to face her and sat down.

"I've come for two reasons. The gift Otis discussed with you in London has been provided for. The papers drawn. With your signature, or the provost's, whatever the church chooses, the funds will be transferred immediately." She drew a folder from her handbag and laid it on the desk.

Will Gordon's eyebrows rose. "The gift?"

Eve was not sure what to say. He could not possibly have forgotten. "After your visit, Otis told me about the damage to the bells. The ceaseless bombings. He was quite adamant the bells be repaired. He said the two of you discussed a generous gift. I was not certain he had arranged it before he died, so I asked our barrister to make the necessary inquiries and draw up the papers for the fund transfer. They have my signature. I hope the amount is sufficient for a full repair." Eve opened the folder, withdrew two pieces of white paper, and handed them to the Reverend Canon.

"Of course, of course. The bells." Will Gordon opened his hands and lifted his chin, gestures of praise and thanksgiving. "The diocese will be most grateful. How good of you to remember Mr. Battersby's wishes on our behalf. The whole of Edinburgh is in his debt." As he scanned the documents, the line of his mouth curved upward. "This is more than adequate, Mrs. Battersby. You've no idea what this gift can mean." He paused. "You say your barrister drew up these documents?"

"Yes, Thomas Jasper. Otis's barrister, actually. Now mine, I suppose. Perhaps you know him."

"Thomas Jasper," Will repeated. He shook his head. "No, I cannot say that we have met. Not that I recall. Odd. Otis and I knew each other but briefly. I knew many of his friends and acquaintances, and enjoyed dining at his gentlemen's club when I was in London. The Cambridge, wasn't it?"

Eve nodded and straightened in her chair. She was not there to discuss gentlemen's clubs. "Now, if I may, I have another matter, a more sensitive issue."

He placed the documents on the desk, seemingly forgotten. His eyes took her in, years of training evident in his tone and his posture. "I am at your service." Gordon's voice dropped almost to a whisper.

"This may sound unusual," she said. "You're someone I can trust to inquire about such things." Will Gordon was, after all, the chief reason she had come to Edinburgh. To find someone who knew Otis, who she knew she could trust, who could guide her inquiries. She continued carefully. "I don't believe Otis died of natural causes." She stopped and waited for his response, eager for his counsel.

He sat silent. He tilted back in his chair, expanding the distance between them. Eve noted the change in him—elbows drawn in, chin dropped, nostrils flared—his cordial manner gone. He breathed noisily, and she watched the collar tighten on his neck. *I've shocked the man*, she thought.

She opened her mouth to explain, but he stood, his cheeks and neck now splotches of red. Balancing himself with his hand on the back of the chair, he said, "Mrs. Battersby, I cannot agree with you. You must see the flaw in this thinking. The matter has been settled, has it not, by the appropriate authorities?"

"I don't believe their ruling," she said. She found Gordon's behavior quite baffling, particularly for a senior member of the clergy.

He checked his gold watch and cleared his throat. His neck reddened further, and he placed a finger inside his white collar, pulling fabric away from skin. "I'm afraid I have another appointment waiting. Where are you staying in Edinburgh? I'd like to call on you before you return to London. You must allow us to properly express our thanks for Mr. Battersby's gift."

At that moment, an image of the bespectacled man in the train compartment leapt to Eve's mind. An icy shiver ran down her spine. "I haven't yet found a suitable place," she said. Her eyes fastened on Gordon's hand that now rested on the brass knob. "I won't be in Edinburgh long, just a night or two." The easy lie. She said the words quickly, before it was too late to take them back. "Of course, once I get settled, I'll let you know of my hotel. Shall I call and leave a message with your assistant?" She willed her voice to sound light as she rose from the chair and took a step toward her escape.

His face brightened. "That would be best," he said. "The Caledonian is a short distance away. It's quite the place, a legend of elegance. We could arrange a room."

His offer made her hesitate. "There's a thought," Eve said, knowing she would now find a place as far from the Caledonian as the taxi driver could carry her. "You are so very kind, but I wouldn't dream of imposing. I'll manage. Taxi drivers are very helpful in Edinburgh."

"You will let us know?"

"It will be the first thing on my mind," she said as she slipped past him into the vast expanse of the cathedral, hardly a living soul to be seen now that evensong was done. She did not slow her pace until she fled through the side door and stepped into the light.

iiiii

She perched on the edge of the back seat and instructed the driver to turn up Gloucester Lane north of Queen Street Gardens.

Little wider than an alleyway, the narrow lane wound its way up the south side of a hill—the top of which was said to capture a singular view of the Gardens and the old city beyond. A mere fifty yards from the top, when both she and the driver determined the road would soon run out of pavement, Eve spotted the yellow door of the confectioner's shop. The innkeeper told her to watch for it. Behind the shop, a narrow white post stood alone, topped with a freshly painted arrow, green and white, indicating the steps to the inn's front door. Eve now understood the innkeeper's emphatic alert to look for the shop out front. The inn could not be identified from the street. Perfect. Not a soul can find this place without instruction. She motioned the driver to stop.

Typical of other homes in the city, the plain box-like structure sat two stories high, plaster on its exterior, a light tan paint with trim in a darker taupe, ivy climbing the trellis that framed the front porch. An orange light glowed from one of two front windows. Eve climbed the dozen steps and rehearsed her introduction. The taxi driver followed, her leather bag in hand. When he reached the top step, he tipped his cap and deposited the bag on the stoop. She rang the bell, heard its harsh jangle somewhere inside, and waited.

The sounds of footsteps, then unlatching, unlocking. The woman who stood aside the highly polished door was tall and angular, sharp bones jutting from chin and shoulders, a deep dimple at the base of her neck, stress lines on her forehead. Eve was most struck by the deep hollowness of her eyes and her hands—the large, rough hands of a laborer.

"Oh dearie. You've arrived so soon. Come in. Finishing my tea, I was, and readying for a bit of a party this evening. Any bags for you? Yes. I see the one. That's all you've brought? What a lovely hat you're wearing. Mind the cat. She's an ancient one. Found her in the bin at the back of the shop, we did. Digging for breakfast. A real dear, she is. However did you find us? I should say me. However did you find me? Husband's gone nigh on three years. Hard to say me when for forty years, the word was we. Worked together, we did. He minded the shop. I minded the inn. The love of my life, he was. Up and left without a word. Up one morning and . . . Could be under earth, for all I know. You'll not be wanting to hear my difficulties. Will you? You've plenty of your own, I'm sure now." The woman looked at Eve expectantly.

"Yes, I have arrived," Eve said, "with only the one bag." She pulled on the strap. "As I mentioned on the telephone, the station officer gave me your inquiry number. I'm looking for an out-of-the-ordinary location. The gentleman suggested that Mrs. Fleming at The Gloucester Inn may have a vacancy."

"He's a dear, that one. A bit scatty, but knows my difficulties, he does, and sends business when he's able. Set that bag inside the door. We'll have it straight to your room, we will." She wiped a bony hand on her apron and thrust it in Eve's direction. A knot under her chin held a flowered kerchief tight on her head. Eve detected no trace of hair beneath the lilac tulips.

"Agnes Fleming, that's who I am. Agnes to friends, neighbors, and custom. You are a pretty one. My daughter, Katherine. Kate. My only daughter. She's a looker. Can't say where she got it. Her father wasn't hard to look at. But me? Never a beauty, was I? Not at any age. A bit of tea for you, now? Or a rest? A long day of traveling for you, I'd wager. On the train, you say? And you'd be coming from where?"

"From the south," Eve said. "A pleasure to meet you, Mrs. Fleming." The oily hand, brown-spotted with age, smelled of grease and eggs. Remnants of her tea, Eve supposed.

Agnes Fleming pulled Eve gently into the high-ceilinged entry, directing attention to an elegantly furnished parlor. A pair of porcelain Staffordshire spaniels adorned the mantle. The draped doors of the open dining room suggested a formal dinner, white linen set with full places of china and silver.

"Agnes. Agnes, it is. Here now. We—I, mean to have four rooms vacant for the whole of the week. The south corner shows a clear view of the gardens. A lovely sight, it is. Two wee rooms in the back with a fine view of the river. The front corner with a view of St. Mary's. If you don't mind the bells, that is. All on the first floor. Not much of a climb. Doors face into the hallway. Loo on the landing. Breakfast at eight o'clock on the chime. Custom are welcome in the parlor until nine in the evening. Six Scottish pounds a night. Forty, if you stay the week. Breakfast will set you back an extra pound a day. No visitors without my knowing. No loud noises or music. Some folks enjoy their smokes, don't they now? I'll not keep them from their habits. And you'll be staying how long?"

"How long?" Eve repeated. She had not thought to rehearse the answer to this question, since she did not know precisely the length of her stay. "We'll start with a week," she said. "I'll pay in advance, including breakfast."

"That settles it, then. A week, you say. That would be a blessing. It would indeed." Agnes Fleming's voice grew hoarse. She brought the edge of the apron to her lips. "The war changed us all, it did. Nary a body venturing too far into the world. We have our lonely weeks here, we do."

How many times today has someone talked of the war? Harry. The Reverend Gordon. Mrs. Fleming. "You mentioned the bells. Would they be the bells of St. Mary's Cathedral?"

"Aye. We've two St. Mary's in our Edinburgh. You'd think the dear founders wise enough to keep from confusing our wee minds. But who's to criticize? Not Agnes Fleming, a mere innkeeper. Me mother's grave be saved. The Episcopal St. Mary's resides on Palmerston. Not too far from here, is it? The Catholics own St. Mary's Metropolitan on York. Near the railway station. You'll not see a view of that one from here."

"I'll take the St. Mary's room," Eve said, her hand on the banister, her body aching to find a bed and lie down. "Before I leave Edinburgh, I'd so like to hear the bells. I'm hopeful they'll be repaired soon."

Agnes Fleming smoothed her kerchief with both hands and looked sideways at Eve. "Repaired, you say? Why would they be needing repair? The whole of Edinburgh hears them every morning."

A cough caught in Eve's throat. "I was told the bells were damaged in the war. Bombed more than once. That they needed extensive restoration."

"Whoever said a thing such as that would be thinking of the church bells in Gorgie. Poor little village. The bells took a few bombs, indeed they did. Evacuated the place for a wee bit. But not our St. Mary's bells. They're safe and sound, they are. Not a scratch or a crack on the lot. Sure, our Edinburgh spent its time in the shelters, we did, when the sirens sounded. On hard wooden benches we passed many a night. Wasn't all bad, no it weren't. We ate our treacle puddings and sang along with old Willie Carrick's accordion. Mind, the German pilots were after the docks and the bridges. Not our bells. But you haven't laid eyes on the room yet, have you? Have a look, will you, before you decide on which pillow you'll be laying your head for the week. I'll just be putting your name in the book, miss." Agnes Fleming, pen in hand, thumbed the edge of the guest book page and waited.

In the back of her mind, a warning. A slight hesitation. "Eve Kicklighter," she replied. She knew Herbie wouldn't mind.

Chapter Seven

13 May 1949, Edinburgh. Near noon, Harry awoke. Hungry and eager to escape the inn's chill and odor of cheap ale, he unfolded the new shirt and pants he'd bought, dressed quickly and walked the short distance to the Caledonia railway station and adjoining Caledonian Hotel. The Caley—as locals called it—anchored one end of Princes Street, an imposing facade of square red bricks and pink columns, symbol of turn-of-the-century Scottish industry and progress. Stone statues of saints, naked to the waist, sat on marble pedestals above the entry doors. Before climbing the stairs to enter, Harry glanced at his reflection and straightened his hat.

"Another fine afternoon," Harry announced to the doorman. "After last week's dismal weather. A pleasure to see you again."

Years of surveillance taught Harry Douglas two essential rules: First, examine and commit to memory each target's layout. More importantly, pretend you know everyone, and everyone knows you. Act as if you belong.

"Aye, sir, a wee bit of sun warms the soul. It's good to see you, sir." The doorman, elegant in full morning suit and neck ascot, tipped his top hat, and held open the door as Harry stepped into the cool elegant interior.

At a slow pace, Harry strolled the lobby. A line of crystal chandeliers hung overhead, evenly spaced, the length of the room's vast expanse. Around him, patrons sat on darkly rich satin sofas and armchairs sipping tea, reading books and newspapers. The pianist played a Strauss waltz. Snippets of conversation followed him past vases of yellow primroses, their aroma sharp and sweet. Gilded mirrors and heavily brassed doors lined the walls. Two silver-haired men slept in heavy wing chairs, eyes closed, heads drooping onto their chests, faint snorts at alternating intervals. When he had seen enough, he turned a corner and headed down a wide corridor to the lounge area, sure to have a newspaper, a cup of tea, and a tasty lunch plate. Afterward, he would find his way upstairs to the suite level where he assumed the game would be played that evening.

Harry first needed to confirm that the game's host and organizer, one Donald Hamilton, had arrived. If Harry knew anything about anyone, he was more than certain Donald Hamilton had booked the hotel's best suite. Every night for a week in Gibraltar, they had played seven-card stud. Thus, he was in no doubt of the game they would be playing tonight. Harry never cared enough to establish the extent of Hamilton's wealth, nor did he particularly like the man, but he recognized Hamilton was accustomed to the comforts of money and what money could buy. His host could lose a bundle and still be in the game. Harry's thousand-pound buy-in, on the other hand, had to last him the week. An ample profit at the end of it would carry him comfortably back to London.

Harry approached the intricately carved desk that served as the registration area and stood, arms crossed, waiting his turn with the clerk. A large man in a straight-backed chair leaned forward across the desk, the length of his forearms fairly covering it. The man's back was to Harry, his chin down, so Harry caught only the odd word of their conversation. When the man concluded his inquiry, he turned his head. In profile, Harry noted the high white collar, the finely streaked gray hair. Vaguely familiar. Where? He shook his head to jar the memory.

The clerk, facing the man, opened a large book and perused several pages, tracing the tip of his finger along each line as he proceeded down the page. When he reached the bottom, he said, "Sorry, sir. The name Batttersby does not appear on our registration list. You did say Eve Battersby, sir?"

At the sound of her name, Harry took a step closer.

"Yes. I am confident Mrs. Battersby said she would be staying here. I met with her only yesterday," the man insisted, a snap in his voice. He thumped two big fingers on the registration book.

"Of course, sir. Let me look again. Perhaps I've missed it." The young man again examined the pages, holding the edges aloft while he scanned them a third time. "Afraid not, sir." He closed the book and placed a hand upon it, a signal the search had ended.

The big man breathed deeply and pushed himself from the chair. "It's important I get in touch with Mrs. Battersby when she arrives." His voice rose, the tone harsh, making his point. "I'll stop by tomorrow. You know where to find me."

The man turned to leave, and Harry studied the full picture of the man's face, red-faced with annoyance. The tailored black suit, the cropped hair, the breadth of his shoulders and chest struck a chord of recognition. The man nodded at Harry as he brushed past.

The clerk spoke to his back. "Indeed, Reverend. Perhaps tomorrow, sir."

A disturbing image took shape in Harry's mind. He was sure he knew the man. An old assignment, was it?

"Sorry to keep you waiting, sir. How may I help you?" the clerk asked.

First things first. "Yes, you can. I ran into Mr. Hamilton, Donald Hamilton, earlier in the day. We have an appointment for lunch. His suite number, please." Harry did not bother to sit down. He stood behind the chair.

"Mr. Hamilton is settled in Suite 536, sir. You'll find him on the fifth floor."

"Thank you," said Harry. He took a step to leave, then turned back toward the clerk. "One more thing, if you please. The man you consulted with before me. I haven't seen him in years and didn't recognize him until he'd gone. I don't think he recognized me either. It's been years, before the war, even. Is he still at . . ." Harry snapped his fingers and furrowed his brow.

"Reverend Gordon, you mean? Oh yes, he's still at St. Mary's."

"St. Mary's, you say?" said Harry.

"Oh yes, sir. Dr. Gordon is the Reverend Canon at St. Mary's Cathedral. Down the street and around the corner, it is. Follow the spires."

Harry thanked the young man once more. "See you this evening." He took the elevators to the fifth floor and located Hamilton's suite, storing its location for later that evening, then left the hotel by one of the side doors. Out in the street, Harry's stomach rumbled, but he walked directly to the Kenilworth, taking the shortest route through the narrow alleys, an urgency in his step. He was counting on Mick MacLeod to remember a man named Gordon. To fill in the blanks of that operation.

Eve? The Caledonian? Is that where she was headed? What was she doing with the likes of Gordon? A Reverend Canon, my ass.

When he arrived at the Kenilworth, he found the drapes drawn and the door locked—the lunch hour over, the dinner crowd not yet arrived. Harry banged on the door until Kate MacLeod's striking face appeared at a side window. At the sight of him, she glowed, her mouth open in surprise as she backed from view. An instant later, he heard the clattering of stools and the bolt lifted. The door swung wide, and Kate threw herself into his arms.

"Harry. My God. Where have you been?" She led him to a table in the back, sat down opposite, and brushed a dust fleck from his shoulder. "You've lost weight."

A radio played softly in the background, a mournful Celtic tune.

"Mick says you got yourself invited to a fancy game tonight." Kate grabbed the hat from Harry's head and placed it on the peg above her head. "What are you playing? Can I watch?"

"They'd find you hard to resist." Harry loosened his tie, unbuttoned the top button on his shirt, and leaned back, lacing his fingers behind his head until he was comfortable.

He liked Kate MacLeod. A lot. Not simply because she was a beautiful woman. Her beauty was indeed the most obvious part of her. Slim and graceful, a face straight out of Hollywood glamour movies, black hair with curls that rested on her shoulders, a smile that knocked you down, and a laugh that lifted you up. From her Scottish mother, she inherited skin the color of rose petals, a blush on each cheek. From her English father, deep-set hazel eyes. But mostly, Harry liked Kate MacLeod because she was Mick's girl and made sure you knew it. Right away. From the start. Harry had gotten that message. Transmitted and received.

"But that would help you, wouldn't it?" she teased.

Harry changed the subject. He never dwelt on an upcoming game, particularly one he needed to win. His palms got wet every time he thought about the table fee in his pocket. "How's your mum, Kate? Haven't seen her since the war ended, the day you and Mick moved north."

"Same as ever. Thinner by half. Running the inn by herself takes a toll. Seems to enjoy it, as long as she doesn't have too many guests to look after. Not much chance of that these days." Kate walked around the bar and filled two glasses with pale ale. "She does the occasional rehearsal dinner and anniversary celebration. Hosted one last night, even. She'd love to see you, Harry. A shame to leave without a visit. If she knew you were here, she'd fly down Gloucester Hill and plant a wet kiss. And pray to the good Lord above for more. A willing sinner for handsome Harry, she'd be."

"Guess I'd forgotten she's still the innkeeper on the hill," Harry said.

Eyeing him over the beer, Kate asked, "How long are you staying, Harry?"

"Can't say for sure. This fellow, the host, can play for days at a stretch. Money and time to burn."

"And you, at the Mussel Inn?" Kate wrinkled her nose. "How do you stand the smells?"

"It's not too bad. Especially if I'm here instead of there," said Harry. He took a gulp from his beer as Mick came down the stairs toward them, his arms out, his mouth in a wide yawn. Although Mick had gained a stone or two since they worked together, he presented the picture of health—trim, muscular, upbeat. Able to flatten a man with one blow, then offer a hand to help him on his way.

Mick rubbed his eyes and sat down. He wrapped his arms around his wife and kissed Kate's neck. "Hey, old chap. Can't stay away, eh? We're about to heat the evening soups. How about a taste for you?"

Harry had missed Mick MacLeod. "I'd like that. If you can sit for a few minutes, I need you to remember a case we worked on. London. Early '45, I think. Near the end. Things were hot, and they were wanting anything on the big krauts—finances, travel applications, relatives, contacts in Britain."

"Before the Nuremberg searches?"

"Yeah, months before. I know we got the order as early as December '44 to prepare for the trials. There were the arguments for and against. Stalin for quick execution of all German staff officers. Churchill for trial, the Moscow Declaration. Just war criminals, not common soldiers."

A Churchill fan, Mick nodded at the sound of his name.

Harry knocked his knuckles on the table, trying to recall the details. "This job happened a bit later than that. You remember, we went to Spain, nosed around, asked about those living in Madrid at the time."

"Belgian, weren't they?" Mick asked.

"You're right. Daye was Belgian," said Harry.

"Pierre Daye. God. Haven't thought of him in a while. Wasn't he sentenced to hang in '46?" Mick straddled the chair, leaned his chin on his arms.

"Firing squad. But we lost him. Escaped to Argentina in '47. Probably still there," said Harry.

"I remember," said Mick. "Isn't that why we went to Madrid? To get a read on their process. How they got to Madrid, who provided money, credentials, where they went after."

Mick got up and paced. "Give me a minute, Harry. Early '45. Madrid. Yeah. We were trying to figure how the Nazis got their escape money. Swiss accounts? British enablers? That the case you're after?"

"That's the one. We spent days chasing our tails, and finally cornered that clerk at the Palace Hotel. What did he tell us? Who did we see there?" Harry looked at his hands, as if they held the key to a distant memory.

"Not the clerk," said Mick. "It was the bellman. You mentioned the word Nazi, and he rolled his eyes. Once he started spilling things, we couldn't shut him up. Definitely not a Franco enthusiast, that one. Must have been a resister, I'd wager. He told us they spoke English. Two fellows. He carried their bags. In the elevator, they told him they were from London on holiday. Then they asked him how to get to Kraucher's Restaurant, and he knew."

"That's the one, Mick. We caught a break with him. We booked a room across the street and parked ourselves on the second floor, on the Palace's north side. Observed that side entry all night." Harry finished his beer.

The more Mick spoke, the faster and louder his voice became, "There were two of them. They were hard to see because they were standing inside the glass doors. Then the third one showed up with the valise. Outside. Just after dawn. A bit of light on the street for us. Enough to make out their faces. Number three stood there, like he was waiting for a taxi. Numbers one and two stepped outside, and we got a solid look at them through the glasses. A couple of photos, even. The valise changed hands. Number one, big guy with graying hair, reached inside his coat and passed a thick envelope to number three. A car pulled up. Out of nowhere. At dawn, mind you. Number three slid in. Took all of forty-five seconds. But we had him full-on. Full body. Full face."

"Not two days later, we got him," said Harry. "German camp commandant. Intercepted at the Madrid airport. But what about the Brits he paid off? Did we identify them? Any arrests made? What happened to those two? And the payoff?" asked Harry.

"The right questions. No answers. No arrests made at the time. Not that I know. What's going on, Harry? Why now? This have anything to do with the Spanish passports you asked about yesterday?"

Harry struggled to make connections between the man at the Caledonian registration desk, Eve Battersby, and the passports. He figured there had to be one. There's generally a reason for coincidences. How much should he say? He decided to ignore the passport issue for now. "I saw one of those chaps today. At the Caledonian. I'm sure it was him."

"You mean a guest at the hotel? A staff member?" asked Mick.

"Neither. I noticed this fellow at the registration desk. Big fellow. I inquired. The registration clerk told me his name is Gordon, none other than the Reverend Canon at St. Mary's Cathedral."

"How did the clerk know him? And what was he doing at the Caledonian registration desk? St. Mary's is within a hundred meters of the hotel. Are you sure?"

"Yeah. I'm sure. That's why I'm here. To know I remembered it right. Hard to believe a clergyman, a big shot at that, is part of a Nazi ratline. But I can't forget that fellow in Madrid. Broad shoulders and chest, solid neck. I remember thinking I wouldn't want to tangle with him. Same big thick face, clean-shaven, full head of steel-colored hair. He's the one who traded the valise for the travel papers."

Harry walked behind the bar and washed the two beer glasses while Kate wiped them with a towel and set them on the shelf next to the others.

"I thought you were done with it, Harry. Why is it important?" she asked. "We all did things in the war. Things we wouldn't do again. Why not leave it alone?"

Kate did not get an answer from him. They were quiet for a while, the occasional street sound echoing in the empty room. Harry considered whether to say more. He was not sure himself why he was dredging up past work. Spies. Half-truths. Deceptions. Shadows. It used to be his work. Much of it dirty. Most of it better left alone.

Call it instincts. Things didn't fit. Maybe they fit too nicely. The man he hunted four years ago was then a facilitator for Nazi relocation. More than a facilitator. A Nazi smuggler. A paid collaborator. Now, he turns up as a high-ranking clergyman. The perfect cover. Harry had followed dozens of leads involving war criminals who left Europe for South America posing as priests—with proper documents and letters of recommendation. Chances were good that Gordon was still in the ratline business. Not the kind of business you duck in and out of. The money was good. Real good. Fortunes taken. Fortunes made.

Today, Gordon had stood ten feet in front of him. Asking about Eve Battersby. He was more than insistent with the clerk, intimidating even. Gordon was convinced she planned to register at the Caledonian, irritated she was not there. Seemed bent on tracking her down. What else? The man on the train. Stealing documents, Spanish passports, from Eve's bag. German-made hat.

German-made eyeglasses. Definitely knee-deep in the business. A player. More than an errand boy, but a lowly worker all the same. Too many coincidences.

Where was Eve? What had she got herself into? It suddenly struck him she might be involved in the whole nasty business.

Chapter Eight

The railway station agent had been right. The inn was everything Eve needed. She slept soundly and warmly, better than she had in months, the soft hiss of the radiator a gentle mask for the Monday morning noises of Gloucester Lane. It was after ten o'clock when she awoke, famished. She remembered eating nothing yesterday or the day before. She buttoned her blouse and stepped into her skirt, her image in the armoire mirror hopelessly gaunt. She studied her face, her cheekbones more obvious than usual, the shadow from her jaw line harsh against her stem of a neck. She looked breakable. What was Harry's descriptor? "Mighty attractive"? Not likely.

She descended the stairs for breakfast, resolved to feast on Agnes's cooking, no matter the options. One of those full English breakfasts perhaps? But this is Scotland, isn't it? What day? May 13? The kitchen was warm, its open shelves cluttered with knick-knacks—a collection of salt and pepper shakers, jam jars, and cream pitchers. On one wall, under a bank of low windows, a line of pegs hung with damp cloths and towels, no doubt set out to gather the stove's heat. On another, a door that led to a well-stocked pantry filled with neat rows of canned fruits and jams. The scent of cinnamon reminded Eve of her late-night cooking sprees on Bramerton Street. She wondered what the cats were eating these days. Agnes had left a terse note: Gone to market. Hot cereal on the stove. Fruit and cream in the icebox. Bread for toast in the breadbox. Tea water in the cooker.

Eve filled a bowl with cinnamon oatmeal and warm cream, wandered with it into the parlor, and tucked herself into the cushioned window seat, the blinds opened sufficiently to allow shafts of sunlight to shine through. A glossy mahogany box on the sill caught the sun's reflection. Inside a poem, Robert Burns' "My Heart's in the Highlands." She read it twice, loving the rhythm and rhyme.

Absent the ticking of a wooden clock and the clattering of her spoon against the bowl, the room was quiet. Serene in greens and blues. A wide sofa with matching armchairs near the fireplace. Against the far wall, a game table and four padded chairs. She had noticed none of it last night when she arrived. Only one light had been burning, and she had been tired—worn out from the long, eventful train trip and that curious meeting with Will Gordon.

Already, she felt better. Away from London. No one in the world knew where she was or where to find her. Away from intruders and stalkers. They were, after all, real. The man on the train proof of her suspicions. She leaned her forehead against the glass. Who was he? Why take one envelope and nothing else? Could he have survived that dreadful, desperate leap from the train?

Safe, fed, thus restored, she could finally think clearly. Her doubts about Otis's death the only thing to consider. Where to begin? Nothing in life had prepared her for detective work. She would figure it out as she went along. Questions. Attempts to answer them. The answers were in her bag, she was sure of it. The photos and her journal. Those odd-looking papers. *Begin with the journal*, she told herself. Relive each day. Draw it forward. The photos will help. Then whatever comes next, whatever that is. She would stay until she knew something. Not everything perhaps, but something.

Eve returned the breakfast bowl and spoon to the kitchen sink, turned off the cooker, and climbed the stairs to retrieve the journal. Before she went to bed last night, she had unpacked a few items—the journal and papers overpowering the bedside table. There was the problem of the money. She had to decide where to put it. The armoire's bottom drawer, perhaps? There could be no bank account. She had to avoid prying bank officers. The coat was too heavy to wear for any length of time. She had a hard enough time sewing the thick wads of cash into the lining. She, of course, had given no thought as to what to do with the money once she got to where she was going. She supposed she could simply hang the coat in the closet and buy another, unbasting stitches and grabbing a stack of bills when needed. For now, that seemed the best approach.

At some point, she must find a pair of comfortable shoes, suitable for walking, and a new trench coat. On the way to the cathedral yesterday, the taxi passed a department store. Jenners, on Princes Street, she remembered. A shoe store on Palmerston, the same street as the cathedral. She dared not go there, fearing a second encounter with Gordon. Not only had he lied about the purpose of Otis's gift, she definitely sensed an underlying alarm at her comments about Otis's death.

This morning, she planned to find a sunny spot with a view of the gardens and review the honeymoon journal, cover to cover. It was easy to assume she was Agnes's only tenant, the house largely to herself. Since her arrival, she had encountered no one else. With Agnes's permission, then, she would spread the photos on the game table, place them in some sort of order, chronologically perhaps, then set about examining them thoroughly. During their honeymoon, she had gone mad with the camera, shooting everything from a striking yellow umbrella to reflections in the Prado's entry doors. Once at home, Otis had chided her, good-naturedly, for boring their friends with such images. She loved the early shots of Madrid, especially the white-tie dinners at that restaurant on Alfonso Calle, the owner a genuine character. A charming man. What was his name? The same as the restaurant, she thought. Balding, an exaggerated chin, long ears, light-gray eyes. Greeted guests as they arrived. Knew their special tables and what they drank.

Journal in hand, Eve sank into the plump pillows of Agnes Fleming's green sofa. Her hand flat on the journal's rich brown cover, thumb poised on the edge, she hesitated. A cup of tea steamed on the tea table in front of her. Off in the distance she heard a train whistle. Conscious of the quiet, she wondered, not for the first time, whether she was prepared to embark on something as important as Otis's death. Something that could change her.

¡¡¡¡¡

May 2, 1948: Pure poetry. Madrid amazes me. Arrived Palace Hotel before noon. Elegant to the last detail. Every sense alerted. On the street, explosions of color, sound, and scent. Mimes on every corner. Pretty dark-haired girls in fitted blouses and tight ruffled skirts. Guitarists, strumming on the streets, singing. Quick clops of castanets. Pigeons on the fly. Pesetas swiftly changing hands. Streets tangled with donkeys and horses, buses and cars. Dust. Odors of old garbage, garlic, and gasoline. City gardens a breadth of color.

Every day was like no other. For nearly two weeks, she and Otis lived at the Palace, their mornings spent sprawled in cafes along the Paseo del Prado drinking espresso and laughing at the life that burst around them. They passed hot afternoons in the shaded bleachers at the bullfight arena and late evenings with pitchers of martinis at the Anglo-American Club, Otis discussing literature and politics with members of the British Council. One morning, an official-looking black car, Spanish flags flying from its bumpers, picked them up at the hotel and drove them to a rural estate. An ambassador, she was told. Near noon, Reiner Reinhardt led them on a tour of the estate's stables, hunting lodge and library, each room filled with paintings of the Dutch Masters. To Eve's surprise, Coco Chanel joined them for lunch, on her way from a meeting in Paris, she said, back to her home in Switzerland. Coco, dressed in signature black and white, chattered in both French and German. Though Eve deciphered only a few sentences, she was easily aware of the more than casual relationship between Coco and the ambassador.

It was the nights she remembered best. Three separate times, they dined at Kraucher's Restaurant. Kraucher. That's his name. Otto Kraucher, who showed favored guests to their special tables. Sparkling champagne buckets. Fresh bouquets of fragrant white roses. A menu of wild game—partridge, duck, roe deer—and creamy desserts served on gleaming silver platters. The waiters overly attentive. In German, Otis and Otto Kraucher held long conversations while Eve admired the Persian carpets and talked with other patrons who stopped at their table, many of whom knew Otis, a sense of camaraderie among them. As if they had been acquainted for many years. In whispers, a wicked twinkle in his eye, Otis identified ambassadors and journalists. On one occasion, they dined with another man. Rolf something. Confident, full of stories, handsome strong jaw, an ugly scar on the left side of his face. He had admired her feathered hat and, shortly thereafter, joined Otis outside for a smoke. She could almost see him. Otis said he was an Austrian administrator. A vague familiarity. She had seen that face a second time. But where?

iiiii

For the next few hours, Eve read and reread the journal, reliving Madrid's markets and bullfights, the smell of the sea at San Sebastian. When she finished reading, she smoothed out a piece of paper and drew a simple chart. On the left, she wrote and underlined the names of people she remembered. On the right, the places they had met and the locations of those meetings. In parentheses, she added other details. Otto Kraucher (spoke German), restaurant owner, Madrid. Reiner Reinhardt (spoke German, French, ambassador, wealthy art collector), rural estate, outside Madrid. Coco Chanel (spoke French and German, on her way to Switzerland, possible lover to ambassador), rural estate, outside Madrid. Rolf Fleiss (spoke German, long facial scar, Austrian administrator), Kraucher Restaurant, Madrid.

Satisfied with her progress for the day, she folded the chart in half and tucked it in the journal's front pages. Beside her, the telephone jingled.

"Hello. No, Mrs. Fleming is not at home. Doing a few errands, I think. Her daughter. Tomorrow, you say, around midday. With a friend. Of course, I'll give her the message when she returns."

Eve noted the time of the call and, on her path upstairs, left the message on the entry table.

Before she lay down for a nap, Eve lifted two envelopes from the bottom of her bag. One thickly stuffed with pictures of her honeymoon, the other thinner and somewhat lesser in length, mysterious for its hiding place in the Bramerton basement pantry. She stacked them on top of the bureau. For tomorrow, another day of detective work.

Chapter Nine

14 May 1949. At the far end of the parlor, Eve studied each row of photographs on the game table, her favorites arranged chronologically on the top row. In this one, they were leaving Chelsea Old Church. Here, they were arriving in the Palace Hotel lobby. In another, Otis was standing in front of Kraucher's Restaurant, a new acquaintance on his right. In this one, they were talking with their handsome host and the famous Coco at the estate outside Madrid.

On a second table, abutting the first, lay a dozen black-and-white photographs—facial portraits, uniformly square, youthful men, some of early middle age. She picked up each picture, examined front and back for marks or identifiers, and replaced it face up on the table. As a group, there was something eerily similar about them. As she set down the last picture, she heard the tinkling of the bell from the foyer, the sound of the door opening and closing, the fall of footsteps.

"Mum. We're here." A feminine Scottish brogue sang out. "She's in the kitchen, I'll wager."

Ah, Agnes's daughter, Kate.

Two shadows filed past the glass-paned double doors that separated the parlor from the entryway. Eve did not wish to interrupt her work or be compelled to provide an explanation for the photo assortments. Nor, for that matter, did she want anyone to know where or who she was. Better to stay out of sight, she decided, focused on her task.

In one of the photos, she noted a tiny mark. Holding the portrait in one hand, she picked up a magnifying glass from the side table. The glass held steady, she moved the portrait to and fro under the magnifier, turning toward the window where the light was best, until she distinguished an odd-looking line on the man's face. A scar? Yes. The face in the portrait looked somewhat different from the man she had met and dined with in Madrid, the hair slicked back, the brows heavier, moustache. The name written on the back of the photograph was clear. One Rolf Fleiss. A further notation, Machinist. A flash of memory. Hadn't Otis introduced Rolf as an Austrian businessman? What was his portrait doing here?

The parlor's pocket doors slid slightly open, and Agnes Fleming slipped through the narrow opening. "I don't mean to disturb your work, Eve. But, with a free minute, would you care to meet my daughter Kate and her friend?"

"Of course," said Eve, not at all sure she did care to meet them, but she laid the magnifier and the photograph aside and walked to meet Agnes in the middle of the room.

Sliding the door farther apart and waving to her guests, Agnes added with a laugh, unable to hide her delight, "Kate's brought with her the man I aim to marry one fine summer day in the shade of Edinburgh Gardens."

Eve's heart jumped when Harry Douglas crossed the threshold. Their eyes met and held for an instant.

Then, Eve turned to the pretty young woman approaching her. To Kate MacLeod, she said, "Pleased to meet you, Kate.

"People do find each other, somehow," she said, extending her hand to Harry. The warm pressure of his fingers, the long half second before letting go. She wondered when and where he had acquired the fresh shirt. "I had no idea you were betrothed."

"You know Mrs. Kicklighter, then?" asked Agnes, curious, her head tilted in Harry's direction.

Harry, one eyebrow raised, a slight smirk upon his face, bowed his head and said, "Mrs. Kicklighter." He emphasized the name and paused. "We met on the train from London."

"Briefly," Eve said quickly. "We shared the same compartment."

Kate MacLeod looked from Eve to Harry and back again. She grinned, grabbed Eve's elbow, and led her into the dining room. "Let's have our lunch, then, and hear all about it. Right, Mum?"

Each found a place at the table. The cool afternoon air breezed in through the window. Amidst a clatter of pots and pans in the kitchen, Agnes marched in carrying a steaming tureen of fresh turnip soup. From there, Agnes served leg of lamb with a light mint sauce, roasted potatoes, and rice and sultana pudding. She had made a substantial effort, Eve noticed, arranging everything carefully on sparkling china and gleaming silverware.

From the first mouthful, Eve neatly sidestepped inquiries into her own background. She simply ignored their questions. Thwarted, Agnes and Kate turned their attention to stories of Harry's associations with the MacLeod-Fleming families and his decade-long partnership with Mick MacLeod in the British Intelligence Service.

"I think Harry and Mick were the last ones out of Milan," said Kate. "Worried me to death. Didn't hear from them for weeks."

Harry poured a fresh glass of Irn Bru for Kate and Eve. "Agnes mentioned you have work to do in Edinburgh. How long will you stay?"

"It's not clear how long the work will last," said Eve evasively.

"She's paid a week in advance, she has," said Agnes.

"You must come for dinner before you go. Back to London, is it?" Kate looked at Harry. "Tomorrow? Or the day after? You'll meet Mick. An early dinner before your game, Harry?"

"The Caledonian doesn't start until nine." He looked at Eve.

"Is that where you're staying?" asked Eve, troubled now. She pushed her chair back from the table.

"Not staying. Just there for the game," said Harry, running his finger around his plate, savoring the last of the mint sauce. "We won't be dining at the Caledonian," he added. "Kate and Mick own the Kenilworth on Rose Street."

"An early dinner the day after tomorrow will be fine," said Eve, exhaling in relief. She patted her lips with her napkin and placed it on the table. "Delicious lunch, Agnes. Thank you for including me. If you'll excuse me, I must get back to work."

After a few minutes, Harry followed her into the back corner of the parlor. "So, here we are. You never cease to surprise." He took in the line of photographs. "What's all this?"

"As usual, you're awfully inquisitive." Eve replied, her body partially shielding the tables from view.

"As usual, you didn't answer my question," said Harry. In a quieter tone, he said, "I need to tell you something. It may have nothing to do with what you're doing here, but I think it's important." He stepped around her and took in the two photo arrays. "Do you know a man named Gordon?"

"Why do you ask?" She wished suddenly for a cigarette.

"Yesterday, he inquired at the desk of the Caledonian about your room number."

"How do you know this?" she asked.

"I stood not five feet from him and heard him do it. Made the clerk look twice at the register. Said he'd check back today. What's going on, Eve?"

"Nothing's going on. I met the man in London. He's an acquaintance of Otis's. After I left you at the railway station, I met with him. An appointment at St. Mary's Cathedral. I thought he could help me with my inquiries, but I was mistaken."

"Why would he think you were staying at the Caledonian?" asked Harry.

"He suggested it, said it was 'quite the place.' He must have assumed I'd take his advice. But I chose not to and ended up here with Agnes," said Eve.

"Under the name Kicklighter. Who the devil is that?" asked Harry.

"Kicklighter was once my name," she replied.

"Along with Battersby and Pierce? C'mon," said Harry, a hint of exasperation in his voice.

"God. Why do you remember everything I say? It's not normal." Dramatically, she collapsed upon the sofa, hoping to change the course of conversation. "This whole business is very confusing. I need time to figure it out. That's all I'm after. Why doesn't everyone just leave me alone, and give me time to think?"

"Because you're in danger, Eve." Firmness in his voice. "There's a lot I don't know about you and your husband—husbands, apparently—but I know enough to be concerned. You would be wise to be concerned, too." He stared into her green eyes, worry clear upon his face. "I'd like to help. I've encountered this Gordon in the past. I understand he's a big shot at St. Mary's. That's not all he is. Definitely not all he appears to be."

"He frightened me," said Eve. "I got a strange feeling during our meeting. For some reason, the image of that man on the train sprang into my head. The gift of fear, some call it. It's the reason I'm here instead of the Caledonian. I thought it best to use another name. So Gordon and the man on the train, if he's still alive, couldn't find me. If either of them came looking."

"That was smart. What was the topic of your meeting with Gordon?" asked Harry.

"Several days before he died, Otis told me he promised the Reverend Gordon to pay to repair the bells of St. Mary's. The sum was quite substantial. Otis said he planned to come to Edinburgh to deliver the check personally. In the many obligations to be settled on Otis's behalf, this one had gone unnoticed. It seemed extremely important to him, at the time." Eve paused before continuing. "When I delivered the check, it was clear Reverend Gordon didn't know what I was talking about. He lied to me and to Otis. I don't know what he will do with the money. Not that the money is important. It simply makes no sense." She paused as if searching for another thought. "I thought I could trust him. A clergyman, after all, and an acquaintance of Otis's. But by the time our meeting was over, I felt confused and, truthfully, very much afraid."

"You're right to feel afraid. Now tell me about these passport photos. Where you got them. What you're doing with them." He settled into the chair and took some time looking at the photos.

"Of course. They *are* passport photos. I knew there was something familiar about the lot of them. And they go with," she stopped, puzzled at the implication.

"The blank Spanish passports." Harry finished her sentence. "Where did you get the photos?" he repeated.

"I brought them up from our basement, along with other papers." She spoke slowly. A door opened in the back of her mind.

"Other papers? You mean like travel documents, certificates?" asked Harry.

"I'm not sure what they are. Some of the lines are blank. I'll get them upstairs," she said.

After Eve explained everything to him, Harry asked, "Would you say they were hidden? In a hiding place?"

His question made her freeze. "I'm not sure I like where this is going, Harry." *And I'm not at all sure I want your help*, she added to herself.

"Let's see what you have. We'll figure it out," he said gently. Then, his tone serious again. "Before you go upstairs, do you know who this fellow is?" He picked up the photo labeled Rolf Fleiss.

"Yes, we dined with him in Madrid. He and Otis talked about being officers in the war, on different sides. At first, he seemed quite nice. Until he had too much to drink. Then, he became a bit loud. Raved on about needing something immediately. Otis tried to calm him. When he grabbed Otis's jacket, Mr. Kraucher escorted him outside."

"At Otto Kraucher's Restaurant? And I suppose you stayed at the Palace Hotel?"

"How did you know?" asked Eve.

"I know both locations well. They are well known in the intelligence community." Harry held up the portrait. "This man is not Rolf Fleiss. His name is Walter Dannecker, an SS colonel. Not a regular army officer. A commando with a reputation for cruelty. Famous for his daring exploits and this arced scar on his face. Tried in 1947, sentenced to twenty years in prison, he escaped from Darmstadt internment camp in early 1948. To be sure, he needed something in a hurry. Papers to flee the Continent before his recapture."

"You're talking about Nazis, for heaven's sake," she said, grabbing the photo from his hand.

"I don't mean to be blunt," Harry said, "but how well did you know your husband's activities?"

"Otis couldn't possibly know anything about this. We were simply having dinner in a lovely restaurant on our honeymoon." She realized her hands were shaking.

Harry tried to take Eve's hand, but she pulled it away. "That may be true. But hear me out. Your husband traveled frequently to Madrid."

"For his business," she interrupted. "He sold ties. Are we finished?"

Harry had already determined Otis Battersby sold more than ties. "You and your husband stayed at the Palace Hotel, a known place of residence for Nazis and collaborators on the run. You dined, several times you said, at Kraucher's Restaurant, a known rendezvous point and money-laundering site for the Nazis and Argentine fascists. Your dinner guests included this man, a war criminal traveling under an alias. You have in your possession blank travel documents, items normal people do not keep hidden in their basement. Your husband is dead. You know something about it is wrong. There are patterns here. These are dangerous people. Don't fail to notice that."

She wanted to flee. She did not—would not—believe Otis was involved in such monstrous things. She tore her hands free, pushed Harry away. Her voice rose along with her anger. "Stop this. Not another word about my husband. About whom you know nothing. None of this has anything to do with him." She spun on her heel and made for the stairs. Over her shoulder, as she went through the door, she said, "No wonder they threw you out of the service."

She waited upstairs until she heard them leave. Then, Eve left the inn and walked quickly toward Princes Street, in the direction of the commercial area. Dressed only in a light blouse and black skirt, she carried a small handbag. Her heels clicked sharply on the pavement. She told herself to calm down, but she could not. The very idea. Otis was an officer, for God's sake. He would have mentioned something. Anything. Nazis. How dare Harry?

After a short time, she found the sign she was looking for, entered the tobacconist shop, spotted the rack of Gauloises. "This weather is warm for May." The cashier spoke into the register drawer, not looking at her.

"Yes, isn't it? I'll have two packs, please, and some matches." Eve placed a one-pound coin on the counter.

"I think it will be at least 26 degrees today," the cashier mused, then, finding no one there, called out, "Madam, you've forgotten your change."

Before Eve reached the next street corner, she had finished one cigarette and lit up another.

She browsed in the clothing department at Jenners, forcing herself to think only of lovely dresses, comfortable shoes and a suitable spring topcoat. An hour later, laden with an arm-load of impulsive purchases, in search of a fashionable bar, she remembered the North British Hotel at the top of the Edinburgh railway station, and hailed a taxi to drop her at the entrance.

The lounge, dimly lit, filled with dark wing chairs and solid antique tables, smelled of peat and expensive tobacco. Businessmen in groups of two or three lined the perimeter space. The more casually dressed, presumably tourists and travelers, sat at tables in the center of the room. Away from the door, Eve found a stool at one end of the bar. At her direction, the barman filled a cocktail glass with single-malt whiskey, added two drops of sweet vermouth, and a twist of lemon.

"Let me know if you want a refill," he offered.

"Not if, when." She leaned toward the flame, and the barman lit the match for her cigarette. "Check back in twenty minutes." Very quietly, she hummed a nameless tune, emptying her mind of Harry's voice. She tried to block it out, the sharp gnawing inside her. Even the heady smoothness of the alcohol could not disguise it. She stared at the cigarette in her hand, glanced to either side of the bar, wondered how much she did not know and whether she could face an ugly truth.

Chapter Ten

Harry squared off his handkerchief and regarded his reflection. The mirror's diagonal crack cut across his body, separating the deep blue of the new blazer from the crisp white shirt on his chest, breaking his tie in two places. A fitting image. He told himself he had done the right thing, trying to protect her. Not entirely noble. More like trying to impress her. Nonetheless, he knew he was all too right. At some point he would have to figure out a way to tell her exactly what he suspected about Otis Battersby and his dealings in Madrid.

For four years, it had been his life's work. He considered himself expert on the Nazi underground, their places of business, escape routes, portholes in and around central and northern Spain. Concealed in the borderland between France and Spain, they traveled safe routes through the Somport and the Roncevaux passes, arriving in the dead of night, border guards and train inspectors bribed into silence. Weeks, sometimes months, later with new identity papers folded into their breast pockets, they crept away on ocean liners and airline flights, fake pasts concocted by Spanish and Argentine diplomats and highly placed clergymen, the occasional helping hand from the Red Cross. Juan Perón's 1946 presidential victory in Argentina increased the ease of their exodus.

He knew the Palace Hotel well. For endless hours, he had stood in its shadows. In San Sebastian at the Hotel Terminus, he had taken photographs as guests arrived by railway and taxi, and departed by ship from the Puente Christina docks. He had spent hours in surveillance at Kraucher's Restaurant, famous for its secret microphones that captured conversations of foreign visitors, the bar a perfect cover for exchanging smuggled Swiss bonds, converting them to Spanish pesetas, then to British pounds.

He had filed and reviewed countless reports of people and places involved in the ratline business. Everything for sale. Passports. Birth certificates. Visas. Work permits. Contacts. Those with the biggest bankrolls first in line. Harry and his British equivalents took bets over their morning tea: "What price an Argentine visa today?" Big money. Chances better than even, Eve Battersby's husband in the thick of it. A people-smuggler. A profiteer. Who was Harry Douglas to destroy a woman's loving image of her dead husband?

He had heard the arguments for mercy over vengeance, the wisdom of letting matters rest, its strongest proponents seated at Buckingham Palace and among the British House of Lords. But he did not buy it. The men he was after tortured and murdered thousands of innocent people, many of their victims shoved into unmarked graves without name or origin. He saw the photographs of Buchenwald and Dachau and witnessed the reality of Neuengamme near Hamburg. Pits full of bones and blackened corpses. He was there at its liberation by British soldiers in April

1945, responsible for interrogating the remaining guards and camp personnel. They were relieved that the British—not the Red—Army arrived first. The Russians would have shown them no mercy. It was there Harry realized the enormity of their crimes. To think they would evade justice sickened him. Evil must be fought. Those who provided safe haven or played a role in their freedom, he would not spare. They, too, should have their reckoning.

He tightened the knot in his tie and stooped beneath the crack for a better view. His body was tense, unhappy. He made a fist and struck the frame of the door. No doubt, he missed the intelligence service. It was everything he had ever wanted. It would never disappear from his thoughts. This afternoon confirmed it once more. But tonight he was a gambler. A restless wanderer, a character aiming for a score. He would make himself agreeable to whomever sat at the table.

Last night, as was his plan, Harry held back, finished in the middle of the pack. His thousand-pound buy-in, and a necessary surplus, intact. For a change, he liked the others. Most of them. Except the Frenchman. Serious players. Amiable enough. All of a certain class, more than able to manage the table fee. He filed away each player's habits, accessible when the right time came.

Paul LaFont, smooth Belgian wine merchant, bushy moustache that disguised a cleft lip, a tendency to mumble his bet. Blinked furiously when he liked what he saw.

Oliver Drake, stuffy Dover shipbuilder, thick eyeglasses and meticulously manicured nails. Examined them an instant longer when unsure whether to fold or stay.

Pierre Bergeron, arrogant French industrialist, a more frequent player than the rest, making him harder to read and more careless with his bets. Used his cigarette holder as a prop before a big play.

Lorenzo Scarpa, burly Milanese construction magnate, never looked up from his cards, spoke only to place his bet or to his sullen companion seated at the door, away from the action—whose only responsibilities were to light Scarpa's cigars and fetch cold towels to wipe the man's forehead after every hand.

Their host, Donald Hamilton, stately Scotsman of considerable wealth and old-fashioned courtesy, proud veteran of the Royal Scots Regiment, renowned for scrupulous manners and expensive iced bourbons. A gentleman who never told the same story twice. Harry suspected he was a good warrior in a fight, though definitely a poor player at the table.

No clear winner the first night, though Scarpa's chip count looked highest, Drake's lower than the rest. At the end of the night, no one counted. No cheaters among them. At least none that Harry could discern.

Harry drew back the curtains and pried up the sash, inhaling a breath of damp air. A light drizzle clung to the windows. At twenty minutes to nine, Harry turned off the light, grabbed his hat and went downstairs to hail a taxi. He welcomed a warm spring rain, and he was tempted to walk. But a damp hat and coat would generate questions, and he did not wish the others to inquire about his lodging arrangements.

He arrived in time to ask at the desk whether Reverend Gordon had returned.

"Aye, sir, you're in luck," said the clerk. "The Reverend Gordon is in the cocktail lounge, waiting for a lady. You should find him there. "

Waiting for Eve? He hoped she was not that foolish. What have I done? A knot in his stomach, Harry checked his watch. Ten minutes. Time for, at the least, a look.

The bar was not crowded, and Harry spotted them right away at a table near an alcove in the wall, engaged in conversation. The two were seated opposite one another, the woman's back to Harry, a broad-brimmed hat covering her head and much of her shoulders. Gordon lounged in the club chair, twirling a pair of eyeglasses in his left hand.

Harry sat down two tables away, close enough to overhear, far enough not to draw undue attention. He pretended to check his pockets. A quick glance in their direction caught her profile. Then she turned, and he caught her full face. Not Eve. Thank God, not Eve.

The woman wore a finely tailored spring suit with mid-calf skirt, matching silver bracelet and necklace, fashionable low-heeled shoes. Not a natural beauty, but attractive—pale complexion, angular jaw, full mouth painted a dark red, a chic dark bob, slim. One elbow on the table, she stared at the bright red tip of her cigarette. The fingers on her other hand drummed the table.

Gordon spoke. "Hotel registers? Yes, the major ones at least. No sign of her. Too many inns in the center city to cover. I'll have Karl check the railway stations. Tomorrow's outbounds. Not that he wants anything more to do with trains. He'll want a bonus for that last job. Where are you staying?"

"At the North British. Atop the railway station. Easy in and out. No word on the man with her on the train? Of course, we've not much to go on except Karl's description."

They lifted their glasses silently and drank. The woman took small sips from her glass, long puffs on her cigarette. Head tilted, she shot the smoke toward the ceiling. Then, crossed her legs and smoothed her skirt—just so. "We need those travel documents. Everything else is in place. Names, places, dates of birth invented.

Payments already in the account. Have been for months. No installments with this bunch. They're getting nervous. They've been told—as have we—that Perón will pass the general amnesty for illegals in July. We promised to get them there by then. For a tidy extra fee, of course. Miguel Fonde's agency is expecting them. I've arranged accommodations and passages to Argentina the first week in June. Just the six men. Out of San Sebastian. Families to follow. Thoroughly planned, but they need time to get there. Damn it. We need those passports and identification documents. All of them."

The woman grabbed Gordon's hand. "My God, Will, everything was going smoothly. The network tight. No holes. Until Otis decided—" She broke off the sentence. "For God's sake. What was he thinking? Where did she find those passports? We couldn't find them, could we? The bonds the big boy promised us for our trouble, where are they? Perhaps little Miss Texas is planning a travel agency of her own."

"No," Gordon said simply, releasing his hand from hers. "We've encountered a bit of a bump in a long, prosperous road. From her remarks the other day, she knows next to nothing. She is suspicious about Otis's death, that's all. We can fix that."

"I'm not convinced," the woman disagreed.

"Do you suppose she's gone back to London?" asked Gordon. "Karl follows her habits. He must have an idea where she would be."

"She's got to be in Edinburgh somewhere. Not Karl. She'll recognize him. Leave it to me."

Harry stiffened and studied the tabletop, careful not to look in their direction. When they turned their attention to the barman to order another drink, he slipped away. Their exchange alarmed him. Christ. It's Eve they're after. Karl, the man on the train. Son of a bitch. He must be in Edinburgh. How long will it be before they find her? What are their plans once they do? They're not throwing a party. Who is that woman?

He had to warn Eve. If they find out where she is staying, Agnes, too, could be in harm's way. At a break in the action, he would call Mick.

Chapter Eleven

Eve lowered herself into the tub, the water as hot as she could stand. Her brain, addled by three whiskeys and a full package of cigarettes, was good and drunk. Upon her return to the inn, Eve had parked herself on the stairs, unable to lift her leaden legs high enough to climb one more riser. Agnes had led her to her room and drawn her bath while Eve placed her recent purchases in the armoire and, on drunken impulse, rearranged her overnight bag. At the bottom of the bag, she found three additional photographs—the first, a grim face, baggy eyes, fleshy jowls; the second, a young man, considerably more handsome, white skin, dark slicked hair with a severe center part, light eyes; the last, a stout man, thick neck, close-cut blond hair, a thin-membraned wart on his chin. Like the photo Harry identified, all carried labels on the back. She recognized their faces, if not the names. Brief flashes of memory. Nothing exact. The younger man had lunched with them one day at the Prado Cafe and joined them for an afternoon bullfight. The other two, together, were frequent visitors at their dining table. In a fit of temper, she snatched the photos from the bag, crumpled them tight in her fist, and hurled them into the wastebasket.

The questions remained. She could not discard them so easily.

She let the water close in around her, soothe her. It will change me. Learning something troublesome about Otis. Broken trust is rarely repaired. Three failed marriages have shown me that truth. What do I know? Nothing really. Am I in a state of ignorant denial? I want to understand. Nothing will be too much, if only I know. Had I known Otis so thinly? Never. Could it have been simply a few months of mad desire? Eve was more than familiar with that sensation. Even so, today she could not discount Harry's remarks. Tomorrow. Tomorrow she would find a way to prove them wrong.

She awoke in the night, trembling, her head aching. She grappled with their faces, their easy laughter. She had not understood their jokes, but they had been kind and attentive. More so to Otis, touching his lapel, whispering to him, filling his glass. She had thought them businessmen, wealthy art patrons of Madrid. She heard the strong resonance of Otis's voice, saw his lips moving across the table, telling her as much.

Why do I question the truth of it now? If those men wanted something as significant as their freedom—as their lives—why would they want to see Otis dead?

On unsteady legs, she walked barefoot to the window, parting the sheer curtains. The house was dark and quiet. By the light of the streetlamps, the spires of St. Mary's Cathedral loomed, heavy shadows in the night.

One deception. But whose? The Reverend Gordon's or Otis's? If one, there must be others. She had opened the door. She now had to decide whether to step over the threshold.

It was only the hour and blackness of the night that kept her from walking out and boarding the next train back to London.

!!!!!

15 May 1949. She arose early, anxious—excited even—to get started. After a quick breakfast, Agnes gave her directions to *The Scotsman* headquarters building on the North Bridge. Her new boots and coat, comfortable and light, allowed her to walk the considerable distance between the inn and the newspaper archives. The morning was cool, gray clouds low in the sky, air moist on her face. She left from the back door of the inn, followed the cobblestoned path from Gloucester Lane, and descended onto Queen Street. Steeper at the top, the lane leveled out as it proceeded south to the Queen's Gardens. From there, she walked east for the length of George Street, emerging at St. Andrew's Square with a clear view of Princes Street, the north end of the North Bridge. She had not expected to see the North British Hotel on the corner. Having taken a taxi to the hotel bar yesterday, she paid little attention to its route. After a few drinks, she scarcely remembered the return ride to the Gloucester Inn. Now, here stood the North British, convenient enough for a second visit after her work. She rubbed her temples and resolved to switch from whiskey to martinis.

She approached *The Scotsman's* magnificent old Gothic building—its thirteen-story pale-gray facade as formidable to Eve as the business inside. Each floor twelve windows across. The American press and the newspaper trade intimidated her, particularly after Nolan Pierce's run-in with the law. The persistent investigative reporters who uncovered Nolan's embezzlement, as well as the company's illegal record keeping, encamped across the street from their Dallas home until Nolan was led away for trial. While she was not overly fond of Nolan Pierce—a good-looking charmer with a Texas drawl and dozens of pairs of handmade Lucchese ostrich boots—she could not think kindly of the newspaper business that exposed his guilt. Nolan marked another mistake in her long list of lovers. And husbands. Repeatedly, she seemed to confuse good looks and good character. After a certain age, did such distinctions matter? In any case, she wasn't much good at either. Finally, Otis had seemed the exception. The primary reason, perhaps, for refusing to believe the worst of him.

She climbed the broad stone steps of the towering headquarters. The building was nearly a block long and almost as high. Behind her, horns blaring, engines rattling, the morning traffic crisscrossed the North Bridge. In the doorway, she stood a moment to secure the envelope of photos and notes she clutched in her gloved hand. In her bag, she carried a notebook and collection of pencils. At the top of the stairs, she made her way through the grand wooden doors into a cavernous entrance hall, marbled and brightly lit, smelling of old paper and floor polish. As she walked, the heels of her boots rang out against the floor.

"Which floor, madam?" asked the guard to her left. He and a similarly uniformed colleague stood inside a massive semicircular desk looking as if they were surrounded by the stump of an ancient oak.

"I'm looking for the newspaper archives, the library," she said.

"Very good, madam. The library is located on the fourth floor. Exit the lift. Turn to your right." The guard pointed to the stand of elevators.

"Do you happen to know the time the library closes?" she asked.

"I do, madam. Announcement is made at half five. The library is locked tight precisely at six o'clock."

"And the rest of the building?" she asked.

"After six, the building is restricted to staff members." The second guard handed her a badge. He watched as she pinned it to her coat.

"Yesterday afternoon I inquired to set aside a list of research materials," she added.

"The fourth floor it is, madam. You'll find the research department in Room 406."

The elevator creaked upward. When Eve exited, she was overwhelmed by the labyrinth of corridors, a maze-like entanglement. Turning right, as instructed, she walked a little way down and found herself standing in the doorway to Room 406. Endless rows of long dark walnut tables, shaded reading lamps at regular intervals, filled the room. Wooden benches on the perimeter. A vast space. Here and there, patrons sat or stood at the tables, poring over books and newspaper pages. She located the research librarian she had spoken to the day before. The librarian sat behind a large steel desk pecking at the keys of a bulky typewriter, a single sheet of paper in the roller. When the bell sounded to mark the end of the row she was typing, the woman tilted up her chin, and looked at Eve.

"We have a full collection of both *The Scotsman* and *The Times* of London," said the librarian. Mrs. Cora Kilbride, a small woman in an official-looking jacket and skirt, made slighter by the room's enormity, eyed Eve over the rim of her glasses. She wore a brass name tag with deeply etched black letters. "Mrs. Kicklighter, is it? Your request covered the later period of the war, 1943 to the present, for both Edinburgh and London. Is that correct?"

"Yes, if I may start there," said Eve.

"That's not a wee bit of reading you'll be doing. How long do you plan on staying with us?"

"Until I finish my research," Eve replied. She patted the envelope in her hand.

"We are here to assist. May I ask if you are searching for a particular question?" the librarian inquired.

Eve was still unsure about the questions to the answers she sought. "Oh, just odd things. I need to look through a number of items to be sure." She sounded less purposeful than she intended.

Mrs. Kilbride drew in her chin and nodded. "Well then. Let us secure a vacant set of tables." In front of her, she pushed a library cart, four shelves thick with folders. At a table situated in the middle of the room near a bank of windows, she unloaded the cart, placing the materials in chronological order, January 1943 to April 1949, in a row along the whole of the table's surface. Then a second row. And a third. When she finished, she made a brisk walk back to the beginning of the line of folders and drew a large round black stamp from the pocket of her skirt. She held the stamp's handle high in the air, poised and ready to strike.

In that voice reserved for official government business, Mrs. Kilbride announced, "On this date, 15 May 1949, these materials are hereby granted to you in loan, madam. They shall not be removed from this space. You are responsible for their care until such time as they are returned to the archival library. With permission, you may leave them in their present state of arrangement overnight." The librarian then marched down the rows of folders, stamping in dramatic fashion, the upper right outside corner of each. A quick thump accompanied each pump of the librarian's arm. At the end of the last row, the stamp disappeared into the librarian's pocket. Without a backward glance, she wheeled around the now-empty cart and marched away.

Only then did Eve realize the scale of the task before her. She had to laugh. She had not envisioned the extent of it. She chided herself for neglecting so basic a thought. Indeed, she should have counted the number of days, hence newspapers, from January 1943 to April 1949. Two thousand three hundred ten, to be exact. At least the folders were organized by week. Three hundred thirty. She needn't look at them all. Not if she found right away what she was looking for. But what am I looking for? The photos. Of course. I'm looking to match the photos. Or recognize a face.

With a quiet word of resolve, she removed her newly acquired coat, draped it on the back of an adjacent chair, sat down, and opened the first folder, arranging its contents, seven thin folded newspapers, on the surface of the table. Carefully, she unfolded each paper and scanned the pages for pictures and headlines. For the most part, the articles included only text. Photos on the front page generally showed damage from bombings or images from the battlefronts. In the interior, pictures of local young men as they enlisted or packages sent by their families. The occasional drawing or comic appeared on the back page. As for headlines, two-thirds of them related to the war's progress. The remainder—rationing, weather, community events, recipes.

This may not be too very difficult after all, she thought. A couple of days will suffice.

By the time she reached the folder for mid-June 1943, Eve had settled into a steady rhythm. While she found nothing of personal interest, she at least felt comfortable in her method. She managed to learn quite a lot about the conditions of the war, its progress and its effects on the Scottish and English populace. In spite of herself, she was intrigued by the information she read, and disturbed by how much she did not know. More so, by the silence with which she had accepted it.

The clock over her head read half past one. Eyes weary, Eve walked to the end of the third table, surveying the long line of tidy folders, marveling at the hours involved in their organization.

Seated once more, she picked up *The Scotsman* folder for mid-July 1943, laid flat the newspapers for each date, scanned the headlines and the photos on the front pages, then, one by one, opened the interior pages. Accustomed to quick scanning, she at first passed over the photograph at the bottom of page two of 14 July 1943. A second look caused her pause. Three familiar figures emerged. Smiling for the camera, the men sat together around a restaurant table, drinks in hand. A lengthy caption beneath the picture explained. "The Reverend Canon Will Gordon of St. Mary's Cathedral, Edinburgh, dined with Captains Otis Battersby and Thomas Jasper of London. Friends since childhood, the men met last evening at The Caledonian's Pompadour Restaurant for cocktails and dinner reminiscent of prewar Edinburgh. On a short leave from their posts, Captains Battersby and Jasper are assigned to the 10th Armoured Division (formerly the 1st Cavalry) under the command of Major-General Horace Birks."

White-knuckled, she gripped the page and reread the caption, assuring its meaning. On impulse, she jerked out of her seat, snatched the page, almost ripping it from the adjoining pages, and walked hurriedly to the research desk.

She pointed to the photograph. With an unsteady hand, she held it out to the librarian. "Do you know this man?" Eve's voice carried throughout the cavernous room. A dozen heads lifted.

The librarian surveyed the room. Wrinkling her brow, she brought an index finger to her lips and nodded. "Yes," she whispered.

Eve waited. Sensing another question and a semblance of self-control were required, she asked, more quietly this time, "Who is he, and how do you know him?"

"As the caption reads, he is indeed the Reverend Canon at St. Mary's Cathedral where I am a member and attend services," the woman replied. She laid her hand beneath Gordon's photo. "His hair is a wee bit grayer these days. For a man his age, it is unusual."

"Do you know the other two men?" Eve continued.

"No, madam," said the librarian. "Once again, their names are listed here. I've no reason to doubt the text as written. Do you?"

Eve sighed heavily, the beginning of a film in her eyes. "No, no reason at all."

No reason other than the Right Reverend lied about knowing Thomas Jasper. Childhood friends. The three of them. From Otis's remarks, she had the firm impression he considered Will Gordon no more than a brief professional acquaintance. Another lie?

In her notebook, she jotted her findings. She wanted to record everything she could remember. After her notes, she added three questions. Now that Otis is dead, what is the relationship between Thomas Jasper and Will Gordon? Why did Gordon lie to me about knowing Thomas? What was the money for Gordon really about?

iiiii

At half five, when the closing announcement was made, Eve tidied the stacks of folders, packed her bag, donned her coat and gloves, and headed for the elevator. On her way out the door, she handed her badge to the guard. "Save this one for me. I'll need it tomorrow," she said.

"No luck today, madam?" he asked.

"You might say that," said Eve with a faint smile. She remembered Harry's comment on the train. Luck has nothing to do with it.

Chapter Twelve

"You know what they say about chasing green-eyed women, Harry. It's madness." Mick MacLeod wiped a few drops from the counter and placed a glass down hard, emphasizing his point. Mick had always enjoyed intruding on Harry's love interests.

"No chasing intended. No madness involved. The woman is in danger. I'm sure of it. At least three people are trying to find her. I'd like to know why." Harry described the exchange in the lounge to Kate and Mick, but neither had any notion of the woman's identity. "I don't want any of them showing up at Agnes's inn asking questions. They said they had tried all the hotel registers. If they're serious about finding Eve, someone will be scouring the inns for her."

"No worries. I called Mum this morning. Told her what you said. You know she'll not be giving information about any of her guests," said Kate.

"And Eve? Did she tell her?' asked Harry.

"Mum said she'd already gone for the day. Off to *The Scotsman* archives this morning," replied Kate.

"*The Scotsman*?" said Harry. "The big Gothic next to the Waverly railway station?"

"That's the one," said Mick.

Mick barely finished his sentence before Harry jumped from the stool and bolted for the door.

"Where the devil are you going? You've not finished your beer. Harry. Harry. The building will be closed at this hour," Mick called after him, his voice trailing off at the sound of the door slamming shut.

In one dismissive motion, Kate flung the soapsuds from her hands. "Madness it is. What's come over the man? A bit crazed, he is." She turned her head to her husband. "To be sure, she is a green-eyed beauty, Mick. But, our Harry. For all his fineness, he's always been a bit of a rogue."

Chapter Thirteen

As he ran, Harry gripped the crown of his hat. He had to intercept Eve, but the light had grown dim and the wind whipped his eyes so that, on the opposite street, he could not distinguish one pedestrian from another. When he reached *The Scotsman's* entry steps and stopped to catch his breath, it was after six o'clock. The building's doors locked, he could make out a faint lamp in the ground-floor windows. He pounded on the doors, hoping to rouse one of the guards.

Even if she's not here, they have to know what time she left.

The pounding brought no response. After a few minutes, he turned back to the bridge, retraced his steps, and skirted the traffic.

She had to come this way. At least over the bridge to the station. Then, she would turn to the left. Here, onto Princes Street.

A sharp cold rain began to fall. When he saw the North British Hotel's red entry flags whipping overhead, he slowed his pace, looking for the nearest entry. He would take shelter until the rain stopped. He shook the water from his hat and surveyed the lobby, eyes adjusting to the half-light, hoping to catch a glimpse of the woman he had seen last night at the Caledonian. Unlike its busy lobby, this one was near empty, only the bellmen milling about.

Following a trail of voices from a hallway to his left, Harry arrived at the entrance to a lounge area. A higher-end watering hole than the Caledonian. Men in gray suits. The well-heeled crowd ran two deep at the bar, smoke curling above their heads, drinks in hand. A friendly nod from the bartender and an anonymous nudge from behind propelled Harry forward so that he found himself wedged between two stools, leaning over the bar counter.

"Macallan, neat," said Harry, straining his voice to be heard above the din.

"I figured you for martinis, very dry, Mr. Douglas," said a familiar voice. From her seat at the end of the bar, Eve met his gaze, raised her glass in his direction, and took a sip.

"You figured wrong. Not the first time, I might add," said Harry.

"Is that some sort of apology?" she inquired.

"Not likely," he replied.

"Now that we've cleared the air, what are you doing here?" Eve edged aside so that Harry could stand in the space next to the stool.

"What are *you* doing here?" he moved closer, catching a whiff of her perfume.

"I'm having a martini, don't you see? Maybe I'm having two. Maybe I'm having a martini every hour," she said, her voice flat, her hand shaking as she set the glass on the counter. "Now you. I asked you first."

"I'm having a whiskey." He stood silent for a moment, watching her fidget, then added casually. "And I'm looking for you."

"I thought we discussed all that nonsense yesterday," she said, holding his eyes.

"You were angry. Understandably. I said too much," said Harry.

"Now that really does sound like an apology," she said, a playful note in her voice. "You came all the way here to say that?"

Without a hint of humor, he said, "There's more. I understand you spent the day in the newspaper archives."

"I did," she said. "Tomorrow as well."

"Find anything interesting?" he asked.

Her frivolous tone disappeared. "I did find something curious today, but I'm not ready to talk about it. I have to think about where it might lead. I may need your help later. If you're willing. If you're still around," she added.

Her not-so-subtle inquiries brought no response. Instead, he said, "Eve, listen to me. You must let me help you. There are at least two people looking for you. For what purpose, I don't know. One of them is this Will Gordon. The other is a woman. Last night, I overheard a conversation between them. It was clear they were speculating where you might be, whether or not you had returned to London."

"A woman. What sort of woman?"

"Definitely sounded as if she knew you and your late husband. Has to be from out of town because she said she was staying here at the North British," said Harry. "Lucky I found you before she did."

"What in God's name does she look like?" Eve asked.

Before he could launch into a description, the bartender handed Harry his whiskey. "She's slim. Wore a wide-brimmed hat and traveling suit, stylish. Nothing fancy, but classy. Silver jewelry. Again, nothing showy, but good quality. Short dark hair, cut properly, curls around her face. Red lipstick. Pale skin. Unblemished. Attractive face."

Not beautiful like yours, he thought. *No comparison*. "Smoked cigarettes."

"Anything else?" Eve asked.

"Nice legs," he added.

She sniffed, narrowed her eyes at him, and took another sip from her glass. "Good lord. That description sounds like half the women in London, or Edinburgh, for that matter. Although the Scots are a very long way from fashion conscious. Was there an accent? Low country? Midlands?"

"Funny thing. I'm pretty good at picking up on those. I couldn't tell from her speech pattern. She spoke with almost stilted precision. As if she had taken elocution lessons. Definitely British," Harry stopped in mid-sentence and nudged Eve's shoulder.

Through the smoky haze that billowed up from the bar, Eve and Harry watched as Myrna Stewart walked the length of the room and back, seemingly searching for a vacant table or chair. Finding every seat and much of the standing room occupied by men in business suits, she approached a smartly dressed young man near the door and held out her hands—a gesture of concession. With the young man at her side, Myrna turned and scanned the room once more, pointing here and there at tables where patrons talked or lounged. In any case, unready to depart.

An instant before Myrna looked in Eve's direction, Eve swiveled her stool away, unnerved, hiding her face. Harry stepped sideways, positioning himself in front of Eve, blocking her from Myrna's view. She could not possibly identify him.

"That's the one," he said under his breath. "Don't move. They've done searching and gone back to the entry."

Eve snatched up her bag and slid from the stool. "I must get out of here."

Harry held her wrist and laid it gently, but firmly, on the counter. "Steady. Don't rush. Wait until we're sure they've retreated from the entry. Then, I'll lead the way."

Harry settled the tab. Eve slipped on her coat and stood behind him, shielded, willing her feet not to flee.

"Who is she?" he asked, guiding her toward the exit. The doorman closed the door after them. Quickly, they descended the steps and crossed the street toward St. Andrews Square. The rain had stopped, leaving, in the faint twilight, dozens of purple clouds on the western sky.

When they reached the Melville Monument in the center of the square, Eve found a dry bench under the pergola and eased herself down. "Her name is Myrna Stewart," Eve said. "She's the woman you saw last night with Gordon?"

"The very same. Tell me about her. Everything you know," said Harry.

"I can't, Harry," she said quietly. Shattered by the day's events, she sat with her hands in her lap and began to sob. "I'm completely ruined. I don't know anything. I came here because I loved Otis. To settle things for him. But nothing is as I know it. I'm beginning to believe I haven't any idea about Otis's work, or life, for that matter. And whatever I think I know about Myrna Stewart is likely to be wrong."

Harry bent to her. With a flourish, he shook the handkerchief from his pocket, and wiped her face. "What did you find today that disturbed you?"

"A newspaper photograph of the three of them. Otis, Thomas, Gordon. Drinking, dining, laughing. The caption named them childhood friends." She drew a deep breath, "He lied. For what reason? I would have believed anything. Do you suppose he knew I wanted everything he said to be true?"

When Harry did not answer her question, she slid sideways, and Harry sat down on the bench. It was almost nine o'clock. In ten minutes, he would be late for the game.

"Tomorrow, I can meet you at the archives," said Harry. "We'll work together. Now, I'll get you a cab back to Agnes's."

She refused both offers. "I'm perfectly capable of finding a cab. Or walking. After I sit for a few minutes," she said.

Reluctantly, he stood and stepped back from the bench. "Eve, be careful."

"How many times have you told me that, Harry? Go." She pointed in several directions. "Go," she repeated.

Before he rounded the corner, he caught a last glimpse of her silhouette, motionless on the bench. In retrospect, he should have insisted she take a cab back to the inn. He somehow understood her reaction would be anything but positive.

Chapter Fourteen

The square was still and dark, the night air cut with the sweet scent of fresh honeysuckle. Last calls surely done. Unlike London's private clubs, alive with patrons until dawn, Edinburgh's pubs closed before midnight, the city's streets emptying shortly thereafter. Parking lots bare. Businesses shuttered. Trolleys stored for the night. Cabs in under abundance.

Her fingers and toes were cold, but Eve decided to walk, unsure how long she had dozed. By the light of the full moon and the intermittent streetlamps, she was relatively certain she could find the route. Up to Queen Street. A path up the hill through the Gardens. Gloucester Lane at the far end.

A chance to put the day in order, undisturbed.

The nap had cleared her head, distanced her—not entirely, she knew, but somewhat—from the raw sting of betrayal. At any rate, she resolved to put aside her feelings and examine what she had discovered thus far. She reminded herself that when she chose to pursue this investigation into Otis's death, she had made a private promise. She would not go back on it. When things got tough, she would not dash for the quickest exit. She would track the story where it led. No matter the outcome.

She wondered how she had been so wrong. How she had allowed herself to be deceived. How many betrayals were left to discover?

On the corner, she passed the imposing yellow columns of the National Portrait Gallery and crossed to the north side of Queen Street. Beyond the sidewalk, the Gardens' pebbled paths forked left and right. She took the left fork and, on a slight incline, proceeded up a hill through a stand of trees. Within a few yards, the faint glow of the streetlamps disappeared into the chestnut boughs, and she found herself guided only by the moon's pale light and the scrunch of gravel under her boots. At the top of the low hill, the path divided once more—one heavily wooded, one lightly so. The heavily wooded path lacked all light, and so she chose the moonlit way, though now unsure that its direction would take her on the western course she required. The path was full of shadows, and she planted her feet deliberately, feeling her way. She could no longer see the street, but she heard the clink of a car door closing, the high sound of a far-away siren that sounded like an air raid warning. How on earth did she lose the path? She listened harder for sounds to orient her way. In the almost eerie silence, she heard a hushed shuffling and, afterwards, the soft twittering of night birds in the trees.

Less confident now, she stumbled forward a few steps on the dimly lighted path until she became aware—ahead or behind, she was not sure—of the low murmur of conversation. She stopped to make certain. Yes, ahead, two voices. Buoyed by the thought of assistance, her pace quickened. The faint beam of a flashlight shone on the path, and she discovered, to her relief, a uniformed constable standing behind the beam, in the middle of the path.

When she approached, she called to him, “You are a welcome sight. I fear I’ve taken a wrong turn. Can you direct me to Heriot Row? Or Queen Street? I need to get to the west end of the park.”

He turned to face her, and in a thick Scottish accent, replied, “Of course, madam. May I inquire what it is you’d be doing in the Gardens at this early hour? Edinburgh is safe enough, but there are dangers about, natural and otherwise. A single lady such as yourself rambling about in the wee hours. You must take better care.” He eyed her up and down, taking in her handbag and coat pockets.

“Is it the wee hours, Constable? I must say, I’ve lost track of the time.” Eve had no desire to admit she had fallen asleep on a park bench. At the same time, she did not want a police constable to assume she was posing as a night burglar. “I’m trying to reach Gloucester Lane. I’m not familiar with the Gardens and mistakenly thought I could walk straight through from one end to the other, east to west.”

“Follow me, if you will, to the gate on the north side. From there, it’s a short walk to the west end on Heriot Row, which is lighted, madam. Without the fog, you’ll easily find the way.” When they reached the gate, he opened it to let her pass, then stood on the curb and searched the deserted street—first left, then right. “Not many cabs in the small hours, madam. You’re all right, then? I can walk you to the corner, if you’d prefer.”

The small hours. A charming way to describe them, she thought.

“You’ve been more than helpful, Constable. I’ll be fine from here. You’re right about the streetlamps. I can almost see the lane up on the right." In the renewed light, she saw he was a smooth-faced young man, evidently new to the job and lowest on the duty schedule. She thanked him again and turned away before she thought to ask, "When I came upon you, I thought I heard two people talking. Was I mistaken?"

"No, madam. You'd be correct. Indeed, there was a man on the same path, just ahead of you. Said he was out for a stroll. I detected a bit of an accent. A foreign visitor, I gathered. Said he favored the early morning calm before the day's calamity begins." The constable touched his nightstick to the tip of his helmet. "A fine day to you, madam."

Eve felt the air disappear from her lungs. She had to get away quickly. She pulled her coat around her, tightened the belt at her waist, and squared her handbag on her shoulder. She searched the sidewalk and the street. Narrower than Queen, famed for its long crescent row of stunning townhouses, Heriot Row was all the same deserted, save an orange tabby meandering diagonally from one corner to the next. A tall hedgerow lined the other side of the street, and Eve thought it wise to keep to the south, adjacent to the park, until she reached the turn for Gloucester Lane.

At a brisk pace she walked, head down, afraid now of what or whom she might encounter, envisioning in punctuated scenes, the man on the train—his brush past her through the compartment door, the wrestle with Harry, the man's abrupt disappearance out the open door.

Surely, he's not the same man. In the small hours, one's imagination runs wild.

In any case, she knew he could not be outrun. Just ahead, on the left, a thick cluster of trees jutted out, a bulging trunk carving a half moon and a ripple in the sidewalk. To avoid it, she slowed and stepped onto the grass between lamppost and walkway. Soft from the evening's rain, the grass gave way, and Eve lost her footing, teetering on the edge of the curb. She slipped awkwardly onto the street and felt her ankle turn beneath her. When her knee hit the pavement, she cried out in pain.

In the dreary orange glow of the streetlamp, she scooted to the curb and gingerly pulled off her right boot. Rubbing her ankle, studying the ugly scrape on her knee, cursing the hour, she knew she could walk no farther. Already, she was unable to reapply her boot. She hoped the young constable's rounds brought him somewhere near her position. Otherwise, she anticipated watching her ankle swell and waiting for the morning dew to soak her through. *I should have taken Harry's suggestion*. The thought of yet another man hovering about—saving her, smothering her—stopped her cold.

At the very least, she thought she could hobble onto a garden bench and wait for the cab drivers' early shift. Not ten yards ago, she noticed a bench set back between the trees. Supported by one good leg, she inched her body up the lamppost. The bare toes of her right foot rested on the base of the post. She moved the foot and placed a limited amount of weight upon it.

"Ow, ow, ouch," she yelped. Each footstep was an effort. Cold trickles of sweat ran down her back and under her arms. Despite the painful throb in her ankle, she managed to weave her way from one tree to the next until she reached a tapered wooden bench wedged between two elms. She held on to a branch so she would not trip in the dark. Only after she eased down upon the seat and peered at her naked foot and ankle did she realize she had left her boot under the streetlamp. When she raised her head, she caught a slight movement among the trees to her left.

So swiftly done, she was not sure she had seen it. She closed her eyes, then opened them again. From the shadows came a quick regular inhalation, as if someone—or something—were out of breath and panting. Her heart nearly stopped when she saw the dark figure emerge, approaching her directly.

"Would this belong to you?" he asked.

Chapter Fifteen

The jarring pounding awakened her. She had been dreaming of him, and the immediacy of him at her door drove her body up from the bed. Sleepily wrapping the robe around her, scuffing into her slippers, she turned the knob and opened the door.

"Jesus, Karl," she grabbed his arm and pulled him smoothly into the room, "You've awakened the entire floor with that thumping. What in heaven's name are you doing in my bedroom at this hour? It's got to be four in the morning."

"You disappoint me, mein liebchen," he sneered. "You speak as if I've never before entered your bedroom."

"Forget that," she snapped. "What did you find?"

Karl sat at the foot of the bed and shook out a cigarette. "I spotted her and the scrapper on the street. Followed them to the square. They were in a hurry, so I figured to follow them to a hotel. After a few minutes, he left. Alone. Walked west to the corner. Odd. She stayed, asleep on the bench until after two. Then, she headed north through the Queen Street Gardens. I thought she had a meet. Early morning. No one about. Could have been a buyer, an informer. The Gardens are private. Just right for that sort of thing. She entered through an unlocked gate on the southeast end. I stayed back in the trees. Bad luck. I ran into a copper and had to come up with a line. After that, I was forced to take a different route." He shrugged. "When I doubled back, she was gone."

He struck a match, held it out, and inhaled until the cigarette tip burned red. Myrna moved closer, slid her right hand along his thigh, and lifted the cigarette, touching his wrist with her warm fingertips. She crossed the room to a side table, poured two glasses from the half-empty bottle of Dalmore, and held one out in his direction. In the mirror, she twirled a curl into place and caught his eye.

"So you lost her. We have no clue where she's staying. I told Will to let me handle her. She believes I'm her lovely friend. It's never dawned on her that Otis was mine. She was merely the cover when things got tense in Madrid. Never knew how trivial she was, poor dear." Myrna turned to face him, the gap in her robe widening, exposing the sleekness of her legs. In so many ways, she enjoyed tormenting him. She sat down and crossed her legs. A slipper dangled from her toes. "Who is he?"

"I don't know." Karl lit a cigarette for himself and inhaled, holding the smoke in his lungs until he felt the searing heat fill his chest.

"You must have some idea," she said. "Those wartime intelligence skills haven't completely disappeared." She smirked and twirled the swizzle stick in her whiskey. "Or have they? The seasoned assassin now an impotent bird. Judging from that nasty bruise on your cheek, your fall from the train caused a bit of damage. Is it possible?" She looked at the ceiling, silent for a moment. "Is he handsome? The one who threw you off? Could he be useful?"

"Never saw him until our encounter on the train. Confident chap. Not one to back off. A Yank, from the accent. North American, at least. He didn't throw me off. I jumped." He crushed out the cigarette in the ashtray he held in his free hand. "You think he wants me to dig around?"

"How would I know what he wants from you? You'll have to ask the Power Meister himself. He sent me to talk to Will, find Eve, and bring her back to London. From there, he will sweet-talk her into going back to America. After he's wrested most of Otis's money from her. Then, we'll get on with our business."

"Why not get rid of her permanently? That's the easier way." He stared at her legs and gnawed on his thumb.

"Because she's got Otis's money and God knows what else. Right now, she's simply an annoyance. Will's convinced she doesn't know anything. We expected you to scare her off, but look where that reasoning got us. You can't even recover the passports and travel documents. Not to mention those bonds we're owed. Why he keeps you around, I'll never know." She slumped further into the chair and turned toward the mirror, legs splayed, blowing smoke at her reflection, never taking her eyes from the mirror.

"Where did you get those glasses? They're hideous." She stood, turning her back to him, dropping the robe from her shoulders. She stretched, took one last drag from the cigarette and, on one foot, twirled around to face him. With a flick of her wrist, she tossed the burning butt into his open palm. "I need a bath."

His fist closed around the red-hot remnant, and he held it for a moment, squeezing the life from it before dropping it to the carpet. Slowly, he removed his eyeglasses, placed one lens in his mouth, and blew on it. He took the handkerchief from his pocket, wiped the lens clean and followed her into the bath.

Chapter Sixteen

"Why do you keep showing up?" Her voice caught on the phrase. She had planned to sound much braver, but her state of mind matched the tone of her voice.

"Just lucky, I guess," he responded, handing her the boot.

"How did you find me?" she asked wearily. "I was trying to be invisible."

"Don't ask directions from young constables," he countered.

"If I were a suspicious person—which I didn't used to be, but find that I am becoming so—I'd think you've been following me. First, the inn, then last night at the bar, now this. How else could one explain such coincidences?" Eve tried to stand.

Harry bent over her, took her elbow and helped her as she rose on one leg. He knew he had to level with her, at least in part. "No coincidence. Simple explanation. I was concerned. What sort of chap leaves a woman sitting alone on a park bench on a stormy night? I almost lost my shirt thinking about it. Couldn't concentrate. Game over, I stopped at Mick's. Agnes had called him earlier, worried when you didn't turn up. So,

I went to Agnes's, backtracked to St. Andrews and picked a street. Before I'd gone too far, I ran into a bobby, asked a few questions, and circled around the Gardens until I found something."

"Someone should have warned me about Edinburgh's closing times. No cabs. No trolleys. Not a soul on the street. I got a little lost. What if I had decided to spend the night at some frivolous activity? Stumble home in the early hours a happy woman?"

"I hope you got all that frivolity in before you broke your ankle," he said.

"It's not broken," she snapped. "I slipped off the curb in the dark. That's all. Nothing that can't be fixed. I'm back to work tomorrow. Today, I mean. Just help me get home—to the inn." Inexplicably, she wrapped her arms around him and said, "You're always rescuing me, Harry. I hate that."

Harry scoured the street. "Take the day off. The whole of the day. Tomorrow I'll go with you to the research room," he said. A lone cab, the morning's first, appeared on the opposite side, and he whistled for it.

"I have an appointment with the Prints and Photographs section," she said. "They're expecting me. I must be there by ten o'clock. Else they're gone, off to Glasgow for the week." She did not intend to spend the day with her foot propped on a pillow.

A thin morning light shown through the trees as he helped her into the cab.

"Eve, stay inside. I'm serious." He held her wrist, insistent.

"I'll give it some thought," she said.

iiiii

"She's okay. Cabbie took her to Agnes's." Harry leaned against the doorjamb and loosened the knot in his tie. He had been reluctant to let her go, could not dismiss the knowledge of potential danger.

"You always were a sucker for a good-looking woman." Mick sat up, rubbed his chest and yawned.

"It's not like that. Not this time. It's not that empty. There's something about this husband of hers." Harry clapped a hand on Mick's shoulder and dropped into the adjacent chair. "C'mon, you need to sleep. It's after dawn."

"Still time for a nightcap, chum." Mick walked to a cabinet behind the bar, uncapped a bottle of Glen Grant single malt and poured them both a drink. He placed the bottle on the table between them. "How's the game?"

"No concentration tonight. Couldn't make any ground, but didn't lose much. Tonight's the last round. I think Hamilton's had enough."

"You really make a living at this?" Mick cocked his head and stared at his friend.

"The truth? I do. Not much purpose to it. Nothing but patience and watchfulness required. And a grand tolerance for whiskey and smoke-filled rooms. We came away from Ethiopia with those skills, didn't we?" Harry drained his shot, and Mick poured him another.

"Ethiopia," Mick almost spat the word. "Those dilettantes in Section Six."

Harry shook his head—no need to explain. There were stories he and Mick kept between themselves. Did not talk of. He still felt the burning in his throat.

It was October 1935 when Mussolini's elite Alpini forces attacked Ethiopia, dropped poison gas on tens of thousands of men, women, and children. Then they raped and slaughtered thousands more. Some, including Harry, called it the real beginning of World War II, a first test of Italian and German warfare. Five years later, in September 1940, Harry and Mick provided advance information to British forces at the Battle of Dakar—though it did little to save them from defeat. Through December, they had been assigned to Khartoum to gather information for the Gideon Force—the mix of British and Africans who, by May 1941, drove out the Italians and reestablished Haile Selassie as emperor. While they were not witness to the early years of that war, Harry and Mick saw enough of its results, the massacres and bombings. Mick blamed much of the suffering and use of the banned poison gas on the upper echelons of British government, arguing it sacrificed the Ethiopian people for its alliances in Europe.

"Hadn't thought about Dakar in a while. Khartoum either." Harry's voice softened. That day in Dakar, vivid and searing, would follow him into the ground. Caught in the memory, he felt the trigger on the tip of his fingers, the weight of the rifle on his shoulder. Mick on his right, firing like a madman, round after round, keeping the Alpini force from them until Harry could send their dispatches. Then, keeping each other alive through the night. Wave upon wave of men, falling as they ran. Unremittingly, as though it would never cease. The powerlessness of it, though he was the one with the rifle. The dead silence that came after nearly ruined him.

"Let go of it." Mick smiled slowly at his friend. "It's done."

"Ghosts catch up with you eventually," said Harry.

"That they do, but not today. Get some sleep. She'll be doing the same."

"She's not easily persuaded." Harry tapped his fingers on the table.

"You're not her keeper," said Mick.

"Not trying to be. She needs protection. They're capable of anything. You know that. She doesn't."

The two men sat together, shoulders hunched, finishing their drinks.

Finally, Mick said, "I'm done. Lock the door on your way out." He headed for the stairs. When his foot reached the first step, he turned and grinned. "You always were a stubborn sot."

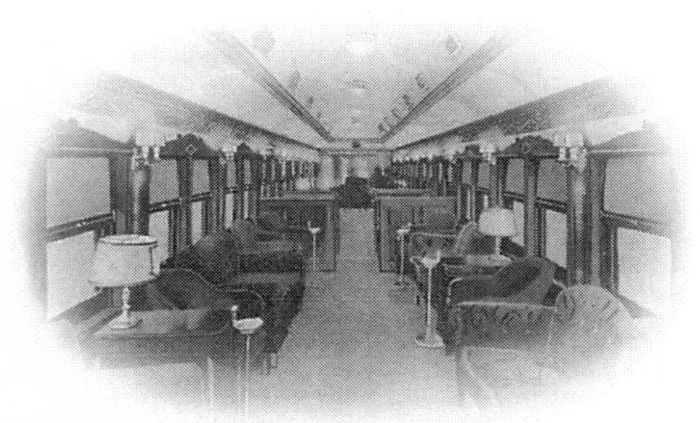

Chapter Seventeen

16 May 1949. The day arrived with a slow steady rain, a constant patter on the glass. At precisely half past nine, Eve limped down the walk to the waiting taxi, Agnes's best umbrella in hand. Eve's data journal, crammed with notes and photos, bulged from her bag. Initially, Agnes mounted mild resistance against Eve's departure, arguing for a warm cup of tea and a cozy spot on the parlor settee. In the end, however, Agnes—amateur herbal therapist—wrapped Eve's ankle in strips of soft flannel lathered in restorative balm, then phoned for the taxi and held open the door as Eve promised to return by early afternoon.

Eve felt a new urgency about her quest. The curious arrival of Myrna Stewart. The discovery of the friendship among Otis, Gordon, and Jasper. The familiar faces in the passport photographs. Although she did not discount Harry's remarks about Nazi connections, she was not ready to believe Otis's involvement in such things. Or that their life together had been no more than a brief exquisite fantasy. It would require Otis to be someone else entirely. Harry was, after all, a spy—trained to see the dark side of the world. Eve wanted today's appointment to provide a clear path for her investigation. In truth, a source of vindication for Otis. Moreover, her own marital judgments.

The Prints and Photographs Research Room was located at the end of a long dark corridor. A sixtyish woman, small of figure with close-cropped gray hair, stood next to a row of file cabinets. Her glasses hung from a thin strap around her neck, and she held a bundle of folders in both hands.

"Aye, you're right on time, dearie," she said as Eve approached. "I'm Vera Barclay, *The Scotsman's* librarian responsible for photographs." Without ado, she identified the point of their meeting. "The files you requested have been organized by date and topic. The early years are arranged on the table in the small reading office to your right off the main reading room. The last batch is here." She handed the bundle to Eve. "Should you need further assistance, please inquire. Closing hour is promptly five o'clock. The quarter-hour bell serves as our alert."

Eve shifted the stack of folders in her arms. "I hope not to take much of your time. You've done more than enough. You can help me with one thing before I begin. Is there a small shop in the building? A place for a cup of tea and a sweet?"

"Aye, a cup of tea is yours for the asking. Just down the hall a bit. A sweet will be harder to manage. You might know that sugar is in short supply. Since July of '42, well-nigh seven years now, our sweets are rationed. In January, the government, bless their souls, lifted the ration. Two weeks ago, the quota was again placed upon us. Our collective sweet tooth far outstripped the wee supply. I do believe we, to a citizen, myself included, overstocked our pantries, fearful of another round of limits. Not that anyone can blame us, you see. We lived without for so long." Vera opened a drawer and withdrew two small objects wrapped in waxed paper. She opened Eve's palm, placed one within it and folded Eve's fingers around it. "It's lovely to share," she whispered conspiratorially, a mischievous smile lighting her face.

Inside the tiny office, made even smaller by its two exit doors, one to the outside corridor, the other to the main reading room, Eve hung her coat and scarf on the door peg. From her bag, she withdrew the dozen small passport photographs and lined them up across the top of the table from left to right. In a second row, she arranged the larger photos she had taken on their honeymoon.

Was it merely a year ago?

Before shifting her attention to the research folders, she withdrew a small magnifying glass from her bag. Carefully, she examined each of the photos she had brought, making a note or two on the back as she recalled a particular detail.

She licked a finger and turned the initial page of the research folder. Nothing of interest in the first two. Once more, she shuffled through them to be certain she had not missed an important image or news item. She found one photograph marked March 1944 particularly stunning. Its caption recounted the shooting of 335 hostages by Nazi storm troopers in the Ardeatine Caves near Rome. Described as a spectacular act of violence, it apparently served as revenge, retaliation for a bombing attack by Italian partisans in Rome. The Italian people described it as the worst symbol of Nazi barbarism.

Eve wondered if Harry had been involved in tracking those killers.

In the third folder, near the end, she stumbled quite accidentally upon an extensive article about the postwar discovery of the art collections of Adolf Hitler and Hermann Goering. Tens of thousands of priceless sculptures, oil paintings, and other artifacts—stolen from museums of occupied cities or confiscated from wealthy homes—were discovered in mountain retreats and underground mine shafts. Accompanying the article was a series of photos showing the works still unaccounted for. For a closer look, she moved the photos of each work under the direct light of the desk lamp. One image stopped her cold. The painting revealed a young woman peering at a letter held close to her face, the only light emanating from a high window on her right. The painting was familiar. The caption explained that the painting had been removed from the collection of one Ernst Franken, a wealthy Jewish industrialist whose Dutch family had been taken from its Amsterdam home in early 1942 and not heard from again.

A surge of nausea swept through her.

When she first met Otis, that very painting had been hanging in the foyer of Otis's Belgravia townhouse. Repeatedly, she had admired it upon entering. When they moved to Chelsea, she placed it above the mantel in her sitting room. It now hung in her Holland Park house.

Tears rose. Ever so slowly, Eve wrapped her arms around herself, a child once again. In that small space, she rocked to and fro in her chair, weeping silently. Her mind tried to frame this new discovery, put it in order, connect the painting with the whole of her life in London. She understood nothing, save the horror that must have accompanied its acquisition. Her own ignorance, cause for shame.

In time, she raised her head, unfurled her body. In clenched fingers, in both despair and rage, she read the article again, studied the dreaded photograph. She wanted to tear the paper into small and smaller bits, set it afire, destroy the words and the image. She could pretend she had never come across the article, and decide that, over time, the story of the painting's rightful owners would disappear from memory. Instead, she placed the article carefully alongside the other items.

A special intensity now drove her. She focused anew, obsessively perhaps, on the folders, studying the news articles, reading, rereading, educating herself, intent on seeing further than her own needs.

One such item, accompanied by several photos of German officers in uniform, interested her: "The Iberian peninsula has become a postwar Nazi refuge. Though the Spanish population struggles, its fascist government finds work and housing for former German officers of the Third Reich. Known as *The Iberian Way*, a network in Spain has managed to provide false identity papers and help for thousands of these men."

False identity papers. She flipped through the photos and compared them to those on the table. She could not be sure; two or three looked similar. The stacks piled higher. She lost track of their order, and her notepad overflowed with summaries and dates. As she wrestled with the details in her memory, she understood she had moved beyond her initial denials. She was at least considering possibilities. Although she still did not know who or what killed Otis Battersby, a clearer picture was emerging.

The afternoon wore on, Eve withdrawn in her shell of concentration. The light bothered her eyes, and she felt the beginnings of a fierce headache. She longed for a cup of tea and a brief respite. Like spring rabbits, the files seemed to multiply. At some point, she could not remember which pile she had reviewed and which she had not. She pushed herself back from the table and switched off the lamp. In so doing, her shoe heel caught on the table leg, and as she steadied herself, one hand came to rest on a folder entitled

Rainbow Tour Summer 1947. Onto the floor spilled several dozen photos of the same woman, a stunning beauty named Eva Perón, the first lady of Argentina. Eve spread them, one by one, on the table. The lengthy newspaper accounts chronicled Perón's European tour. Arrival in Spain. Dinner in Madrid with Franco. Motorcade through Spanish villages, throwing pesetas to children. Papal visit in Rome. In France, a promise of Argentinean wheat. Holiday in Switzerland.

Eve lifted the larger photos, inspecting each. She remembered hearing of Juan Perón's election to the Argentine presidency. At the time, it was the scandal involving his wife that had caught Eve's attention. Here she was, Mrs. Perón, representing her husband's new fascist government.

Six photos in Madrid. Their captions identified Eva Perón, places she visited, members of her entourage. In the background of one photo, Eve recognized the Palace Hotel. The photo was badly creased, as if it had been examined and folded repeatedly. Under a heavier file, she sought to flatten it, easing her thumb carefully along the vertical crease, revealing the top-to-bottom scene. Halfway down the photo, she paused for a quick intake of breath. Oh God. Her eyes darted to the caption. Mrs. Eva Perón, first lady of Argentina, on her way to visit the city of Bilbao, accompanied by shipping magnate Señor Alberto Todero, London clothier Mr. Otis Battersby, and his personal assistant Mr. Karl Wolff.

Bile rose in her throat, and she fought an impulse to vomit. The photo slipped from her hand, floating above the floor as if time had stopped and held it there, suspended, air crumbling around it. She felt as if she were melting away.

Karl Wolff. The thief on the train. The man stalking her home. Personal assistant? That explained, she now understood, how he came to know and use the name Pierce.

Here was the first obvious acknowledgment, one she could not refute. She had met, married and eventually loved a man she thought she knew. She had no idea who Otis Battersby really was. Nor the level of his deceit. She had been led and misled. His secrets revealed, he had plucked out her soul.

The closing bell, more like a low-intensity buzzer, sounded in the corridor outside the office Eve occupied. A moment later, Vera Barclay appeared. "Fifteen minutes until the closing hour. You must be exhausted, spending the whole of the day in this wee place. Did you find what you needed, dearie?"

"More than enough and not quite enough," Eve replied, "if that makes any sense. My view of the world is in disarray." Disarray. Not nearly what she felt. She cleared her throat. "Might I reorganize and replace these files for you?"

"No, no. Can't have you doing my job. Tomorrow is soon enough. That leaves you a minute to freshen up before they throw the likes of us into the street. I'll retrieve my bag and wait near the lift." Vera walked back toward the research desk, leaving the door to the reading room slightly ajar.

Eve packed her handbag and made her way across the narrow corridor to the loo. Having spent most of the day propped on a pillowed stool Vera had provided—"Keep that foot elevated, dearie, and you'll be good as new"—Eve's ankle felt considerably better, the occasional twinge a faint remembrance of injury. As Agnes had promised, the herbal remedy indeed worked wonders. Not a hint of swelling or discomfort.

When she emerged into the hallway five minutes later, the light had grown dim, a single bulb casting shadows down the corridor's entirety. She expected to see Vera standing opposite the lift, but a mumble of voices alerted Eve that a visitor was present in the main reading area. She sidestepped through the corridor door into the office to retrieve her coat and scarf, intending to remain there until Vera was ready to leave. The conversation continued, however, one voice intensifying, the other barely audible. Eve moved to the reading room door and looked through, squinting against the poor lighting. When she saw a man's silhouette standing near the exit door, she had the first hint of apprehension.

In a far corner, Eve saw Vera button her coat and fold her arms, place her handbag deliberately over her wrist and hold it primly in front. Unhurriedly, almost sweetly, as if she were stalling for time, Eve heard Vera say, "No sir. You may not have a look around just now. It is closing hour. This room is open by appointment only. You may return tomorrow after an appointment is made. You may have heard the closing bell. As you see, I'm on my way to the lift."

It occurred to Eve that Vera had directed her voice, low and firm, toward the half-open door where Eve was standing. In response, Eve quickly stepped back so as to remain unseen to anyone on the other side. A deep, heavily accented voice drifted through the room. "It is important, madam, that I am permitted to come in."

"I assure you, sir, there is no one here but I. Everyone has been instructed to exit the building. Precisely at five, the guards check each floor. The lights are showing last bits before they are extinguished for the night. Walk with me to the lift. We'll go down together." Vera's tone lightened. "Else, you'll be stuck here with the likes of me for the whole of this night. I dare to say, that is not an ideal thought for a handsome young lad like yourself." Vera gave a quick laugh. The man stepped forward so that his profile moved into Eve's line of vision, her view of him keener through the slit between the door and the jamb. Karl Wolff. The name she had learned just hours ago. It was the first time she had heard his voice.

Vera seemed to move closer until Eve heard the rattle of the door handle. She watched the door close against the jamb, and heard Vera's words drift away. "It will be my pleasure to show you our collection tomorrow, sir."

Eve looked slowly around the room and listened for a moment until the fall of footsteps echoed in the outer hallway. Tensed against the wall, she felt a terrible chill. As she waited for the whirr of the lift descending, her teeth began to chatter uncontrollably, and she wrapped her coat and scarf tightly. How did he find her? Her thoughts went to Agnes and the inn.

After waiting interminable minutes, she stepped into the nearly black corridor. It frightened her, but she kept walking in the direction of the lift, intent on reaching the ground floor, focused on eluding him. It crossed her mind that he would linger outside, wait for her to emerge. She would need to find another exit. Surely, there were alternatives. When the lift stopped at the ground floor, she held back inside the car until she was sure no one stood on the landing. She knew the guard would come to investigate the open lift door, secure it for the night.

"Madam," the guard blurted, a surprised expression on his face. He was the young man she had spoken to yesterday at the information desk. "You've missed the closing bell."

She pulled him inside the lift, placed two fingers over his lips. "Please, I mustn't go out the front door."

"But, madam, that is the usual route," he said politely.

"Is there another exit?" she asked, almost dizzy with alarm. In a whisper, she hurried on. "I need your help in getting safely out of the building." Her grip tightened on the fabric of his uniform.

The young man's eyes finally brightened in understanding. "Perhaps there is an exception to be made." He bent around her, glanced left and right around the lift cage, as if a secret plot were hatched between them. In a hush, he said, "At your service, madam. Follow me. A service tunnel leads down to the car park. If you will descend a steep set of risers, I'll take you there straight away." He gave her arm a reassuring pat, took her by the elbow, and made to leave the lift.

"Wait. One moment more." She stood in place, holding fast to his arm. "Tell me there's no one in the lobby or thereabout."

"Not a soul, madam. The other guards are securing the floors."

Relieved, she gathered her courage. "I'm in your debt."

"Off we go then, madam. Mind the steps."

He led her down a long dim hallway and descended a few stone risers until they reached a door marked Private Entry. Alone, Eve walked outside into a narrow alley, high dark walls on either side. A warm wind snapped the door closed behind her. The car park with spaces for a dozen cars, no more, now almost empty, stood ten yards ahead. Farther in the distance, to the right, the Waverly Bridge. *If I cross on foot, I will be exposed*, she thought. Abruptly, the alleyway ended, the late afternoon sun warm on her coat. Before she left the reassurance of the door through which she had come, she wrapped her scarf around her head, fluffed out its edges and tied it under her chin, concealing much of her face and hair, but not so peculiar-looking as to draw attention. To broaden her figure, she unbelted her coat. For a change, she wished it were raining so she could hide amidst a sea of black umbrellas. How to appear less noticeable? She remembered the way in which Agnes and Vera held their pocketbooks, thinking at the time how clearly that simple gesture defined them. In front of her body, Eve draped the straps of her handbag over one forearm, bent at the elbow, held snug against her waist. The other forearm covering the first, securing the bag to her body. A stern message to pickpockets everywhere.

Buoyed by her summoned confidence, Eve stepped from her shelter and deliberately shortened her gait, one an older woman might use. She forced herself to amble unhurriedly, limping ever so slightly, across the car park's expanse and onto the bridge. The sidewalks were full of people, grocery bags and briefcases in hand. Trains moved beneath her in and out of Waverly Station. A group of young girls skipped across the bridge, arm in arm. She tried to blend into the street activity, walking a certain way, not swinging her arms. She had a notion of eyes upon her, but she walked steadily, her eyes ahead.

On the face of it, she was a local woman making her way home. The sound of purposeful footsteps unnerved her, and she hunched up her shoulders and set her course for the far side of Waverly Bridge. Halfway across, out of the corner of her eye—she dared not look fully around—she glimpsed a man of familiar build. Not too fast. Slowly. She wanted to run. Instead, she lowered her head and turned slightly, her shadow elongating. She pretended to search her handbag for a lost item. As he brushed past her, she noted only the gloss of his shoes.

On the far side of the bridge, she spotted the back door of a bakery that fronted on Princes Street, the door open to ease the oven's heat. Stepping across the threshold into unexpected darkness, her senses sharpened to the smell of fermented yeasts and the feel of warm air. Two oversized floured hands emerged from the shadows. A flat white apron followed. "Hello lass. You've found the back door, have you? A bit dangerous near these ovens. Sit down here afore you fall into a hot cavern. A toasty golden crust you'll have." The baker mopped beads of sweat from his forehead and offered her a backless bench next to the door.

Eve sat down, legs quivering, and started to explain. "Sorry. I saw the open door and couldn't resist the aroma." The heat was heavy, and she sucked in the moist air, relieved to be out of sight of the street.

The baker wiped his hands on his apron, tore off one end of a freshly baked loaf and placed it in her hand. "I'll wager, by the looks of you, you could eat the whole of this," he said, turning at the sound of the front doorbell.

"I never got around to eating a proper lunch." She sat very still, nibbling at the edge of the bread, listening for the customers at the front entry. After a few minutes, she rose, steadier than before, and walked the length of the counter from which the baker was removing half a dozen fresh teacakes. She waited while he tended to three customers—four raisin scones, a dozen shortbread cookies, a loaf of cinnamon bread. "I'll take two loaves, if you please, one rye and one cinnamon." For Agnes's breakfast. "One of these pear tarts, too." *I must thank Vera Barclay*, she thought. Eve would call Annie and instruct her to buy ten pounds of granulated sugar and mail it to Vera. Sugar was readily available in the states, only 85 cents, small price for what Vera had saved her from today. The baker wrapped and bagged Eve's order, eyeing her as he placed her purchases on the counter.

"Mind these loaves cool a bit before slicing, madam. Twenty minutes, at the least. The rye especially needs to cool if it's to last."

"Light rye is a favorite of mine," she said.

The baker unrolled a second strip of white paper, placed a shortbread cookie inside and handed it to Eve. "Aye, I've made more of it since the war and after. It keeps a long while, this bread. Not much variety to it. Hard to get the kimmel lately, no caraway. A course, the patrons won't buy the pumpernickel. German bread, they call it."

For another moment, the baker chatted about sourdough starter and rye meal. Then, Eve picked up her packages and bid him good day.

When she set foot outside, she felt the same strange chill she had felt earlier on the bridge. Careful to maintain her pretense, she began to walk west in the direction of the inn, scanning the street for a taxi. Coincidentally, she arrived at the corner of Princes and Hanover Streets just as a city transit bus boarded a handful of passengers. She joined the queue, stepped aboard, and made her way down the aisle to a seat at the rear. She sat down and laid her parcels aside, gloved hands tightly clasped in her lap. She did not care where the bus might take her. She merely needed escape to some nameless yesterday. Before she knew of art thefts, cave massacres, and treachery.

As the bus rolled away, she looked back over her shoulder. There, on the opposite curb, hands in pockets, newspaper under one arm, stood Karl Wolff.

Chapter Eighteen

She allowed herself a moment of glee at her successful deception. Good grief. What am I thinking? The man is pursuing me. Relentlessly. To what end? There's the question. To what end? How could he know to search *The Scotsman* archives? Is he examining every building in the city, hoping to strike gold in one? What did Harry say? Will Gordon and Myrna Stewart had explored the hotel registers.

In any case, she could not ride city transit indefinitely. Jostling the bag of baked goods, her notebooks, and Agnes's umbrella, Eve disembarked at the next stop and hurried into the side entrance of the Caledonian Hotel. With minimal exposure to the street, the doorman could hail a taxi that would take her back to the inn. Quickly, she organized her parcels, slid the scarf from her head, retied it around her shoulders, shouldered her purse, belted the coat, and exited through the hotel's front doors, looking every inch the out-of-town guest, fresh from a lavish shopping excursion. She arrived at the doorman's station, made her request, and retreated to the hotel canopy to await his signal. In less than three minutes, a black cab swung into the hotel driveway, and Eve stepped forward. A moment too soon. When the cab door opened to discharge its passenger, she regretted her haste.

"Eve. Oh my word. It *is* Eve Battersby. In Edinburgh. What a delight. Thomas will not believe it when I tell him. He wondered where you got off to. He thought perhaps you packed up and went home to Texas. It is Texas, isn't it? That scarf is lovely. Wherever did you find it?"

"Myrna," Eve hesitated, thinking furiously. "Yes, here I am. I've come to Edinburgh to conduct a few matters of business." Myrna would have talked to Will Gordon. "And a bit of sightseeing. What brings you here?"

"Clients. Thomas collects them here, there, everywhere. Estate planning. After the war, everyone is planning an estate. Mounds of signatures needed."

"That means considerable business travel for you," Eve said.

Myrna continued, "When did you arrive? Where are you staying? Here at the Caledonian? We must have cocktails and dinner." Myrna bent to check her image in the cab's side mirror, brushed a stray hair back under her hat and ran a finger along one superbly thin half-moon brow.

"What about tonight? We'll catch up on your plans," Myrna blocked Eve's path to the taxi's entry door.

"Sorry. I have another engagement this evening." Eve remembered her promise to meet Kate and her husband—and Harry—at the Kenilworth.

"Why don't I join you?" said Myrna.

"I'm free tomorrow evening," Eve blurted. She had no idea why she suggested it. If Myrna detected this obvious diversion, she gave no sign.

"Splendid. Tomorrow evening at seven. Cocktails and dinner here. The Pompadour on the top floor. It's heavenly."

"It's settled, then, tomorrow at seven," Eve mumbled, her gaze resting on Myrna's gloves. Turquoise lambskin. Fine stitching. Five tiny buttons at the cuff. The sudden revelation stunned her. She turned her head away and climbed quickly into the waiting cab. She gave the address and sank against the seat, heart in her stomach. Today, in a thousand small ways, she had been shocked, wounded. Thrown in unexpected directions. There was no getting around it. But this one. This was the deepest wound.

iiiii

"Is she here yet?" Kate wiped the front of her apron, one hand after the other. "Mum called ten minutes ago. Said Eve was exhausted. Maybe not exhausted so much as distant, Mum said. Not a word when she returned. Went to her room and closed the door. Mum said she heard the lock click. Then, a sort of wailing that went on for some time. Came down only to meet the taxi."

Surrounded by strangers hunched over their pints, Harry sat at the bar watching the door. "She'll be along," he said, wondering what Eve had discovered that had so disturbed her.

Kate had reserved the private table in the alcove under the stairs. Earlier, she set out plates and silver on a creamy embossed cloth, selected a French table wine saved for special occasions, and cajoled—with promises of a week's worth of free ale—Louise Ross and husband Roy into minding the bar and waiting tables for an hour. Kate wrapped an arm around Harry's shoulder. "Any subjects to avoid?'

"How would I know? The woman's a fount of surprises and contradictions," said Harry.

"Exactly why you're intrigued, Harry Douglas. Don't argue yourself out of it," Kate said. "It's mighty obvious to anyone who cares to notice."

"Discuss whatever you like. Not that you'll get a straight answer." Harry breathed out and turned toward the door. "Remember, I've got to leave before nine. Final game at the Caley."

iiiii

Eve stopped just inside the entry of the dimly lit bar, eyes searching for a familiar face. She was not entirely sure the taxi driver had dropped her at the right place. She told him she wanted to go to the Kenilworth. The driver swore something under his breath, lurched off up Gloucester Lane, swung around at the crest of the hill, and roared back down at what she considered, dangerous speed. After wandering along Princes Street for fifteen minutes, the driver screeched around a corner, stopped abruptly, flung open the back door, and pointed to a location on the opposite side of the street. He waited impatiently while she paid the fare, an extra shilling for his trouble. He hopped back into the cab, swerved into oncoming traffic, and left her on the curb. She managed to scoop up an armful of notebooks and papers, now strewn in an untidy heap, before being dumped out of the taxi.

"Eve, are you all right?" She sensed Harry's presence at her elbow.

She nodded in the direction of his voice. At that moment, unbelievably, she was.

"How's the ankle?" he asked.

"Better. Not as bad as I'd imagined. A slight twist is all it was," she replied. "I've had it propped up all day."

Harry led her into another room and around a corner to a small table set for dinner.

"What's all this?" he gestured at the armload of paper. "We're having dinner. Kate spent half the day cooking and baking."

"Of course we're having dinner. But, afterwards, I need you to look at my notes." She shoved the plates and silver aside and heaped the overstuffed notebooks on the table. "Quite remarkable. I don't know what to think. You're better at these historical things. You'll have a look, won't you?" Eve could not stop herself from talking. "The first one is here in this notebook. No, maybe this one." Her eyes darted from one to the other. She felt somehow undone, thoughts flying in all directions. She pulled on a thick black corner, the books and papers spilling onto the floor. She stooped to retrieve them, knocking a portion under the table. "Oh God. What a mess. Give me a minute."

Without a word, Harry opened his hand to her, and she took it. He sat her on a chair, handed her a wineglass filled to the rim with a deep burgundy. He knelt on the floor, organized the scattered papers into two neat piles, folded them into the notebooks, and placed the whole of them on a sideboard next to the table. Across from Eve, he sat down, carefully replaced the plates and silver to their original locations, and picked up a second glass, half empty now. "These people are my friends. They've made special arrangements for this evening. Before I leave, we can talk about the things you need to talk about." He glanced at the notebooks, took a small taste of the wine, and added, "Looks as if you had a rough day."

She felt her eyes fill with tears, but she bit her lip and cleared her throat. *You have no idea*. "Good grief. I'm starved," she said. "Dinner sounds wonderful."

iiiii

It was after eight o'clock when Kate removed the empty dessert dishes and offered a bit of chocolate to her guests. A variation of

Blue Baron's "Cruising Down the River" played in the background.

"A bit tame for our Kenil, isn't it now?" said Mick, cocking his head toward the radio cabinet.

"A half hour of romantic tunes won't drive the regulars to The Rose and Crown," said Kate. "Their drinks are dear and poorly drawn." She smiled at him. "It's a wee pleasure to sing a lovely lyric—something other than a Celtic jig. The occasional love song might quiet the lads and their darts."

The meal had been perfect—Kate's leek soup, fresh Scottish salmon, roasted potatoes, baby sprouts, and raspberry pudding. Famished, unlike her appetite of the past months, Eve had savored every bite. Moreover, she had valued meeting and getting to know Mick and Kate MacLeod. Mick, a workingman's man, authentic, witty, preoccupied with football and whiskey, enamored with Kate, in clear command of his ego, and possessed of a genuine affection for Harry. Mick reminded Eve a bit of Rip Dexter—Rip's better qualities, that is, the mental and physical toughness. For all his athletic bravado, she never considered Rip Dexter anything but harmless off the field. Mick MacLeod, on the other hand, in the right situation, could take care of himself. He would not shrink from danger. Nor, Eve was even more certain, would Harry Douglas. She wondered why she had not encountered such men before.

iiiii

After two glasses of wine and Mick's stories, Eve was calmer than when she had arrived. Still, she was desperate to get Harry's view on her day's discoveries. The facts did not fit. She knew she would not sleep until she could link them together. Never mind the color of Myrna Stewart's gloves. Never mind what she thought had been love.

"You saved the best for last, Kate. I'll dream of that pudding," said Harry. "Do you mind if Eve and I sit for a minute? She's got a question we need to settle before I leave."

"Leave? Where are you going?" Eve asked.

"Game starts at nine," said Harry. "I'm heading out in thirty minutes. It's the last night of play."

"You promised, Harry. I need to talk to you. It's important." For the last two hours, Eve had been more than patient. She had played her part. She was not leaving without Harry's help. "There are things I need to know. You'll have to skip the game."

Quietly, Mick and Kate slipped away from the table.

Harry shook his head. "I came to Edinburgh to work. The game is my job. Besides, I don't just skip out. Not after I've made a commitment."

"But you made a commitment to me. At the beginning of the evening," she argued.

"You're right. I did. I will fulfill that commitment. We can meet tomorrow at the inn. Before I catch the train."

She had not thought of him leaving altogether. "The things I found today are disturbing. Shocking, really. You can't go tomorrow," she insisted. "I was followed. By the man on the train." She waited for his reaction—a mere raised eyebrow—and said, "I need your advice. I'm having dinner with Myrna Stewart tomorrow evening."

"How did that happen?" he asked.

"I couldn't say no." She sped on, not wanting to relive the encounter. "What about later tonight? When your game is over? I won't sleep."

"That's no good. We won't finish until three, four in the morning," he said. "What about breakfast? I'll come to

Agnes's at eight. I'll bring Mick. The three of us can come up with something. Then we'll talk about how to handle dinner with Myrna."

It was the best Eve could get from him. Why this sudden rush to leave town? "You said you had a few minutes. Listen to these notes, two in particular, and think about them before tomorrow." She reached for a notebook, found the passage, and read the headline about the stolen artwork. The horror of it struck her anew. "The paintings shown in the article," she paused. "One of them hung in Otis's home. Another, I recognized from the Spanish estate we visited. There may have been more than one." She flipped a few more pages and read the caption from Eva Perón's photograph that named Otis and Karl Wolff. "The picture plainly showed Otis and the man on the train. The same man followed me today."

Harry listened intently, then took the notes from her hand. He had a long, careful look at those Eve had marked. "You're right. What you found is significant. You have quite a lot here."

"Being in the middle of it," she looked away, "it wasn't that obvious." For some reason, she wanted to apologize. At least, say something in way of explanation.

"We're all victims of where we stand, who we're with," he said, concentrating on closing the notebook. He handed the notebook to her. "Did this man, Karl Wolff, know you recognized him?"

"No, he didn't see me. Not that I know of, anyway. I saw him. At the archives, again on the bridge. And then on the curb after I slipped past him onto the bus." She wanted to boast about her successful disguise, but there wasn't time.

"He's tailing you. Catch a cab back to Agnes's. Stay inside. Do not leave. I repeat: Do not leave the inn. I will see you tomorrow."

For a moment, he said nothing. They sat facing each other, the silence thick between them. Then he stood. "I should go."

She followed him to the door, watched him lift the hat from the rack, one hand smooth back his hair, the other settle the gray Dobbs on his head. Mick approached, their shoulders almost touching, Harry's hat brim and Mick's head inches apart. Two centurions guarding the Queen's gate. With an upturned finger, Harry tilted the brim of his hat, and spoke into Mick's ear. Mick nodded once, and Harry was gone.

Chapter Nineteen

"I was quite the card player in my youth," Donald Hamilton remarked. Harry noted a wistful expression on the older man's face.

"When I was young, I played my share of blackjack," said Oliver Drake. "As the years passed, I found it too solitary a game. I like to see the other chaps around the table. A bit of live action."

The three men stood inside the open terrace door making small talk, gazing at the city's lights, whiskeys in hand, waiting for the others to arrive. A white-jacketed waiter lit Hamilton's cigar, whisked away an empty glass, brushed a speck from the felt-topped table, careful not to disturb the stacks of chips at each position.

"Hope you chaps don't mind. I have invited a new player this evening. We were a man short. Earlier this evening, Scarpa's secretary came round to collect his things. Said Scarpa left for Milan. An unexpected family issue, I was led to believe." Hamilton took a short puff on the cigar, looked around for an ashtray.

"A pity," said Drake. "Excellent card player, though not much for conversation. Is LaFont coming?"

"Paul should be along. These Belgians are usually prompt. Can't say what's kept him." Hamilton made his way across the room to the door, where he stood waiting. The congenial host.

"Let's hope our new player leaves his hot poker hand outside." Drake chuckled once, set down his whiskey, removed his glasses, peered up through the lenses, and replaced them on his nose.

Hamilton smoothed the lapel of his jacket. "Another drink, Harry?"

"Whatever's left in the shaker." Harry heard himself say, gesturing toward the silver container in the waiter's hand. Harry would switch to coffee in an hour. Meanwhile, he would nurse a weak martini.

In a flurry of heavily accented apologies, Paul LaFont arrived, plopped on the double sofa, gulped down a half pint of ale, and set a cigarillo between his lips. Lost beneath the luxuriant mustache, the cigarillo remained unlit while he unfolded a thin, finely embroidered handkerchief and patted his forehead. He turned to Harry. "Good to see you tonight, my friend. Sorry it will be our last. You must visit me in Brussels. We will share a drink or two. My cellar is filled with the finest French burgundies."

They heard a soft—almost inaudible—knock, and the door opened. Harry recognized him immediately. The full head of steel-gray hair, collar too small for his neck, the dark suit snug on his broad frame.

Cigar in one hand, whiskey in the other, Donald Hamilton addressed the group, "Gentlemen, the Reverend Will Gordon will join us tonight."

"Will. Just Will," said Gordon. He smiled and shook each man's hand in turn.

Harry met Gordon's eyes. There was a shrewd intelligence, and something else—hardly spiritual—evident there. Harry thought how much he would enjoy taking Gordon's money. From whichever godforsaken place he had stolen it.

The group finally assembled, the six men acted out the familiar ritual, removing their coats, loosening their ties. With awareness of the others watching, they rolled up their sleeves, postured into their chairs—arms spread, feet planted, ashtrays and drinks within easy reach, a quick count of chips.

To begin the evening, Hamilton's stacks were full. Harry was up two thousand pounds. Bergeron even. Drake and LaFont down. Gordon bought in, put away the monogrammed money clip in the pocket of his trousers. He took considerable time stacking and straightening his chips.

Harry occupied the fourth seat, Drake on his left at number five, LaFont to his right in three, Gordon across the table in chair number one, Bergeron next to him in six. Hamilton always seated himself in the number two spot.

They played a preliminary hand of five-card high-low stud. No bets involved. The game was, to Harry's mind, where it belonged—a warm-up hand. Reserved for the simple-minded amateur. Limited to home games and small casinos.

After the warm-up, Hamilton signaled the waiter to refill everyone's glass. Then, the evening's play began in earnest. As host, Hamilton selected the game. "Seven-card stud, gentlemen. Two down, one up, then opening bets, next three cards up, last one down, betting after each card. Would you be good enough to deal, Reverend?"

After several rounds of aggressive betting, Gordon produced a flush on the first hand. Harry folded out of contention after the fourth round when he saw the Reverend push away from the table, cross his legs, and nod ever so slightly. Will Gordon was bound to go broke before the night was done.

Before Hamilton dealt the second hand, Drake looked at Harry. "I've admired your play all week, Harry. Yours is a splendid table image."

"Table image?" repeated Harry. He tried to keep the sarcasm from his tone and the smile from his face.

"The way one is perceived by one's opponents," said Drake.

"Ah. Of course. Table image." Harry wondered what Drake would make of Andy Blake's table image.

"Big wins can make you walk on water," said Gordon. Harry watched the buttons on Gordon's shirt strain against the added air in his chest.

"And big losses can hammer one into the ground," scoffed LaFont, the unlit cigarillo still between his teeth, his mustache stirring atop the twitch of a Belgian sneer.

Harry expected fast play from Gordon and got it. Over the next three hands, the Reverend bet, raised and re-raised—leaving the other players few options. Apparently, it did not occur to Gordon that slow play built the pot. Mostly, Harry played it tight, got out early and observed—without seeming to look at him—Gordon's give-away mannerisms. Nothing if not predictable. While Gordon maintained the same facial expression throughout play, he was typical of the hot-shot amateurs Harry regularly encountered—overdosed on confidence with a high tolerance for risk. Happy feet and jittery legs meant the strength of his hand had just increased with the last card. The squinting eyes, a finger between the thick roll of neck and the back of his collar meant the cards had not gone his way. Better yet, the Reverend took offense easily.

After each man had dealt at least three hands, the hour was well past midnight. Harry had learned what he needed to know, and his stack still showed a worthwhile, if not handsome, profit. He planned to pass the rest of the night methodically acquiring Will Gordon's money. Every last sixpence.

"Shall we have a break?" suggested Hamilton. "Anyone for a bit of brandy on the terrace?"

Alerted, the waiter lifted a gleaming silver tray from the sideboard. As he moved smoothly about the room, taking orders, filling glasses, the chandelier's crystals reflected the tray's polished edges. *All the luxuries*, thought Harry. Each man selected a warmed brandy snifter, waited in turn for a generous pour of gold liquid, then ambled through the terrace doors, rotating the tightness from their shoulders, moving their necks side to side, a free hand rubbing their eyelids.

The terrace looked out over a darkened courtyard. Gordon walked over to Harry and raised his glass. "Douglas. A proud old name. Families at St. Mary's with the same surname. But, your accent. Hardly Scot. What brings you to Edinburgh? Relatives in the highlands?"

"None that I know. Point of fact, the Black Douglases hailed from the lowlands centuries ago," replied Harry, turning up his glass and taking a gulp. "I grew up in Canada." He felt the heat reach his stomach.

"Ah, Black Douglases. The king's guards. A tough bunch, they were," said Gordon.

"So I'm told," said Harry.

Donald Hamilton cocked an ear and joined the conversation. "A fitting ancestral profession, then. Harry was associated with Section Six. British Intelligence. Nazi hunting after the war. Wasn't it, Harry?"

Harry felt Gordon tense.

"That's right," said Harry. He wondered how Hamilton held such information.

"Anything to do with Nuremberg?' asked Drake.

"I was there," said Harry.

"Didn't try enough of them. Not to my mind," said Drake.

Harry nodded.

Bergeron, leaning on the balustrade smoking a cigarette said, "The racial question compels debate. These men simply held one view and took steps to resolve it. Their punishment—likewise the German businessmen who served their country's needs in time of war—was completely unwarranted. A waste of time and money, tracking and trying them. They were patriots."

Harry was not surprised at Bergeron's remarks. In preparing financial documents for the Krupp trial in 1947, Harry came across Pierre Bergeron's name. He had played a minor role in France's Vichy government, a deputy who collaborated with German industrialists like Alfried Krupp in steel production and manufacturing, much of it at the hands of forced labor. Undoubtedly, in so doing, Bergeron had amassed his small fortune. Harry wondered how Bergeron defined "the racial question." Jews, métèques, Gypsies. Why, after the liberation, had he not been detained? Pardoned by de Gaulle or amnestied under the Fourth Republic? One never knew with the French. Harry decided he would have to pocket the smug Bergeron's money, too, before the end of the night. Of course, Bergeron was a far more skillful player than Gordon, his gestures not nearly so revealing. A worthier opponent. *At least,* Harry thought, *I'll make him think twice.*

Drake was not diverted. "These patriots, as you call them, stole millions in deposits from our government, engaged in forgeries that nearly bankrupted the crown. I'll not excuse a hair on their heads."

Bergeron ignored Drake's remark, delicately cleared his throat, blew a circle of smoke in Harry's direction. "Will I see you in Monte Carlo?"

"I'm headed that way. Catching the train to London tomorrow, then across the channel," said Harry.

"I have my car, if you're in need of a lift," said Bergeron.

"Good of you to offer," said Harry. "I have unfinished business in the morning."

"I must reach Paris before six," said Bergeron.

"Better get on the road, then," said Harry. "I can't be sure when I'll be free to travel."

Gordon stood alone sipping a second glass of brandy. He had remained silent during the conversation, but managed to catch Bergeron as he entered the terrace doors. "After the game, perhaps you'll have time for a drink," Harry heard him say.

"If the hour is right, a coffee would suit me," said Bergeron.

"We might have something to discuss," said Gordon.

Harry stepped farther out onto the terrace. He needed another dose of fresh air.

At Hamilton's lead, the men resumed their places. Over the next few hands, LaFont's luck changed, his short stack gaining altitude. Nothing strong, but enough to keep him in the game. Then, Bergeron hit a hot streak—a couple of full houses and a flush—defying the rules of logic and probability. In the middle of the table, a sumptuous pot would double the Frenchman's stack. The last card, face down, had been dealt and observed.

"Where's your courage, Canuck?" Bergeron placed a sizeable bet and grinned at Harry, the only players left in the hand.

A less experienced player would have retaliated immediately against the derogatory term, done something foolish. The Frenchman, calm and cool, used that kind of gamesmanship. Harry remembered a piece of advice from a grizzled veteran. "Figure out what your opponent wants you to do, then do the opposite." The rule did not always apply, but in this case, it might.

Bergeron edged his chair a little closer to the table and stared at his up cards, a pair of queens—one heart, one spade. Two more spades, a nine and a three. His face expressionless, he played with the tip of the cigarette holder.

Harry held three kings, two up, another in the hole. They would surely command three queens, but lose to a flush. "I'm tempted," said Harry, ignoring the insult, thumping his finger, figuring the odds of a fourth and fifth spade. Four queens out of the question.

Bergeron made a show of lifting the edge of the seventh card, turning his head a fraction, lifting his chin, staring at Harry.

In Harry's experience, the same gestures signaled the winning flush. Bergeron was riding a wave. But the Frenchman was an actor. Unlike Andy Blake who got high from bluffing and making the big call, Bergeron set traps for his opponents. Mined their weak points, cultivated their inadequacies. A seemingly nonchalant student of the needier side of human behavior. Better than any player Harry had encountered.

As Harry decided whether to move in or fold, the waiter approached the table with a fresh decanter of brandy. The other men, relaxed and waiting for Harry and Bergeron to settle the hand, loosened their limbs, nodded over their empty glasses. The waiter stood behind Bergeron and quietly cleared his throat, causing a ruffle in Bergeron's composure. "Mon Dieu," he said sharply. With a flip of his hand, he dismissed the waiter, annoyance on his face. He kept an eye on the cards.

A confident man would have ordered another brandy. It's down to kings and queens, thought Harry. "Call," he said. Chips clattered into the pot. "And raise." Another stack of chips.

The Frenchman seemed more amused than annoyed. A twitch of the lip. A simple shrug. A drag on the Gitane. With one hand, he gathered his cards into a neat stack, folded them facedown in front of him. "Well played, Monsieur Douglas." Resignation in his voice.

Harry nodded, keeping himself in check. He kept everything in check. He used to get a rush from winning a huge pot. Hunger made for poor discipline. The occasional big win had strengthened him, tempered his recklessness. He learned to control the urge to leap from his chair and bear hug the opposing player. *Careful*, thought Harry. *It will not end here. I will see Pierre Bergeron again, likely at a small private table in Monte Carlo. We will shake hands and smile, and I will sit next to him and laugh politely at his stories.*

Unhurriedly, Harry raked in the pot. Then, he rose from his chair, stretched and requested a short break. He followed the waiter into the outside corridor and placed a twenty-pound note on his tray.

Harry reentered the room, surveyed the placement of the remaining players. In the hours before dawn, it was easy to lose track, his eyes mildly irritated from the smoke and the need for sleep. Drake claimed exhaustion and left, reducing the number of players to five. Not the ideal table, but Hamilton insisted they continue.

"One final battle," he declared.

That suited Harry. While he had managed to whittle down Gordon's pile throughout the night, he had not yet maneuvered Gordon into surrendering the remainder of his chips. Drake's chair removed, Bergeron was now seated to Harry's left, Gordon next to Bergeron.

From here on, Harry thought, *it's Gordon's bad luck.*

Yet again, Gordon dealt first. Harry dropped out in the third round, slight hope for anything better than a pair of nines. The second deal, Hamilton's, produced three aces, and Harry hung on until the sixth round, but a straight cost Harry the pot. LaFont's deal worked much the same way. Hamilton's diamond flush beat the table. By the time it was Harry's turn to deal, he had all but given up the quest to flatten Gordon, the cards not falling Harry's way. The deal from Bergeron, however, held a possible straight. Harry's three up cards included a nine of spades, a ten of diamonds, a jack of clubs. By some miracle, Gordon's array showed similar promise—nine of hearts, ten of clubs, queen of spades. Bergeron dealt the fourth card up to Gordon, revealing the jack of diamonds. Three cards along, Harry garnered an eight of spades.

"A second piece of bad luck," said Gordon to Harry, raising his arms above his head, settling them in a clasp behind his head.

"True enough," said Harry. He did not like the man, but would keep his hostility under control until the game's conclusion.

Bergeron dealt a card to himself, swore under his breath.

Gordon laughed, named the highest figure of the night, pushed his wager into the pot.

With a sigh of resignation, Hamilton folded. LaFont followed.

Gordon looked at Harry. "Might as well get out while you can, Douglas. Not much point, is there?"

"There's always a point," said Harry.

"The point of taking my money, you mean?" said Gordon.

"It's well beyond that," said Harry. "Well beyond." He counted out Gordon's raise and placed it in the pot. "The Reverend Gordon's," Harry announced, "and raise an equivalent amount."

"The hour has undone your senses, Douglas," Bergeron gasped, his accent all of a sudden thicker. He folded his cards, slapped them down on the table. "You are indeed a foolish man."

Gordon shuffled in his chair, removed his gold-rimmed eyeglasses, silently counted his chips, and glared at Harry. A hush fell over the table.

Harry met Gordon's gaze. "In," said Gordon emphatically, shoving most of his chips to the center. "You've got plenty of nerve. You're making a big mistake, Douglas. That I can promise you."

"So be it," said Harry.

Bergeron dealt the last two cards, down. Before he looked at his own, Harry watched Gordon's reaction. A dip of the head, nothing more. A slight upward tic at the corner of his mouth. Harry expected him to gleefully grin and rub his hands. Gordon had few chips with which to place his bet. "Check," he said, staring down at the table, unconsciously flipping the corner of the last card.

Harry could make another large bet, force Gordon to dig in his pocket for more cash, but he was not after the money. Just the man.

"Check," said Harry.

Gordon smiled and turned up his last card, the king of diamonds. "A lovely straight, king high," he said.

In turn, Harry turned up his down card, the ace of hearts. Gordon laughed and moved, too soon, for the pot. From across the table, Harry reached out and grabbed Gordon's arm. Too much pressure for Gordon's blood, for he raised up in his chair, tried to fling Harry's hand away. Harry held fast. Staring hard at Gordon, Harry turned up the first card from his hand—the queen of clubs.

"Not good enough," Gordon spat the words. "My king is high." He muttered out of the corner of his mouth, "Let go of my arm."

"Fair enough." His grip tightened. "After this next card."

Harry closed one eye, turned up the corner, then the whole of the second card—the king that lay hidden to all save its keeper. The other men, silent until now, watching the scene unfold, sent up a collective oath at the sight of it.

"Straight, ace high," said Harry. Only then did he loosen his hold on Gordon's arm.

Chapter Twenty

17 May 1949. Harry watched the needle atop the elevator doors arc downward in its descent to the Caledonia lobby. Moments before, he had bidden goodbye to his fellow players, thanked Donald Hamilton for his hospitality, and exchanged his chips for tens of thousands in cash. In need of a burst of fresh air and a coffee, he walked a few blocks, followed his nose down an unfamiliar alley. The café was all but deserted at this early hour. He ordered a cup of espresso, sat down to smoke his pipe and scan the morning's paper. The weather was warm and windy, the rising sun in his face as he inhaled the aromas of fresh brew and tobacco.

For the first time in many months, Harry was relaxed, satisfied with the proceeds of the week's work. There was more money in his pocket than he had seen in the last year—the advantage of wealthy opponents. No longer worried about scrambling for a game he could afford, he could spend the summer and fall in Monte Carlo, finally able to play at the world's most sophisticated tables.

More important than money, however, Harry was convinced he had spent the better part of twenty-four hours playing cards with at least one accomplice—major or minor player, he was not sure—in the Nazi smuggling business. Where else would the Right Reverend Gordon get the kind of money he was throwing around? He didn't make it giving sermons or, least of all, playing cards. Of course, it was entirely possible Gordon was involved in another illegal trade, but the connection with Otis Battersby and the conversation Harry overheard between Gordon and Myrna Stewart provided evidence for the former. Clever. A high-ranking clergyman as cover for Red Cross requests and travel documents, currency exchanges. A perfectly safe way to launder payments, in one direction and another. Who would question such transactions?

Harry told himself he would have to handle this morning's discussions with Eve carefully. It was one reason he had asked Mick to join them. When it came to sensitivity, Harry knew his limitations. He did not yet know what Eve had found yesterday or, for that matter, everything she had brought with her from London. A part of him suspected she would not share all of it. He was surprised she had uncovered as much as she had. After all, she didn't know what the hell she was doing. From what he knew thus far, all roads led to the same conclusion. Eve Battersby's dead husband was paid handsomely to smuggle Nazis and collaborators out of Western Europe, most likely to the friendly fascist government in Argentina. He was certain of that connection as soon as Eve told him about the photo of Otis Battersby and Perón's wife in Madrid. Why would someone want to kill the man? To figure it out, Harry needed more information. Whatever it was, he guessed it would not end well. For all of Eve's declarations, he believed, when it came down to it, she did not really want to know the truth of the matter. More than anything, Harry worried what Eve would think when she learned the truth. Would she blame him for a truth she did not want to believe?

He finished off the coffee and the paper, emptied and cleaned his pipe. It was hours before he was due at Agnes's. Enough time for a shave and a fresh shirt.

iiiii

"I've set them all out on tables and chairs," said Eve. "Organized as best I could last night. Since I was under strict orders not to leave the inn." She frowned at Harry. Dressed in a flowing skirt of forest green and a long-sleeved creamy silk blouse, a thin black patent belt at her waist, auburn hair brushed back from her face, the slightest hint of rouge on her cheek, she looked as if she were on her way to an afternoon tea dance. Throughout breakfast, she felt Harry staring at her. Perhaps he will stay another day. She had taken care to splash one small drop of rose perfume on the back of her neck, another on the hollow of her throat.

They followed her through the double doors into the parlor. Harry and Mick walked the room, inspecting the items Eve had arranged, some effort at chronology evident. Photos, Spanish passports, health certificates, Argentine visas and landing permits, letters of reference. *The total identity package*, thought Harry. Everything save the travel ticket.

"The Spanish passports disappeared off the train." Harry flipped open the cover and leafed through the blank pages.

"There were more," said Eve. "In another envelope."

"And these other documents," Harry touched the stack of Argentine visas, "they were all together?"

"As best I can recall," Eve said. "All in different bowls and chafing dishes."

Mick stopped at a square-looking item on the card table, set apart from the rest—a thick stack of papers bound in opaque paper—and peeled back the wrapping. "What's this?" he whistled. "A small fortune in Swiss bearer bonds. Issued by the Swiss National Bank."

"Is that what they are?" asked Eve, a note of surprise in her voice. "They, too, were in our basement pantry. Stuck under a cast iron skillet. I had no idea what to do with them."

Mick and Harry exchanged glances. "How long have you had them?" asked Harry.

"Several months after Otis died. I was searching for a cooking pot. There they were, neatly stacked, a note taped on top. The handwriting did not appear to be Otis's." Eve remembered the days when she longed for a sign—any sign—of his existence. When she spent long afternoons sniffing every letter in his desk.

She picked up the piece of wrapping that had fallen to the floor and handed it to Mick. "Yes, here's the note. A few scribbled words, a date, a name, perhaps."

Mick examined the half-sheet. Rcvd pmt, 20 Sep 48, Dannecker/Rolf Fleiss. "Some sort of office stationery, faint embossing at the top." He handed it to Harry.

"Received payment on 20 September 1948 from Walter Dannecker alias Rolf Fleiss." Harry's brow tightened in concentration. He scratched the back of his neck, thought about what to say. "You have the passport photo, Eve." Harry riffled through the photos lined up on the opposite table. "Here. The man with the facial scar. Walter Dannecker, the man introduced to you as Rolf Fleiss." Harry snapped his fingers. "Didn't you tell me your husband returned from a business trip to Madrid the day before he died?"

"Two days before," Eve replied.

"And he died on what date?" asked Harry.

"September 25," she answered.

Harry said to Mick, "SS Colonel Walter Dannecker, sentenced to twenty years in prison after the war, but escaped in February 1948. In Madrid, in May of '48, Eve and her husband met him at Kraucher's Restaurant. Dined with him several times, wasn't it?"

Eve nodded. "You're saying these bearer bonds belong to him?"

Mick picked up one of the bonds and showed it to Eve. "A bearer bond is as good as cash. Once it matures—these are ten-year bonds—it is payable to the bearer for the full amount. There's no name on this type of bond. So, whoever presents this particular bond for payment is entitled to 5,000 Swiss francs."

"Sounds like a lot of money," said Eve.

"Depends on the exchange rate. Bonds like this and Swiss francs, in general, are pegged to the U.S. dollar. Check my memory, Harry. As far as I remember from our work on the financial angles, each U.S. dollar is equivalent to around 4.3 Swiss francs, set by international agreement in 1945. This piece of paper would probably get you around 1,100 U.S. dollars."

"Sounds right," said Harry. "You're the finance hound. How many bonds in that pile?"

"Over a hundred," said Mick. "Meaning at least 120,000 U.S. dollars."

"What are the dates?" asked Harry.

"Blessed son of a gun. The purchase date is October 1, 1938," said Mick.

"That's important?' asked Eve.

"Means it matured on October 1, 1948. Six days after your husband died," said Harry.

"There's a stamp in the corner, hardly readable. Let's get the magnifier." Mick held the glass over the image. Eve watched his face fall, his nostrils flare. "Looks like a family surname and city, Berkowicz, Warsaw."

"Explains a few more things," said Harry, eyes narrowing.

"Such as?" asked Eve.

"I strongly doubt these bonds were originally purchased by Walter Dannecker. From the looks of it, a Polish family living in Warsaw in 1938 bought them."

"And then gave them to this Dannecker person?" asked Eve.

"Gave? Not likely. This was a Jewish family. Once those in the Warsaw Ghetto were removed, German officials took their belongings. Money, jewelry, artwork, other valuables."

"I don't follow. How did these bonds, belonging to a Jewish family in Warsaw, end up in my basement?" said Eve.

Mick carefully closed the parlor's double doors. "Agnes doesn't need to hear this."

He began to speak. "Let's suppose I'm a wealthy Jewish businessman named Berkowicz living in Warsaw in 1938. To the south, the Germans have annexed Austria, taken control of Czechoslovakia. There are rumors of violence against Jews, forced relocation. In Danzig, my relatives are frightened. Some of them have fled to England or America. Their city has become unfriendly to Jews and immigrants and others considered by the Reich as undesirable. I've lived in Warsaw all my life. I do not want to leave. I have a successful business, a nice home. I send my children away to relatives in France, just for a little while, until things return to normal. Let us suppose I grow increasingly worried. I want to ensure financial security for my family. I no longer trust my own currency. So, I've taken some of my savings, bought a good number of Swiss bonds, hidden them in a safe place. I feel better, confident now that my wife and I and my parents can leave, if necessary. Then, in the blink of an eye, in September and October 1939, the Germans invade from the north, south, and west. Over the next year, Warsaw is occupied. Eventually, a third of my city, 400,000 Jews, are identified, my wife and I required to wear a yellow star on our chests. My business, my home, its furnishings are all confiscated. We are to be moved to the Ghetto, walled and barbed-wired. Let us suppose, at some point in this ordeal, I seize the opportunity to purchase my wife's and my parents' freedom, perhaps my own. I make clandestine arrangements to approach a German official. I take my Swiss bonds from their hiding place and meet with one Walter Dannecker." He ended on a warning note, stopped and faced Eve.

"And then what? What happened to them?" she asked.

"Any number of things could have happened. I wouldn't know for sure," said Mick. He sat down on the edge of the sofa. "It's a familiar story. One Harry and I have heard many times. From both sides of the transaction."

Eve felt her stomach clench. "That still doesn't explain."

Harry interrupted, "There is a second part to the story." He stood. "If you're willing to hear it."

She hesitated. "You mean I'm not going to like this next part? The part about the basement and my husband."

"That covers it," Harry said.

Torn, Eve paused to look around the room at the items covering the tabletops and chair cushions, the open notebooks, pages she had filled, the time devoted to finding out things that more than troubled her, things that had wounded her in ways she could not yet fathom. The pause lengthened into a heavy silence. Finally, she said, "I want to know what happened to him."

She was not sure, at that moment, whether she meant what happened to Otis Battersby of London or Mr. Berkowicz of Warsaw. She folded her hands in her lap, her voice surprisingly calm. "If Otis Battersby was not the man I think he was, I want to know that, too."

"You're sure?" asked Harry. "We could leave the story here. You pack up, go back to London, fine memories intact."

"Too late for that sweet story," said Eve. "I want to hear the rest of it. No matter the cost." Even as she said it, she wondered if it were true. Am I really finished running away from horrors that may unfold?

"The risk could be high," said Harry. *For both of us*, he thought.

Eve said nothing.

Mick gave a quick nod at Harry. "She needs a bit of background first."

Harry walked to a space near the window, pulled the shade, cleared his throat. "By late 1944, the Nazis knew they were beaten. Italy had fallen to the Allies. The German machine was in ruins, food and supplies scarce. Nothing could stop the Russian advance from the east. The Red Army was determined to march straight to the heart of Berlin. The rest of us were moving in from the west and south. Knowing they were defeated, powerful members of the Third Reich made plans to flee, get out of Europe, take with them the wealth, at least some of it, they had acquired. Given what they had done to the Russians—the siege of Leningrad, the death-squad massacres—leaders in the Reich were particularly afraid of falling into Russian hands. The alternative was not much better. Word was out that the Americans and the British would arrest and try those who participated in the Nazi atrocities—relocations, imprisonments, slave labor, medical experiments, mass exterminations of Jews, Slavs, Gypsies, and other undesirables, as they called them. The Allies wanted to prosecute under the war crimes statutes, crimes against humanity. Consequently, there was a furious amount of activity by those who did not want to be captured, who wanted to escape imprisonment or worse."

"Worse?" Eve tried to make sense of what he was saying.

"Execution," said Harry.

"How do you know all this?" she asked.

"I was stationed, for much of the war, the early '40's, in London. Mick, too. We investigated these types of activities. After the armistice was signed, I went to Berlin to collect evidence for the Nuremberg trials. In the course of that work, I came across all sorts of identity and financial documents. Our investigative team discovered," Harry corrected himself, "not discovered, so much as uncovered, a series of connections—people, places, organizations—that worked to provide false identities, travel routes and papers, for those desperate to escape. Counterfeiters, people smugglers, whatever you want to call them. They all turned out, some motivated by principle or to help a family member or neighbor. Others in it for the money. Big money, as it turns out."

"So this happened at the end of the war and right after," said Eve.

"In truth, these escapes are still being arranged. There were thousands of crimes committed. Thousands of criminals to be captured and tried. Now, four years after the end of the war, captures and trials continue. There is no time limitation on torture and murder."

Eve eyes blazed. "You're all wrong. It's not possible that Otis was one of these criminals. He served in the British military during the war."

Swiftly, Mick got up from the sofa and opened the double doors. "Let's take a break. After a cup of tea, we'll have a look at what we believe was your husband's involvement. These items you've brought will help us put the puzzle together." Mick took Eve's arm, led her into the broader entryway. "And show us what possibly led to his death."

iiiii

Harry continued. "There were several escape routes, known as 'ratlines,' out of Europe. From our research, Italy and the Vatican were the most accommodating to fugitive Nazis and their collaborators. Many made their way to Rome and then, with new identities and papers provided for them, escaped on ocean liners from Genoa. Many went east to Egypt and Syria, some as far as Pakistan. Others went west, thousands shipped off to South America."

"You're confusing me. What does Madrid have to do with this? If they escaped through Genoa?"

"Spain is a fascist country. Franco provided—still provides—friendly haven for other fascists, including Nazis and their friends. A network we called The Iberian Way."

Eve interrupted, "The Iberian Way. I just read a news article about it."

"The Iberian Way," said Harry, "was set up to help thousands of war criminals arrive in and travel through Spain. During their stay, they picked up clothing, relocation papers, and advice on travel routes. It remains a very active network, though not as tightly organized as we—the intelligence services—were led to believe. As early as 1943, Spain was targeted to become a postwar Nazi refuge. Barcelona became the home of a popular organization known by the name '88,' the two numbers standing for the eighth letter of the alphabet 'HH,' Heil Hitler.

"By our reports, Rome and Madrid emerged as the centers for Nazi relocation. In Madrid, Otto Kraucher opened his restaurant, an obvious invitation to fellow Nazis to congregate. The Palace Hotel became known as a luxurious Nazi retreat. Countless 'social assistance groups' were organized. Government offices and immigration officials were sympathetic."

"The Spanish passports," said Eve. "You knew their significance."

"Old habits. Something clicked," said Harry. "Why would some chap on a train steal a bunch of blank Spanish passports? Why would a beautiful woman be carrying them around? I wasn't sure how involved you were or if you played a part in the relocations."

"Then you saw the passport photos, as you rightly recognized them to be." Eve looked up at Harry expectantly, isolated pieces beginning to fit together.

"After the war, there were many organizations assisting escaping Nazis. There were also individuals or groups of individuals helping them. For example, doctors helped SS men remove their blood-type tattoos and furnished them with false medical reports."

"Blood-type tattoos," Eve repeated.

Harry sighed, remembering several he had seen. "The Reich thought it was a good idea at the time. The blood-type tattoo was a small black tattoo located on the underside of the left arm near the armpit." Harry raised his arm to show the spot. "Applied, supposedly, to all Waffen-SS members. The letter—A, B, AB or O—was small in size, but clearly visible. In case of casualty, if the man needed a blood transfusion, his blood type was immediately identifiable. When the war ended, the Allies used the blood-group tattoo to identify Waffen-SS members. This led to their imprisonment, prosecution, and sometimes execution. As you would think, the officers were keen to have the marks removed. And paid handsomely for the service."

Eve asked the obvious question, "What about these individuals who helped with the escapes?"

"I believe your husband was one of those individuals," said Harry. And made a fortune doing it, he did not say.

There was a pause. *I will not cry*, Eve thought. "I need to know exactly why you think so. So I can understand it."

Harry was reluctant to begin the explanation. He wanted to have a clear eye, start at the beginning, lay it out for her. But he did not want to be cruel. He stopped at the table filled with the identity documents, lifted each in turn, stared at it, set it back in place. "The change of identity is a lengthy process, and there can be many people involved. Based on where you found these documents, the fact they were well hidden, the fact that, once completed, they would pave the way for a successful escape to Argentina—no questions asked—I believe your husband helped, or was in the process of helping, the men in these passport photos thoroughly change their identities." Harry picked up the passport photo marked Rolf Fleiss and handed it to her. "In other words, once a Nazi fugitive reached Madrid, your husband helped that fugitive become someone else and move to Argentina."

Her eyes moved from the photo to Harry. "Why are you so sure it's Argentina? You said they went to the Middle East or Pakistan."

"You found the news clippings and photos of Eva Perón's 1947 tour of Europe. There's a photo of Mrs. Perón, your husband, a man named Todero, and the man named Karl Wolff that you recognized as the man on the train. To you, the photo was personal and surprising. I imagine you must have been shocked. To me, the photo meant something larger and more revealing." Harry picked up the notebook, leafed to the page and read aloud from Eve's notes. "Called the *Rainbow Tour*, it was billed as European goodwill from the new president of Argentina, who sent his beautiful wife to charm the important leaders of Europe." Harry laid down the notebook and walked around the table. "We knew the tour as something different. We believed it had a parallel purpose. Namely, Juan Perón sent his wife to meet and court certain leaders of Europe to strengthen fascism in Argentina. To coordinate the loose networks of relocation and make it easier for boatloads of Nazis to relocate there.

"While in Spain, Mrs. Perón met with members of these networks. It is well known that her husband aims to build a strong fascist government in Argentina. He needs the help of other sympathizers. Those with experience. Those who built the fascist military, scientific, and industrial complex in Europe. Juan Perón also wants money, both for his ambitious government programs and for himself. The Nazi relocation business is profitable. Very profitable. So, Perón's motives are both political and financial.

"The fact that both your husband and Alberto Todero, the owner of a huge Argentine shipping fleet, simultaneously met with Eva Perón is significant. Todero's fleet is known for transporting thousands of Nazis to Argentina and other ports in South America. His larger ships leave from the port of Genoa. Smaller and medium-sized ships use the ports of Bilbao and San Sebastian in northern Spain. Before they can board Todero's ships or get into Argentina, legally, they must present the documents you see accumulated on these tables.

"A foreigner is required to present certain items." Harry held up one finger. "First, a passport. Hence, the blank Spanish passports and the labeled passport photos." He stepped to the next group of items. "Then, a landing permit for Argentina. To get a landing permit, one needs an application or a letter of reference." Harry held up the landing permits and letters of reference. "The application is sent to Argentina, approved by the immigration officer there who then informs the consulate in Madrid. A representative—your husband? his associate possibly?—then goes to the Spanish consulate and picks up the approved papers."

Harry's eyes focused on Eve. "You said your husband traveled frequently to Madrid and San Sebastian."

She nodded.

"A visa is stamped on the passport, an identification certificate is issued. One last hurdle is the medical certificate." Harry thumped two fingers on the documents—blank at the top where the name should be, signed at the bottom with an unreadable name, the letters MD following. "Every one of the items I named is sitting on these tables. You said every item was found in your basement. The obvious proof sits here before us. There appears to be a coordinated effort. We can rightly envision the sequence of events. The exit papers, the transport, the welcoming country at the other end." Harry stood over the stack of Swiss bonds. "The payment for services. A sizeable payment, it is, from one Walter Dannecker, now Rolf Fleiss. Surely, meant to be divided among the suppliers of these services."

"You think there are other people involved. People Otis knew," she said. The faces of their friends crowded her brain. "And Karl Wolff is one of them."

"Yes, he's the clear accomplice. But, he's not in a position to make the big decisions. He's hired by others. As you suspected, he followed you, broke into your home, searched for these very items. Karl needs them to follow through with Otis's arrangements with Walter Dannecker. "That man," Harry pointed to the photo in Eve's hand, "could not have received his papers. They are sitting here, piecemeal, in this room. He is still waiting for his new identity. It looks as if he's already paid for it. Karl Wolff had to take a chance, especially when he saw you were leaving London," said Harry. "He followed you to the train station. Then to Edinburgh."

"How could he know?" asked Eve.

"Probably didn't know for sure," said Harry. "But what else could he do? He's getting pressure."

"Pressure from whom?" asked Eve. "I saw Walter Dannecker in Madrid. I can only suppose he's still in Madrid."

"That's where the Reverend Gordon and Myrna Stewart come in," said Harry.

"Good grief. You think they're working together?" asked Eve. "A member of the clergy and Myrna and Otis selling new identities to war criminals?"

"That seems right," said Harry. "The discussion went like this: Myrna said she had to get the travel documents. That everything else was in place. That payments had been made months ago. That they—I assume the fugitives—were aware Perón was getting ready to pass a general amnesty, and they wanted to be in Argentina to benefit from it. They had paid extra to get there before July and were getting antsy. She mentioned Miguel Fonde."

"I vaguely recognize that name," said Eve. "I may have met him in Madrid or at an estate where we had lunch. Yes, I think that was the circumstance. Who is he?"

"As far as I know, Fonde is an Argentine Nazi. Travels back and forth between Madrid and Buenos Aires. Was a member of the SS and then German Intelligence. Story has it, at war's end, Fonde flew into Madrid with a planeload of stolen art. Now he sells it off piecemeal or uses it for payoffs. He was responsible for setting up the first wave of Nazis to emigrate. Been at it ever since. Within the last two years he set up a cover company in Argentina known as CAPRI."

"Capri, as in the Isle of Capri?" asked Eve.

"Not the Isle, no. With generous state support from the Perón government, this CAPRI hands out work permits to new SS arrivals," said Harry. "Did you notice how many of these photos have the word *machinist* written on the back? That's what their work permit will say, though I'd wager, most of them have never been anywhere near a set of tools."

"I seem to recall a small envelope with that word on it," said Eve. She started searching the tables and chair cushions. "Here it is. All capital letters, unusual."

"What's inside?" asked Mick.

Eve pried the lip of the envelope and withdrew two sheets of paper, folded over once. "Appears to be a list of names organized by some sort of heading. Some entries have one name, a dash, then another name. Others just a single name."

Over her shoulder, Harry read aloud. "Gonzalez Catan: Siegfried Uiberreither-Armin Dardieux; Armin Dadieu-Armin Pelkhofer; Bernhard Heilig; Erwin Fleiss; Franz Sterzinger; Fritz Maria Kuper." Harry looked at Mick. "I recognize a couple of things. Gonzalez Catan is the name of a suburb of Buenos Aires, famed for industrial work. Fritz Kuper was the public works inspector for Hitler and in charge of the Nuremberg port. I don't recognize the other names offhand, but I'm betting, if we researched them, these names would all come up SS or Third Reich managers of some agency or another. Perfect credentials for Perón's plans for a new Argentina." There were scores of names on the single-spaced two pages. Various headings seemed to indicate a city or area in Argentina.

Mick nodded at his friend. "You know more than you're saying about this."

Harry shrugged. "I spent a lot of time on these guys. Back to Gordon's conversation. Myrna said she's arranged passage for six men during the first week in June. Out of San Sebastian. She was pretty adamant that she needs these passports and entry papers. I assume that's why she's here in Edinburgh. She seems to think you have them. Or know where they are."

"Did she specifically mention Otis?" asked Eve.

"Yes, I heard his name clearly. Myrna said everything was going smoothly until Otis decided to do something."

"What? What did he decide to do?" Eve touched Harry's arm.

"I don't know. She didn't finish the sentence. Then, she made a remark about wondering what Otis was thinking." Harry omitted Myrna's mean-spirited comment about little Miss Texas. No cause to add insult to injury. He did not remove Eve's hand. "Specifically, she mentioned payment with the bonds. Most likely, those on the table."

Eve sighed. "They were looking for them, I suppose. All the while, sitting under an old cooking skillet." Eve almost laughed at the absurdity of it. "So, it's true. Otis was involved. He provided these identity packets. Took money for it. Works of art. Stolen money. Stolen art." She pushed their original owners from her mind.

"You knew it all along," she added.

No point answering that. But Harry could not dismiss it forever. She would come back to it. He hurried on, "So, we know there are at least four of them on this side of the operation. Karl Wolff, Will Gordon, Myrna Stewart, and Otis Battersby. Could be more. We have an idea of their roles, everyone except Gordon. Stewart, the travel arranger. Battersby, the documents and pick-up man. Wolff, the enforcer and general errand boy. Gordon, the money launderer? Can't see Gordon as the big-decision maker. Too remote. Too hot-headed."

Harry was on a roll and could not stop himself. "For all their fine organization, they miscalculated. A nasty wrench in the cogs. Battersby died before the rest of them knew how to access these documents. Left them scrambling to find them. Leads me to believe his death was indeed unexpected."

"You think it's true, then, the way they said Otis died." Eve furrowed her brow.

"Or," Mick added, "if you will allow another view. The rest of them thought they knew where the documents and such were and then could not find them. Double-crossed, perhaps. A form of self-preservation—or revenge—on Battersby's part."

"We have to know for sure who else is involved. They didn't think you'd be suspicious about his death, Eve," said Harry. "If you hadn't come to Edinburgh, mentioned your concerns to Gordon, they wouldn't have known."

"My mistake," said Eve grimly. "One among many."

"I overheard Gordon saying you didn't know anything about Otis's death. Suspicious was all. 'We can fix that,' I remember he said."

"How is that going to work, do you suppose?" asked Eve. "Perhaps they're planning to kill me, too." She said it very slowly, the thought settling.

"You're having dinner with Myrna tonight," he said.

"Indeed I am."

"Do you know what she's up to? Could be dangerous. Why not cancel?"

Her voice hardened. "Trust me. I will not."

"Let's talk about it," said Harry. He knew it could go all wrong.

Chapter Twenty-One

There would be talk of Otis. She had to prepare herself. Her performance must be flawless. She could not be hasty or impatient. She had to appear comfortable, relaxed, move naturally as though she knew nothing of false identities or escape routes or Swiss bonds. Disregard fresh wounds.

Eve dressed carefully. Her impulsive shopping spree had garnered more than a few suitable choices. Immediately, she discounted the summer pastels. Too charming. What about the red charmeuse? Too formal, although the fabric is heavenly. The gray cashmere? Too stuffy. I'll sweat to death before the soup arrives. The brown tussah? Silky, the right fit. Soft and elegant. Myrna will drool over it.

Opting for vanity over comfort, Eve blessed Agnes for her doctoring skills and tucked her toes into the three-inch rust-colored glossy heels. What are taxis for?

On her way down the stairs, she stopped on the landing, inspected herself in the gilded mirror, where the light caught in her hair. Eyelashes curled to perfection. A hint of lilac perfume. Cheeks slightly rouged. Eye shadow contrast on both lids. Lip color too light. She darkened the final coat until a spot of luster disappeared.

She knew she would be studied. They were nearly strangers, but Eve knew she had encountered her share of Myrna Stewarts. Women who spent a great deal of time sizing up others without seeming to do so, watching without being seen watching, judging the color of your manicure and the cost of your jewelry, figuring which Sloane Street shops sold your handbags and shoes, noticing where your husband placed his hand.

Harry's words echoed in her mind. "Put decency and intelligence aside. The people you're dealing with are cruel. More than cruel; they are vicious. They deal in violence. Go with your gut. Know when to leave." Perhaps, after all, I have not known women like Myrna Stewart. Most certainly, Myrna Stewart has not known anyone like me.

Eve belted her coat, drew on the turquoise gloves, pulled them down tight over each knuckle, stared at them a moment too long, resolved not to care. This evening, they would serve their purpose. They would separate lies from truth.

The summer evening was just beginning to lose its light. A soft rain dampened the pavement. She stepped into the taxi and pulled the door closed.

iiiii

The restaurant was busy, tables and bar full of customers, filling every space. Myrna had been right. The Pompadour was heavenly. From the large windows, breathtaking views of Edinburgh, street lights glimmering far into the distance. Peach-colored walls. Raeburn portraits, Mackintosh landscapes. Low-hanging chandeliers reflected in gold-trimmed mirrors. Pedestals of fresh floral bouquets.

The room seemed familiar, somehow, to Eve.

In search of privacy, the black-suited maître d' seated them at a table in the far corner, a view of sky and rooftops, the street six levels below.

"I specifically requested a table overlooking the Cathedral," Myrna protested to the waiter. "You people are always getting it wrong. I don't know why I come back here time after time. In the future, I shall rethink my choice," her voice loud, harsh, the pearls at her throat quivering.

Myrna's short rant prompted the young man to scurry off in search of drinks. Eve and Myrna faced each other across the white linen-draped table. Myrna picked up her purse, riffled through it, found what she sought, offered Eve a cigarette.

"We all mourn for Otis," she said, easing her pale-green silk skirt aside, crossing one leg over the other, openly studying Eve's face, surveying every inch of Eve's body.

Eve had not anticipated the remark or the overly blunt visual appraisal. Grudgingly, she admired Myrna's confidence. Pushed into silence, Eve lit her cigarette and lowered her eyes so she would not have to think of something to say.

The waiter arrived with the drinks. One elbow on the table, Myrna held the cigarette between two willowy fingers, her chin up, willfully staring at Eve. From the pocket of his waistcoat, the young man produced a bronzed lighter, bent toward Myrna. She took a long puff, blew a line of smoke through her pursed lips.

"I'll need more than this," Myrna said, waggling the glass of whiskey. Her eyes never turned toward the young man. "Before we order dinner." She had not consulted Eve, although Eve was much too preoccupied to be concerned with what she might eat.

"Few people outside Edinburgh know," Myrna said, "about this place. Incredible food. Exemplary service. So glad we could meet tonight. What a surprise, running into you yesterday. I had no idea you were in the city." Myrna's dark hair fell across her eyes, and she flicked it away with her thumb, the burning ash from her cigarette forming a fresh spot on the cream-and-gray patterned carpet.

"No reason why you would," Eve said, lying smoothly.

"I hope you're getting out more. We've worried about you. Cooped up in that townhouse all those months," she smiled pleasantly at Eve.

"I didn't consider it 'cooped up' as you say." She realized now that by sequestering herself—never leaving the Bramerton residence, putting Thomas off for months—they were denied the opportunity to search her home. You weren't worried about me. You needed access to your precious papers. "We?"

"What do you mean?" asked Myrna. She clinked the ice in her second glass of whiskey.

"We. You said we worried about you. I'm curious to know who we are, these people who are worrying about me." Eve's voice was sharper than she had intended.

Eve's challenge seemed to surprise Myrna. Her dark eyes snapped. "Why, Thomas, of course." A pause. "And me," she added.

"That's very thoughtful of you and Thomas." Eve smiled sweetly. Thomas. Of course, Thomas is in it. The photograph. Here in this very room. No wonder the room is familiar. "I'm surprised you cared where I was. Or what I was doing. Not many people did. It was a dark time. I appreciate someone," she emphasized the word, "keeping an eye on me." Eve bent to pick up the napkin that had slid from her lap. "It's always a comfort to know friends are keeping a kind eye out for each other," the slightest hint of sarcasm in her voice. She held Myrna's freshly alert gaze, could see her mind's wheels turning. Eve shifted her eyes to the menu. "Shall we order?"

iiiii

They ate the soup course in silence, Myrna heavily salting her portion. She ordered another whiskey. "No ice," she commanded, a new assault on the waiter.

Her third, thought Eve. *I wonder how many she had before dinner.*

After a fig salad, the entrees arrived. Chicken Dijon for Eve, Myrna the fresh salmon. Eve resolved to eat very slowly to prolong the meal and perhaps add to Myrna's alcohol intake.

"Have you heard?" Myrna commented. "Le Maison Chanel has reopened in Paris. On the Rue Cambon. I'm confident the other French houses will reopen soon. Schiaparelli, Vionnet."

"I confess, I haven't paid much attention," said Eve.

They went on for a while, back and forth, Myrna chattering endlessly about the latest French fashion, lines and colors, a new Moroccan designer. Eve felt a rush of fury—talk of mid-calf gowns and geometric scarves in light of the business Myrna conducted—but responded at appropriate intervals. Innocuous banter.

"Not at all."

"I hadn't heard."

"Not in the slightest."

"Oh, do tell me." Anything to keep Myrna talking. Prolong the drinking. Finally, she felt it time to proceed. "What about Madrid fashion houses? Do you travel there often?" She fingered the rim of her glass.

Almost as if she had prepared for the question, Myrna responded, "Madrid, an interesting city. Much more attractive and cosmopolitan than I'd expected. I've been there several times."

"Recently?" asked Eve. "I only ask because I so loved the Palace Hotel and the restaurant variety. Kraucher's was grand. I hope they're thriving."

Myrna put down her fork, suddenly enthused. Easily, she drained her glass. "I stayed at the Palace last week. It's so convenient to the consulate where I had to pick up—" She stopped in mid-sentence, tried to backtrack. "My sister, an item for my sister. My only sister is interested in traveling the Spanish countryside and wondered what she needs for an unguided trip. I told her I'd check on it."

Myrna withdrew a compact from her handbag, patted her nose to take away the shine, rubbed a spot on her cheek.

An awkward diversion, Eve assessed.

Still searching her handbag, Myrna produced a gold key on a wooden ring. "Look at this. How forgetful of me. I forgot to turn it in at the desk. I'm at the other end of this lovely Princes Street, the North Bridge Hotel. Love the atmosphere, except that musty old lobby," Myrna wrinkled her nose. "Where did you say you're staying? Is it near?"

"Not very," said Eve. "I prefer the country."

With the tip of her finger, Myrna stirred her fourth whiskey. "Sounds exhausting, getting back and forth."

"Not at all," said Eve. "Chelsea was such a relief from the London city traffic."

Myrna pretended to smooth a wrinkle in the tablecloth. Eve could tell she was trying to ask the question in a causal, disinterested, offhand sort of way, but the alcohol had taken its toll.

Her words slurred noticeably. "Did Otis happen to leave anything unusual? A parcel? Legal papers? A list of items for review? He often dropped such things at the office. For proper handling."

"I'm not sure. There were some odd articles I couldn't decipher. Nothing I needed. I don't recall what happened to them. Most likely still in a storage box in the Holland Park cellar. I really couldn't say exactly where. Are they important? I could search for them if you like."

She watched Myrna lean forward in her seat. Innocently, Eve took the last bite of her chicken, set down the fork, pressed the napkin primly to her lips.

"Could it be something called CAPRI?" she asked artlessly. "Is that the name? Or have I got it wrong? Yes, CAPRI. I remember thinking what an intriguing name." Eve looked up at the ceiling briefly, chewed on her lip. "Yes, that must be it. I came across this envelope labeled with those letters, all caps. Inside were several papers. A list of names, it looked to be. Definitely foreign-sounding names. They weren't Spanish. Those I would have recognized. These names were more difficult to pronounce. Odd, considering Otis wasn't planning a trip other than his usual back and forth to Spain. You know about those, of course." She leaned in and whispered, as if divulging something secretive. "Oh, another thing," Eve blurted, seemingly unable to control her excitement. "The very strangest item on that list was at the bottom. It was signed by the Reverend Will Gordon."

Myrna frowned. "Should I know him? I'm afraid I don't, but it does sound like rather a famous name."

"Otis knew him," said Eve. "I thought you might. I don't know what gave me the idea that you would. I've met the man twice." Eve's tone elevated an octave. She stared out the window, thinking.

"Yes, twice. He's the Reverend Canon at St. Mary's. Sounds important, doesn't it? Another reason I thought you would know him." Eve smiled. She had to keep the sarcasm from her voice. "I must assume this list is distinctly official. At first, I thought perhaps it would be best to send it to the police or Scotland Yard. Sometimes these documents are important, sometimes not. But since his signature appears quite prominently and I'm right here in Edinburgh, I think I'll drop it at the church." Eve paused. "Before I go back to London tomorrow." Purposefully, she let the news sink in while she rambled on about her new Holland Park residence, the renovations that several workmen were completing in her absence. "I must keep an eye on the tradesmen. The neighbors tell me sometimes they leave the cellar unlocked."

Funny, how smoothly a lie escaped.

Myrna looked sideways at Eve. "Aside from tonight's sprinkle, the Edinburgh weather has been quite beautiful. Why not stay for a couple of days?" she suggested. "I highly recommend the North Bridge Hotel. Ideal for sightseeing, getting away from old memories. It takes time to forget a husband's loving gaze," said Myrna.

"A husband's loving gaze." Eve repeated. The perfect transition. *Time for a brilliant performance*, she told herself. She swallowed hard, turned over a silver spoon in her hand, pictured Otis's gaze, felt his deep blue eyes upon her. For an instant, she let herself believe he loved her still. Or had loved her at all. With an inaudible sigh, directed only to herself, she returned to present business.

Before she uttered it, she sensed something precious about to be lost forever, but she proceeded, not yet fully aware of the consequences. "Make no mistake," she said, "I hoped it would go on forever. Otis and I. But I'm not foolish. At the risk of sounding disparaging to my recently departed husband, Otis gave every woman a loving gaze."

Myrna shifted in her seat, face clouding. The muscle in her jaw twitched. She set down her glass, opened her mouth, as if to disagree.

The hour was growing late, and Myrna's alcohol consumption was at the tipping point. Eve had to push hard. "And a lovely pair of turquoise gloves," she smiled, gathering hers from her bag, laying the gloves on the table, spreading them out, caressing the palm with her fingertips. "Fine Spanish leather. I believe yours have these same exquisite little buttons on the cuff." She paused for effect. "Exactly like mine. Can you believe I found three pairs in Otis's bureau?"

Myrna stared intently at her glass, avoided looking at the gloves, pressed her lips together, said nothing.

Eve tried to look contrite. "Oh. Oh dear. I thought you knew. There you were, thinking you were the only mare in Otis's stable. Besides me, of course. What a terrible thing to do, to mislead someone that way." She spoke softly, lowered her eyes, put her hand on Myrna's. "I've married four husbands, philandering rascals all." *Forgive me, faithful husbands*, she thought. "I know how deeply these affairs can hurt. I am sorry."

A glare of murderous hatred, sparks of rage, crossed Myrna's face—revealing something of her true self. Then, a brittle smile. She snatched her hand from Eve's. Unsteadily, she pushed herself up, threw her napkin on the table, staggered across the room, narrowly missing the largest of the floral pedestals, swerving at the last possible moment.

Eve's hand clutched the turquoise gloves, squeezed them into a fist. She watched Myrna stumble past the ever-vigilant maître d' who offered his arm in assistance. Eve tilted back her chair and dropped the gloves into her handbag. She almost spat on them.

She spied Myrna's still-burning cigarette, the garish red lipstick smearing the edge. Between thumb and forefinger, she picked it up and smiled. She took a deep drag, exhaled, watched the double smoke rings float up and melt among the cherubs on the ceiling.

Eve signaled the waiter, "If you please, I'll have a double gin martini, very dry, up with a twist." No wonder theater people turn to drink.

Chapter Twenty-Two

He checked the water line on the crusted piling, then his watch. An hour past high tide. Perfect timing. Before dawn, the churning water would carry the body into the Firth, wash it away with the rest of the Leith filth. The sea fog was rolling in, thick and dark, choking the air, the streetlamp already hazy. In thirty minutes, the night would be nearly black, nothing to guide him but the reek of dead fish and burnt tar. Luck was with him.

The muddy footpath sucked at his shoes. He would clean them when he reached his destination. Shoulders hunched against the dampness, he set a brisk pace, congratulated himself on his choice of location. Respectable men did not frequent Leith after dark—at least not that they talked about—its reputation for rough slums and prostitution well earned. But this road, this location. To most men, it was safe enough, even at this late hour.

At Great Junction Street, he turned right, made his way to Easter Road, caught sight of the vague outline of the Old St. Andrews steeple, and walked toward it. The squeak of the arched gate announced his entry. He relatched the gatepost. It would offer a warning of the second man's approach. At the end of the railing, he stationed himself in a narrow passageway behind the memorial stone. He stopped in the shadows, out of sight to those who might pass by, though once the fog fully settled, chances were near perfect he would be all but invisible. The stench of urine told him others had stopped here before him. Across the road, the blurred reflection of a third-floor lamp compelled him to move farther along the passageway, up three steps, until he no longer saw the light. He stood motionless and listened, his eyes adjusting to the darkness, the gray stone cold against his back, struck by the absence of sound.

The assignment had been vaguely disturbing. Since the war ended, he had not killed—nor even thought of killing. He did not consider himself an assassin, did not know the job would call for such a task. Until now, he rather liked the job, the duties consisting mainly of covert investigations, the occasional stalking or burglary. He was paid—handsomely, he liked to boast—to do their bidding. Whatever else he did on the side was none of their affair. In truth, he had spent most of his life following orders, for far fewer wages. In the name of orders, he had committed worse sins.

He shoved his hair back and let the memory unroll. A chilly March day five years ago. The Ardeatine Caves. He had learned the brutal price of vengeance that day. The retaliations started at three in the afternoon, finished after dark. More than three hundred corpses. He had used his pistol, others their rifles. He shook away the echoing blasts, the hard pings of the ricochets as their aim faltered, the stunned faces of the men as they fell forward, one by one. They had not bothered to bury them. No one wanted to dig, so they simply blew in the cave. Then they drank. The stink of death upon them.

Instinctively, his hand felt the bayonet knife on his belt, the Mauser casing snug against his ribs. He shrugged. If one did not reflect too long on it, the act was simple enough, particularly when the victim, like this one, was unaware of your intent.

One foot on the wall, he leaned back, withdrew a cigarette. He favored the aromatic Murads, a preference he had acquired during the late 1930s when he found them easily available on the black market, smuggled by ship from Turkey and the Balkans. He turned slightly, shielding the match with his body, aware of the shadow he created. He lit the end of the cigarette, inhaled, savored the rich scent of the first puff. Carefully, with one hand, he replaced the cigarettes and matches in his coat pocket, assured himself they were secure, and settled in to wait.

Ten minutes later, a heavy footfall, the squeak of the gate, the dark bulk moving toward him. Right on time. He drew a last drag, flipped the butt. With the toe of his shoe, he extinguished the cigarette, picked it up, reached up and placed it on the lip of a ledge above his head. He would retrieve it later. He stepped out of the shadows to meet him.

"What is it, man? What's so urgent you've brought me here at this hour?" A silhouette in the darkness, his breath foul as he drew near.

"Orders," he said flatly.

"What orders?"

"I'll show you. Let's walk. It's near the wharf."

As they closed in on the narrow street that led to the waterfront, he looked both left and right, hid the tension he felt. Senses sharpened, he smelled the liquor that oozed from the man's pores, listened to the rhythm of their footsteps on the brick pavement, measured the distance between them, the height of the man's shoulders, the width of his chest. Eyeing him patiently, he wondered how the man had spent the last night of his life.

They were almost there, the spot he had selected. Moving deliberately, he positioned himself to the man's right, unclenched his fist, counted in his head. Five feet to the edge. His fingers twitched as he reached for the hilt of the knife.

A quick step back, his leg kicked out to buckle the man's knee. He heard the bone crack, imagined it splinter into dozens of jagged pieces. Before the man was completely down, he grabbed a handful of his collar and pulled up. The slice clean, soundless, the metallic smell of blood added to the oily air, a hoarse gurgle in the windpipe. He felt the head go limp, and his hand tightened on the collar. He dared not let go until he dropped him into the black water. Straining, he heaved up on the heavy torso, shoved the head and shoulders over the edge, and struggled to push forward until gravity took its course. The rest toppled after, gliding down, the legs lengthening out behind. Half an instant later, he heard the long, low splash.

Chapter Twenty-Three

18 May 1949. News of Will Gordon's death came before noon. Harry arrived at the inn in the torrential rain, drenched to the skin, to warn her.

"Murdered?" she whispered. She was astonished. "Are you sure?'

"It's mighty difficult to slit your own throat," Harry said.

She wanted details, but he had few to give. "He is most definitely dead. As I understand it, early this morning, before dawn, a young fisherman sighted a body hung up on one of the Leith jetties. Harbor police hauled him in and identified him as the Right Reverend Canon of St. Mary's. A bit of a shock. Said he'd been in the water less than six hours. Found his car abandoned on Great Junction Street."

"And how do you know this?' she asked. She was not sure why she thought him capable of such an act. Slitting someone's throat.

"Gordon's an important figure in Edinburgh," he replied. "Leith police immediately set to work, identified those he'd come in contact with the last few days, rounded us up before breakfast and questioned us. Gordon and I had an unpleasant exchange at the table the other night. The detectives were suspicious. I assured them I was not prone to murder, particularly over poker money. Besides, I had won the pot. He would have been the murdering one. They saw the logic in that. By their line of questioning, I guess they're trying to figure out what he was doing on the Leith docks—either last night or early this morning. I'd like to know, too."

Agnes stoked the furnace, positioned Harry in front of it, took his top coat and jacket to dry them in the oven, grabbed his hat on her way.

"Not the hat," he insisted. "I'll set it here, near the vent." With both hands, he held it at the top, front and back, shook the rain from it, reshaped the crown's crease and the brim, then placed the hat carefully on a ledge upwards of the blast of heat.

Agnes appeared with a warm towel, straight from the oven, and a dark wool blanket, fussing around his neck and shoulders. Drier and thus adorned, Harry paced back and forth in front of the windows. Frequently, he stared out at the street, past the water drops pulsing on the windows.

Things have changed, he thought, *a frightening change*. It was absurd to deny it. These are cold, clever people. They lured Gordon to Leith and murdered him. Did Eve's questions spawn such events? Or was it an unrelated plot? Two deaths. Otis Battersby killed months ago, meticulously planned and staged to look like a natural death, his body quickly cremated, the ashes whisked away to a distant place. A neat package. A near-perfect package, save for an observant doctor's experience with war's poison gas. And Eve digging around her basement. Gordon's death, on the other hand, was hurried, sloppy, on public display. A spontaneous act? If not spontaneous, at least one that could not wait. They are afraid of something. Something that could ruin their game, expose them?

"Do you suppose?" Eve gave him a long look.

"Yes, I do," said Harry, his voice sharp, then more restrained. "I'm trying to make the connections. What did you and Myrna talk about last night?"

"Good grief." She covered her mouth with her hand. "I've got the man murdered." She tried to gather herself together. "At one point—I was taking the last bite of my chicken—Myrna asked if Otis had left any papers for Thomas or the firm. I told her I had found a box in the cellar, and I would get it for her. I mentioned Gordon's signature on this list of names, said I was going to see him before I left town." Eve recalled her words: Could it be something called CAPRI?

Harry scanned the street. "Exactly what did you tell her? Tell it as close as you can."

"I told her I came across an envelope labeled CAPRI with several pieces of paper, lists of names. Foreign names. The lists were signed by Gordon. She asked if I had them with me. I told her no, that I had thought of giving the entire envelope to Scotland Yard or the police department because it looked so official and these names might be terribly important. I thought I was being so clever. Then I said, since his signature is on them, Gordon would know right away where the pages should go. That I planned to drop them off at the church." She paused. "Today."

"And she gave no signal that she knew him?" asked Harry.

"None. In fact, she specifically said she didn't know him," said Eve. "I gave her an opportunity to change her mind, to remember. Even then, she was not swayed."

"You could be right," said Harry. "Something about that conversation got Gordon killed. As I said yesterday, CAPRI is an organization set up by Miguel Fonde, an Argentine Nazi, who works directly with the Perón government to bring highly skilled Nazis to Argentina. Leaking the names on those lists would have dramatic effects. If they fall into hands other than Gordon's."

Harry stopped. "No. No, that can't be it. It had to be a cause worth murdering for. Something big. Something to lose. You were taking the envelope to Gordon. Gordon would have the lists, and they—the men named on them and the conspirators—would be safe." Harry snapped his fingers. "Unless."

"Unless what?"

"You found the envelope hidden in your basement. Unlike the other items, there was just the one. It was all by itself. It wasn't set to go anywhere. At least not that we knew of. Or be used for anything but—"

"But what? Tell me. I have to know if what I said caused his death."

"Your conversation had little to do with it. Only incidentally. I think we know what got your husband killed. And then led to Gordon's death. Both by people with whom they were doing business. Nasty business."

"Because of these lists? Nothing else, just the lists?" She could not believe it.

"The lists are a big part of it. By God, it all fits. If I'm right, it's about money and secrets. It's always about money. But this time, that money is rooted in greed and the need for secrecy." Harry threw off the blanket from his shoulders. "Some would say justice. Vengeance, justice. In this case, they may be one and the same."

"Tell me what you're saying. I don't understand."

"By necessity, the people involved in this ratline business are skilled at secrecy, discretion. They're also ruthless. For five years, they've created new identities for criminals and smuggled them across borders and oceans so they won't be arrested and prosecuted. Any number of people are needed to carry out the steps necessary for such an escape. Money changes hands up and down the line. Each cog in the wheel figures out its own means of making money, laundering the profits, assuring the payments look lawful. Your husband's sole proprietorship in a fashionable clothing business, as well as his tie design and manufacturing operations, provided cover for seemingly legitimate deposits and payouts. Who knows how much a tailored suit or custom tie sells for? I'm guessing Otis Battersby filed his earnings, paid the appropriate taxes, kept it clean, looked perfectly legal to any auditor who might inquire about the price of Spanish fabric. He imported supplies. He exported clothing and ties. He traveled back and forth to take care of these transactions. How long did this game go on?"

Thanks to her front-row attendance at Nolan Pierce's corruption trial, she was quite familiar with the creative wrangling of corporate bookkeeping. In answer to Harry's question, she did not know how long. How could she? Somehow, she was certain it had started before she and Otis met.

Harry continued, constantly checking out the windows. "So, not only was your husband the initial contact with the Perón government, he was pickup man for at least some of the false identity papers, and his company legitimized the money flow. Seems to me he did most of the heavy lifting in this operation."

Eve winced at the thought of the Otis Battersby she knew involved in such appalling dealings. A few days ago, she would have thought it an impossibility. She had started this journey loving him. At times, it was still like that. In her mind, theirs had not been a momentary relationship. It would not have a momentary finish. There was no way to make it beautiful again.

"Myrna Stewart does the organizing. Sets timelines, makes travel arrangements, packages documents, handles correspondence. The daily liaison. This she can do through her job as legal assistant and the occasional travel companion." He was careful not to look at Eve when he said it. "From the looks of her, she's learned her way around the shadier sides of life, particularly international business and law. Come a long way from humble beginnings. To which she will do just about anything not to return. Am I wrong?"

"I couldn't say," mumbled Eve. "She wouldn't have killed Otis. She and Otis were . . ." Eve continued, no longer protecting herself. "She and Otis were lovers."

Harry said nothing, just nodded.

"You knew?" she said, a huskiness to her voice.

He studied her, watched the light on her face fade. "Suspected," he replied.

"And you said nothing."

"Not the kind of thing one needs to mention."

"It doesn't matter."

"Betrayal always matters," he said.

"What I meant was, it doesn't matter in regard to Otis's death. A short time ago, I decided it is important to find the truth. If someone killed him, I want to know. I want others to know. No matter where it leads. No matter what else there is to it. Where does Gordon's murder figure in?"

"We'll get to him. First, Wolff. Hatchet man. Brute. Former SS, early escapee to London through an underground network, probably with your husband's help. I suspect that's how they came to know one another. Early on, he changed his identity, removed any trace of past including wartime service, went to work for your husband. Followed orders. I doubt that he killed your husband. Occasionally there is loyalty among thieves and murderers. Most likely, Otis Battersby's death was as big a shock to him as it was to you. He may have had some questions about it. In the end, he figured it's none of his affair. He still gets paid. Knowing what he does about the so-called ratline business, Karl Wolff continues to work for the small and lucrative operation Battersby and his colleagues created. Having said that, I'm almost positive it was Karl Wolff who got orders to kill Gordon last night."

"Orders? By whom? Why? Why? That was the big question on my mind when you started this tale." She gave him an impatient look. "Hours ago."

Some of the facts did not yet fit. Harry could not afford to rush to judgment. Some of his thinking was pure speculation. "All right. Okay. I need to lay it all out. See if it makes sense. Before I get to the murders. The connections are important. A lot led up to those moments."

He stopped, his eyes intense. "You're the next target, Eve. That's why I'm here. To warn you. They're cleaning up. Anyone who can identify them or has seen the names of the men on that list. Anyone who knows such a list exists. The only reason you're still alive is because they need that document. They've been looking for it quite some time. At first, mistakenly, I thought they wanted the whole package of items, all the documents you brought with you. Those items, however, are replaceable. They acquired them once. They'll get them again. It's fine and dandy to gather them all up and use them in the future. But that's icing on the cake. They're really after only one thing. That list. That's the valuable piece."

"And I have it," she said warily. "It's in this very room, and last night, I told Myrna I have it. How stupid of me."

"They killed Gordon because they didn't want him to have those names. Or know anything about them. I'm guessing when he originally signed the thing, he didn't even look at it, didn't know what it was. Maybe he signed a blank document, and the names were added later. If you gave the list to him today, he'd start to ask questions. That's why it was urgent they move quickly."

"What's so damned important about a simple list? That decent people would kill for it?" she asked.

"Years ago, these people put decency aside. They're infinitely more devious than you could imagine. That list is a matter of life and death. If the intelligence service gets hold of it, they will know the fugitives on that list are alive. Their new identities are clearly shown on that list. Those fugitives are either now in or on their way to Argentina, compliments of Miguel Fonde. If that list is leaked, those people are identified. Old names. New names. Country of residence. Possible work location. Then, it's only a matter of time before they are captured and tried, perhaps imprisoned or executed. It was stupid of Fonde to allow it out of his hands. Not only will these people be arrested, Fonde's reputation for safe relocation and discretion will be ruined, particularly with the Perón administration. With his reputation goes his bankroll. Possibly his life. Fonde desperately needs to have that list back. At all costs. Then, to erase all traces of it. And anyone who knows about it."

"So this Fonde is scared," she said.

"Oh, he's not scared. He is angry. Someone has to pay for this, even if it was his mistake. Believe me, people do all kinds of things to each other when they're angry. Especially if they happen to be greedy and powerful."

"Open to blackmail, too, I suppose," Eve said. She had only just thought of it, as Harry was talking. "I understand how you say Gordon was killed because of it. You're saying that Otis came upon the list by accident, by mistake in the course of acquiring these other items? Otherwise, how would he have laid hands on it? Fonde wouldn't have handed it to him."

"A crucial question. One we can't answer."

"Must you keep staring out the windows?" she asked. "It's most annoying."

"Wolff and Stewart are operating on an urgent timeline. They have to get that list before someone else does. If they don't know where you're staying, they only have two opportunities. You said you're going to St. Mary's sometime today and then, most likely, to the railway station. They'll be at both locations, waiting."

"But, if Gordon is dead, I won't be going to St. Mary's," said Eve.

Harry shook his head. "You don't know he's dead. The police department is still investigating. Information about the murder, including the victim's name, has not been released. So, they think you'll show up at the cathedral, hoping to catch Gordon in his office." He continued, "If by chance, they've found where you're staying, they'll be here, soon."

Eve's face went pale. "What about Agnes? I don't care about me, but she's defenseless. Totally innocent. What can we do?"

"When I came in, I told her to call Kate to pick her up. I first suggested a taxi—forgot who I was dealing with. Kate should be here any minute," said Harry, "when the rain lets up."

"I must tell her goodbye," said Eve, "and thank her for everything."

"Do it now, but don't let on. Pretend you're on your way to the station. I'll lock the doors and windows. She usually leaves them open," said Harry.

Eve hurried up the stairs to her room, took a pair of scissors to the hem lining of her coat, and extracted a wad of bills. *Better make it two wads*, she thought. In the kitchen pantry, clanging amongst the pots and pans, she found Agnes. A flowered apron, dull from years of washing, hanging loosely on her body. A catalog of thank-yous. An awkward hug, sharp bones and rough hands. "I left a few things atop the chest of drawers. They're yours. They belong to you now. Please don't send them to me. I don't need them." Eve backed out the pantry door, moisture clouding her view. *After today, I may not need anything at all*, she thought.

¡¡¡¡¡

They decided that Eve would, at half past one, take a taxi to St. Mary's Cathedral. She was adamant that she expose herself to confrontation with Karl or Myrna. In so doing, she was sure one of them would reveal the truth of Otis's death. Equally insistent, Harry was not at all in favor of the plan she concocted, but he agreed to the first half once Eve agreed to the second. In a separate taxi, he would wait across the street, out of sight, while Eve delivered a supposed copy of the CAPRI list to the Reverend Gordon's secretary. While Wolff and Stewart were busy retrieving the list, Harry and Eve would travel together to the Waverly railway station and quickly board the two o'clock express train to London, before either Stewart or Wolff could follow. Upon arrival in London, Eve, using an alias, would check in to a small hotel situated near St. James Park. She would stay out of sight until the following morning when she would request a police escort to deliver her and the contents of her overnight bag to the Foreign Section of the Secret Intelligence Service at 54 Broadway.

"It's a good plan," she said.

"It's a terrible plan," responded Harry.

Years of experience and countless undercover missions had taught Harry Douglas valuable lessons. First, plans—however well conceived and tightly organized—rarely came off smoothly. In his considered opinion, Eve's plan was nowhere close to being well conceived. Indeed, nothing if not ill conceived. Loosely organized hardly covered it. A lot could go wrong. A lot would go wrong. Repeatedly, he tried in vain to explain the dangers and obstacles to her. She reminded him he had intruded on her investigation. He reminded her she could not have discovered what she did without his help. In the end, she would not budge. After an hour of pressing Eve to return to London on the next available train followed by a long expanse of silence, Harry relented. Her husband. Her documents. Her risks. She was absolute in her resolve. Against his better judgment, he forced himself to exercise restraint. He did triumph, however, in one area. She agreed to compromise on the contents of her bag.

At quarter past one, within the span of two minutes amid a brief respite from the rain, a tandem of taxis pulled up to the Gloucester Inn. Harry loaded Eve and her bag into the first, then slid into the second. He directed the driver, a young man named Dirk Clayburn, to stay close on the first cab's tail. At the corner of Princes Street and Palmerston Place, Harry touched Dirk's shoulder, and told him to pull slowly around and park curbside near the corner. Resting his forearms on the top of the front seat, he watched Eve walk, bag in hand, through the double doors of the cavernous church. He checked his watch. If she did not reappear within five minutes, he would go after her.

Two minutes passed. Out of habit, he slipped his hand into his coat pocket, felt for his pipe, his eyes never leaving the entry recess.

At four minutes gone, the corner of his left eye caught a dark color, a slight movement. The image grew larger, closer. His head swiveled. A black Bentley, sleek and quiet, cruised an eastern path up Palmerston Street. At the curb, not more than twenty feet shy of the cathedral steps, barely out of sight to those who would exit, the driver eased up close and stopped, motor idling, front wheels turned a fraction outward toward the street. Had he seen it any other day, Harry would not have given a second look.

Dressed in a pale-gray traveling suit, a stylish pillbox hat and gloves of the same shade, Eve descended the steps, and turned toward him, her hand partially raised in the beginning of a wave. A sigh of relief.

In the flash of the next split second, Harry knew he had made a monstrous error.

Chapter Twenty-Four

Hours later, when Eve recalled it, the first thing that registered when she stepped out of the cathedral was that the rain had stopped, the sky once again cloudless, a spirited blue, a bit of sunlight reflecting off the polished brass when she pushed the door closed.

In one hand, she gripped the handle of her overnight bag, lifting it higher off each step as she went down, its weight now familiar. She made her way through the cathedral courtyard, felt the sun's warmth on her back, and savored the dense sweetness of the Japanese lilacs, more intense after the hard rain. Approaching the sidewalk, she looked toward the corner where she knew Harry would be waiting.

At first, she did not notice how easily the Bentley blocked her path. Not until its rear door swung open was she aware of it. Even then, its presence did not concern her, intent as she was on crossing the street. She would simply go around it. Then, a voice she recognized said, "Eve, get in, won't you?"

She saw then what was happening, realized that her questions, the ones she had brought with her to Edinburgh, would finally have answers. Though in the beginning of her quest, she had never planned to offer her life for them. She almost smiled at the absurdity of it. From what she had learned in the past few days, the man named Otis Battersby was hardly worth the price of mortality.

She ducked her head, peered into the far dark corner of the back seat, and willed an affected air of nonchalance. He looked impeccable, refined, polished. "Thomas, you look," she searched for the right word, "relieved to see me."

Reclining easily against the heavily padded seat, he said, "I confess. I am most happy to see you."

On the far side of the front seat, she took in the driver's familiar profile, the pale hair and dark eyeglasses drawing her attention. The glass screen that divided front and back was drawn up tight. A burl wood tray table, within easy reach of Thomas's right hand, held a cocktail glass, amber liquid at the bottom. His left arm rested on a pillowed support.

Inside her gloves, Eve's palms were sweating.

"Can I offer you a drink," he held up a heavy crystal glass an inch off the tray, just enough to show he was vaguely aware of its presence, "Or are you going to stand on the curb making things difficult?"

She pictured the hollow state of his soul as she decided whether to make a dash for freedom or stand her ground. Not in a thousand years would she give him the satisfaction of seeing her squirm. "I'm seldom able to resist temptation," she said, a tone of false cheerfulness. "I don't suppose you're serving vodka martinis at this hour."

Thomas Jasper gave a bit of a laugh. He slid smoothly to the edge of the seat, a mere three feet from her, so that if he so chose, he could reach out and grasp her. The legs of his perfectly cut trousers set at a right angle in front of her. He leaned forward, bowed his head. When he raised it, his eyes bore an undisguised warning. "You are in possession of several items that belong to me. I'm here to collect them."

Self-consciously indifferent, she said, "I believe we settled that, Thomas. Last month it was. Lest you've forgotten our divine lunch at Simpson's. I distinctly remember your telling me everything in the Bramerton Street townhouse belonged to *me*." The overnight bag now seemed heavier, and she longed to set it down. "I was able to identify one article that may be of use to someone else. You will need to check with the Reverend Gordon about it. You know the Reverend, I trust."

"Of course. He's an old friend," he replied, the present tense knowingly belying the fact of his death. "Now, the documents. You have no use for them. I do."

"And the bearer bonds. I suppose you'll want those, too."

"That is correct." He blinked languidly.

"Since those items belong to me, it is assumedly my choice to deliver them to whomever I choose." She took a step back, far enough away from his grasp. She stared up at the sky, marveled at how quickly it had drained of color. She hoped that her face was not as pale.

"Not everyone has a choice," he said.

She wondered whether Harry was watching, hoped he would not interrupt until she had what she wanted. "Did my husband have a choice?"

A dismissive wave of his hand, Thomas said, "You're asking a question I can't answer."

"I very much doubt that."

"These things happen. It was discreetly done," he conceded.

"Never mind your upper-class protocol and clever talk," she said, "I want to know one thing. That's all I'm after."

"And what might that be?" He asked, studying her.

"You see, I keep asking myself, why? Why did you kill Otis?" she said.

"I suppose you want to hear every detail."

She sensed movement behind her and turned, startled. Without speaking, Karl Wolff lifted the bag from her hand, nudged her forward into the back seat of the car, and quietly closed the door. He reemerged in the front seat and, in a matter of seconds, sped effortlessly away from the curb.

She braced herself against the door. "Where are we going?"

"For a walk," Thomas said, an authoritative edge in his voice.

"Not interested," she said.

"Oh, I think you're very interested. Too interested. A bit naïve, as well. Frankly, Eve, I expected more of you."

The ice in his tone surprised her. The pit of her stomach lurched, but she managed to respond. She remembered Harry's line. "So, in the end, it's about the money."

"Having been given much, I want more. A bit simple, but there you have it," he said.

"I'll have that drink," she said. "Whiskey, if you please."

A look of amusement flickered across his face. "Neat or over ice?"

She made a supreme effort to keep her voice calm and restrain her hand from slapping him. "I've always considered ice the ruination of fine whiskey."

She held the glass in both hands, surprised they were not shaking, breathed in the whiskey's perfume, and gathered her strength. She glanced out the window, spied the railway tracks below as they raced across the Waverly Bridge. She resolved that neither Thomas Jasper nor Karl Wolff was going to detect the slightest nervousness on her part. It was several seconds before she spoke. "As you were saying, Otis's death was about money. He had it, you wanted it."

"You Americans are so simple about such things. Money? It was more than that." He shook the liquid in his glass, a tight smile on his lips.

She pressed on, fearful they would reach their destination before she heard the truth. "I'm not entirely clear on the timing of Otis's death. Why last September? What changed that you felt the need to poison him so thoroughly one fall morning?"

"I don't know what you mean."

"Yes, you do," she snapped. "Before you do away with me, too, I want to hear your explanation."

"You want me to explain what? How a charming fellow you didn't have the first notion about married you, then left you unexpectedly?"

It was a cruel question. But then, he meant it to be cruel. She looked at him coldly. "Precisely," she said. "I want to hear your explanation of Otis's death. The reasoning behind it. The how and the why."

From a recess in the ceiling, a thick leather curtain lowered itself, covering the glass partition that separated the driver from the back seat passengers. He turned slightly to face her. "I'll tell you what I choose. Nothing more." He was quiet for a moment, When he began to speak, he did not look at her, but past her out the window. "Reputation is everything. The success of our business—our relocation business, that is—is dependent on reputation for secrecy, discretion, fair play. For these qualities, we are paid substantial sums of money, and oftentimes, receive goods of enormous value."

She thought of the painting on her wall. "For relocating Nazis to and from fascist countries?" she clarified.

"Nazis, fascists. Who cares? Most people don't know the difference," he said. "As long as they pay, they get what they want. Which—to them—means the chance to live their lives. Granted, a different life in a different place. They, of course, show the appropriate level of gratitude." Thomas sipped his drink. Still, he did not look at her. "As the war was coming to its inevitable end, boyhood friends—we'd spent several summers with them in Bavaria—contacted Otis, knowing he could likely assist those who required it. Due to his clothier business, he has—had—connections the world over. He traveled internationally, ordered supplies, received shipments. Nothing to slipping in an odd extra here and there—fabrics, visas, persons, what have you." He waved it aside. "We settled on delivery procedures, payment schedules, travel departures."

"We?"

"Otis, Will, and I as principals. Myrna does the spadework. Later, once Otis helped Karl escape that appalling British prison camp, Karl joined us. One day in 1946, his name was Rudolf Durr, German prisoner of war, harvester of crops in the English midlands. The next day, he became Karl Wolff, Swedish expatriate, delivering ties and miscellany for Lansdowne Clothiers." He glanced quickly at the curtained partition, as if assuring himself it was locked in place. "Karl was loyal to Otis."

"And now Otis and Gordon are both dead," she said. "Leaving only—"

"You know about Gordon?"

"I do," she said.

"Then, you know you are correct. One principal remains. And two underlings." The corners of his lips curved upward, almost a smile.

"I hardly think Myrna appreciates that title. Underling," said Eve.

"It is, in reality, her role," said Thomas. "Much as she assumes the affectations of London's privileged, she is, after all, simply one of a Yorkshire miner's litter."

Eve felt the car slow, a change of direction. "You talked of reputation," she said.

"Ah, yes. The original thread." Thomas again glanced at the curtained partition, then out the side window. "Since war's end, we've assisted in hundreds of relocations, increased our connections, and collected a host of generous fees and art objects.

"Returning from Madrid one day last September, Otis confided he was in possession of a lengthy list of names. A list of considerable significance, one that identified so-called fugitives and their present whereabouts. This document, he argued, would command millions of pounds. From several potential sources. Dependent on who was willing to pay to keep it from circulation. Or worse, public disclosure. He declined to divulge the manner in which he had obtained this list, but it was clear from his remarks that he and Will, on an earlier occasion, had arranged to acquire it. My understanding was that, at first, he intended to engage in a form of blackmail, selling it back to the owner. In this case, Miguel Fonde. On the other hand, he and Will were convinced that other groups—so-called Nazi hunters, both public and private—would pay an even higher price. With money in hand, he and Will could then abandon the relocation business—leave it to me, as it were—and resume their legitimate professions and business dealings, as if they had never been involved in the whole nasty business."

"You said he gave you this notice in early September," said Eve. "Right before he died."

"You've hit on the proper timeline," said Thomas.

"You didn't agree with his blackmail plan, so you killed him. Your boyhood friend. Your business colleague. Your confidant. That was your solution?"

"You impress me with your grasp of the obvious," said Thomas.

"It's never been my goal to impress you, Thomas," she said.

"What is it, then? What is it you want?" he asked. "Not that it makes a difference to me. One way or another."

"It makes a difference to me," she said. "No matter Otis's crimes, he was murdered."

"Let me be utterly clear," he said. "As you have observed on numerous occasions, I rather liked Otis. Brilliant tennis partner. Swift as a gazelle. Fierce as a doomed warrior. It came as rather a large jolt, him keeling over without warning, our side of the net. But fair is fair, dear Eve. Otis was about to ruin an incredibly lucrative business. As well as my reputation. On the international stage, no less. These Argentines do not forgive such acts of treachery. I would have been ruined. Otis could retreat to his eccentric ties and tailored suits, Will to his pathetic spiritual missions. I would not emerge so fortunate."

The car had stopped. She needed just one more bit of information. "The poison. How did that happen?"

"You are insistent in these questions."

"I am. And will ask them until the truth emerges."

"Ah, elusive truth," he repeated her word, a deadly edge in his tone.

She heard a car door close, the solid thud of expensive indulgence, and felt the car grow lighter. "The poison," she repeated, refusing to be swayed, fighting an urgency to flee, though she knew not where, or how.

He thought for a moment, sipped his drink, sighed, granted her a last favor. "Such things are never hard to obtain. A military connection here or there. A store of confiscated weapons in forgotten warehouses. Currency changes hands between officer and former report. Very little bother, really. A quick cremation. You see the logic, of course."

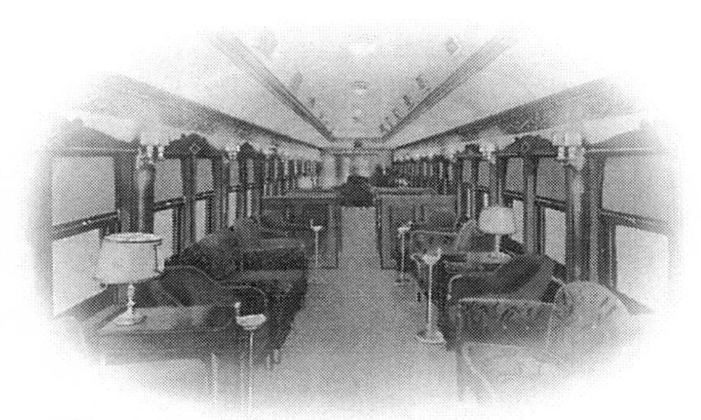

Chapter Twenty-Five

At a sensible distance, Dirk guided them through the dense traffic across the Waverly Bridge and east on the High Street, the massive gates of Holyrood Palace visible at its finish. As they approached the palace, Harry watched the Bentley disappear, seemingly swallowed by the gaping cavity. As they drew closer, however, it was clear the Bentley had not entered the closed gates, but turned off to the right onto a smaller graveled road.

"Queen's Drive, perimeter road for Holyrood Park," Dirk announced. "It arcs around the Salisbury Crags—the cliffs in the center of the park—and Arthur's Seat."

"Arthur's Seat," Harry repeated while his eyes explored the road. "What's that?"

"Highest point in the park. Popular with hill walkers. There's an ancient fort at the top." As they rounded a corner, Dirk pointed out the distinctive summit, a high rock formation, rising some eight hundred feet. "Most mornings, you can't see for the fog, but it looks to be clear at this hour. There," he said, "you can see the track leading up and around."

"Is that the only access road?" asked Harry, calculating time and distance. It was a substantial path winding its way up the western slope. "For walkers only?"

"There's no other direct line that I know. People say there is a set of steps on the southern side. A bit steep. Never used them myself. A might slick today, I'd wager, after the rain," Dirk added.

Ahead, some three hundred yards, Harry spotted the black Bentley, parked off the road, no lights in evidence.

"Cruise by. Slowly. You're a tourist gawking at the crags," said Harry. "Just as we pass, pull in hard and cut off his angle at the front bumper. Meanwhile, while he's distracted, I'll duck out the rear door and go round." He had only one thought, to get Eve out of that car. If he could slow the Bentley's departure even a fraction, he figured to have enough time to grab its door handle and yank.

The taxi crept forward, flush now with the Bentley's back windows. Crouched behind the seat, Harry leaned his shoulder into the taxi's rear door and leapt to the ground. Scrambling for balance, staying low, he circled the back of the taxi, shifting his body sideways, lodging himself between the two vehicles, still out of sight. The Bentley had not moved. Harry drew in a breath, reached out with both hands and jerked on the Bentley's rear door.

Save for the rich scents of fine leather and aged whiskey, the car was empty. No trace of driver or passengers. The front passenger seat held Eve's hat and overnight bag.

Harry felt an instant of relief, followed by momentary panic, then grave premonition. He stood, scanned the flat plain and the sharp cliffs beyond. On foot, in so short a time, they could not have traveled far. Has to be the driver, one passenger in back, and Eve.

Leaning into the taxi's front window, Harry yanked off his tie and shrugged out of his coat. "Straight away, take my case in the back seat and this one," he handed Eve's bag through the window along with his coat and tie, "to the Kenilworth Pub on Rose Street. Leave them with Mick or Kate MacLeod, the owners. Tell them to call the authorities to pick up this car." Harry pointed toward the Bentley. He reached into his pocket, unrolled a stack of notes, handed them to Dirk. "For your trouble," he said. As he backed away, toward the cliffs, he secured his hat and shouted, "How far to the top?"

iiiii

No trees sheltered the path, only barren red-brown earth below and alternating shades of gray rock face above. Standing on the grassy plain, Harry searched the western slope. At an angle, approximately twenty degrees, he spotted them. Clearly exposed, three silhouettes in a straight line, one behind the other, leaning into the mountain track. Harry saw no other walkers or climbers around them, or anywhere else on the cliffs. He focused on the slight figure he thought to be Eve, tethered by some means in the middle of two huskier beings. From this distance and angle, he was not able to identify Eve's attendants. Only that they appeared to be men.

For a few moments, he observed their slow, steady advance, contemplated their destination, wondered if they intended to go the entire distance to the top or stop at some interim point. Dirk had mentioned a rocky clump on the northeastern side, three-quarters of the way up, where the track ended, giving way to a ledge and a narrow set of stairs, hewn from the rock, and leading up a steep embankment to the ancient fort. From that point to the north, the slab broadened into a grassy plateau, providing a wide view of the sea and the wharves of Leith port. To the east was a crumbling cliff of molten rock, a sudden sheer falling away to the green, fertile fields far below.

Harry cuffed his shirtsleeves, shoved his hat down on his head, and checked his pockets. He removed a handkerchief. Fat lot of good that will do. The Wenger officer's knife. He had almost forgotten it. Along the hard steel surface, he found the blades' indentations—the extended main blade a full four inches. Not much, but something. The smaller, thinner blade sharper, more lethal. He had used it only once before and knew its effect. If one found the precise spot on a man's neck.

Scrambling atop a boulder and over a cluster of loose stones, he hoisted himself up to the path's onset. The ascent was steeper than it looked from below. At a jog, wishing he had worn a sturdier pair of shoes and a wind jacket, he set off after them. He hung back, not wanting to alert them to his pursuit, not knowing what he would do once he reached them. He gave them plenty of distance, hugging an inside wall of earth until he could no longer see them. Then, he quickened his pace, rounded a bend in the track, and stopped dead.

The track narrowed considerably, dropping away slightly—no more than a man's height—into a muddy swale on the left edge. To the right, an uneven ridge of rocks, interrupted here and there by a rounded boulder pushing out onto the track. The slope was now an almost vertical incline. Looking up, he saw that he stood almost directly below them. In their line of sight, should the man in the rear decide to look down. Behind a jutting boulder, Harry concealed himself and paused to consider the arrangement of the three figures. They, too, had stopped. The last figure, shoulders hunched, looked back down the slope. Harry thought the man looked directly at him, so remained perfectly still—part of the landscape. His light-colored shirt was sufficiently hidden by the boulder.

The man in the lead moved his head from side to side, seemingly scanning the hill and swale, and then pivoted forward, Eve in the middle. Their progress slowed as the steepness of the climb increased. He saw them far ahead, walking unevenly, the man in back urging Eve forward.

Harry climbed steadily, the air moist on his face, negotiating standing water and rocks crumbling around him. Below, the vast green expanse of the once-royal hunting grounds, the palace to one side, gradually diminished in size. The higher he climbed, the noise of the park faded until no sound existed, save his labored breathing and the slipping stones that fell away under his feet. His scalp was wet with sweat, and he stopped to empty the sharp pebbles and dull water from his shoes. He kept the three in sight.

The slope rose sharper, and the ridge disappeared so he could no longer hide himself against an overhanging crag. He felt a sudden shift in the air. The temperature dropped, and an unexpected wind tore across the open space, making his eyes tear, knocking him off balance. He leaned into it, regained a stable footing, and struggled toward a stony embankment, the wind stinging his eyes. A sharp pain burst in his ears; the cold chilled the back of his neck. Dislodged by a gust of wind, his hat tumbled away down the embankment. He cursed aloud. It had taken years to find and afford the Dobbs.

It was then he saw Eve turn and start back down the path. The man in the lead jerked the rope that held her and pushed her from behind so that she stumbled, legs crumbling beneath her, knees hitting the ground with what Harry imagined was a painful jolt. Roughly, the man pulled her up and shoved her forward, up and hard to the right.

They were nearing the top. Now was the time, he decided, to close the gap between them. To minimize the effects of the wind, Harry angled his body and attempted to increase his speed.

In the distance was the formidable sea. The rugged Scottish landscape struck him anew, and he reasoned he might use it to his advantage. As if reading his thoughts, the sky grew rapidly darker, storm-laden clouds portending another rain. Harry breathed hard, his shoes sliding on the wet rocks piled along the narrower path. He was unsure whether the rain would help or hinder Eve's rescue. At least it would distract their focus.

The three were directly above him now, having taken a sharp turn up the hill toward a broad foot ledge. As stones from their feet dislodged, he flattened his body against the hill, covered his head with his hands. If he forced himself up too quickly, he would be at a critical disadvantage, they occupying the high ground, he out of breath and strength. He would wait to show himself until the ground leveled off.

Glancing up, he was startled to see them some distance to his left on a long, upward slope. He came level with them, found a hiding spot behind a large stone, and saw they had reached a plateau, large slabs of rock above a light green wash. The man in the lead untethered himself from Eve, said something to the second man who pulled her closer to him. The man in front went to stand upon an open flat stone above the grassy area. Harry saw him squat on his heels and examine the edge and overhang, surveying angle and distance. The man stood, shook his head as if annulling an earlier decision.

Harry heard him shout a command to the second, whom Harry, at this closer distance, recognized with stunning clarity as Karl Wolff. "Too risky here," the lead man said. "A few broken bones is all it would be. Use the eastern cliff."

Wolff looked to the east, a sudden jerk in his body a sign of protest. Harry could not hear his words.

The man on the rock replied, "You'll not have to get too close to the edge. A healthy shove, and you're clear of it."

It was then Wolff reached around Eve to untie and disentangle the rope from her waist. He pushed her, a harsh thrust forward. She raised her hands to protect herself, shoved him away, tugged herself free, and prepared to run, until Wolff grabbed her from behind, one strong forearm around her throat. Harry watched as Wolff used his free hand to coil the now-loose rope into a tight circle and deposit it in his pocket. A leap of alarm. They were leaving nothing behind. This is their destination, he realized. They have chosen to kill her here. She walked off the cliff, people will say, blinded by the storm.

He had few ideas about which cards to play, surprise and the knife his only weapons. Aside from the brief tussle on the train with Wolff, Harry had not fought hand-to-hand in a long time. Their encounter had not truly tested his skills—nor Wolff's either, he suspected. Whatever happened next would happen suddenly, unpredictably. Harry was not a natural-born fighter. Instinct and reaction, the memory of experience, must carry him.

From this vantage, he studied the first man. Smartly dressed. Leads the way, gives the orders, delegates the physical contact. It made sense, then, the first man would rely on Wolff for his defense. Only if it proved necessary, to save himself, would the first man risk contact. Chances were better than even, his first reaction would be flight. Eve might be capable of distracting the first man, at least for a crucial moment. The possibility was there.

Before he realized the impulsiveness of his act, Harry was moving up the rise. He drew in two sharp breaths, arms and legs churning, zigzagging up the track, gauging when to turn by the steepness of the path—to the top of the hill. He doubled back, traversed along the cliff top, dropped to his stomach and crept out until he was directly above them, not six feet from Wolff's head. Wolff held a squirming Eve. She fended him off, managing to dislodge his black spectacles. Harry saw the two locked together, Wolff's hand struggling to push up the eyeglasses that were now perched on the end of his nose, ready to fall. Wolff dropped his arm from her neck, wrapped her arms behind her, her wrists and elbows touching. Harry heard her cry out in pain, saw her draw back her foot and kick Wolff hard in the shin. In his move to strike her, the eyeglasses fell, crushed beneath his foot.

The man on the rock kept a safe distance, waving his arms east, commanding Wolff to the edge of the cliff, his voice muffled by the wind that had begun to howl. Harry felt the first firm drops of rain splatter the back of his shirt.

Waiting until Wolff nudged Eve away from his body, Harry rose to his feet, knees slightly bent, arms outstretched, a pale spot on the back of Wolff's head his only thought. He took a half step to the outer edge of the rock, poised to strike, and launched himself up and out, the smaller blade of the knife and the white handkerchief between the fingers of his right hand. It seemed infinitely slow to him, that burst of flight.

A single brilliant flash of light and a deafening clap broke the sky above. Buckets of water, thick and fierce, poured down.

The force of the landing knocked the breath from his lungs. For an instant, he lay dazed, vision clouded, body slowed by the violence of the rain. He made out the bright red beads of blood on the palm of his hand, a slice of flesh beneath. He squeezed the hand around the sodden handkerchief, almost cried out as icy water found the wound.

Shaken alert, Harry glanced up in time to see the sole of a boot advancing toward his nose. He spun to his left, wincing as the flat of the boot caught the crook of his shoulder. He lifted himself up fast, grabbed the boot's heel and pushed up and away. In a blinding rain, he saw Wolff tumble backward and sprawl, knees in the air.

No second to waste, Harry lunged forward. With one pulsating hand, he pinned Wolff's neck to the ground. Slick with rain and blood, the hand soon lost its grip, and Wolff rolled from under him, staggering to his feet.

The next instant, Harry felt the boot between his shoulders, slamming him hard to the ground, sharp pains rolling up his spine. His vision black, he felt two crushing blows to his ribs. Before he hit the ground, Harry managed to throw out his hands and brace himself. On a flat stone, his feet found an inch of traction. He pushed forward as he imagined a racer would do off a starting block. He rose from the crouch, his eyes miraculously regaining focus.

Harry planted his feet in time to swing at the charging Wolff, a bare-knuckled left cross that caught the cheekbone's crest under Wolff's right eye. He heard the bone crack, saw the blood gather, watched Wolff collapse.

When the German staggered to his feet, reeling to one side, Harry thought it was over. The knife in Wolff's hand told a different story. Loosely, the German gripped the hilt, rotating it smoothly in his hand, an easy familiarity between knife and handler. A grim-faced Wolff sidestepped left, then right, then left again. Harry knew at any moment Wolff would lunge, knife poised for Harry's neck or heart.

It would be a matter of strength.

The two men glared across the imaginary circle they had created. Their feet moved on the edge of it, a scant ten feet apart, a pair of awkward dancers stumbling through their exhaustion and the falling rain.

As torrent gave way to light drizzle, Harry shook out his left hand. *Christ*, he thought, *I've well-nigh broken the one good hand I had left.*

What he needed was a weapon, one that came close to matching Wolff's blade. At least he could set his fingers around it, wave it in the air, create a diversion. The Wenger, pathetic by comparison, lay at Harry's feet. It had done its damage; hardly as Harry had intended.

Harry's well-placed blow had pushed up the bone below Wolff's right eye, an oozing bloody lump that blocked the eye's vision almost entirely. Wolff's inability to see was Harry's one advantage. Depending on the degree of his near-sightedness—and Harry suspected it was considerable—life would be a blur, his vision limited to little more than an arm's length in front of his face. With the additional swelling, Wolff had to rely on one bad eye.

Harry took two steps back.

Wolff strode forward in pursuit, but the gracelessness with which he moved confirmed Harry's suspicions. During that moment of adjustment, the hand that held the knife flailed, forgotten at Wolff's side.

By now, Harry's right hand was clumsy as a claw, prickly cold and white as chalk. He could not count on its response. For all he knew, the left hand was worthless as well. He had to catch Wolff off guard, an instant of lost concentration. Harry kept his feet moving.

An upward swipe of Wolff's blade formed a vertical line on Harry's forehead. Tasting blood, he knew enough to move aggressively before Wolff could position for a downward swing. Harry dropped below Wolff's vision, ran at his knee, knocked his leg from under him, and dodged the sweeping blade. Wolff stumbled but did not fall, pivoted, slightly off balance, the steel-plate of the knife handle dangling.

Seeing his chance, Harry grabbed Wolff's wrist and bent it back and up, a grip he had perfected during his first week in training. He used their momentum to run Wolff into a wall of rock. Wolff hit the wall head-on. Incredibly, he bounced off and remained on his feet.

The wall of rock was more yielding than it appeared. Or Wolff's skull was most unusual. Somewhere during the force of the collision, the knife let loose from Wolff's hand, out of immediate sight. He seemed unable to find the blade. Harry heard him swear, saw him tilt one good eye to the ground, and then turn in Harry's direction.

Harry let out a deep guttural growl to drive away the searing pain in his body, all too aware he could not hold out much longer. His ribs ached. He blinked away the steady stream of blood that ran from his forehead. The gash on his palm throbbed to the bone, aggravated by its constant opening and closing.

He did not want to kill the man, but could see no way around it, save his own finish. What strength he had brought to this fight had seeped from his body, the cold further deadening his senses. In a few minutes, he knew his body would give way to violent shivering.

Stalling, he scrambled onto an outcropping of rocks, an irregular wedge a few feet off the ground. *A minor height advantage,* he thought, *too contracted for leverage.* He felt his legs spasm, the muscles drawn in upon themselves.

In their struggle, in the midst of trying to stay alive, the two men had moved back and forth, nearer to, then farther from the cliff's edge. Harry knew only that all exits were blocked. To his back, a rock-solid wall. To his front, the menacing Wolff. To each side, a narrow ledge, constrained by boulders and sodden earth.

The tables had turned. Wolff knew it. Wild-eyed, now hard-pressed for breath, Wolff staggered toward Harry, filling space and sky. Somehow, the German had scooped up the knife, for he cradled it once more in his right hand. A vicious grin parted his lips.

Harry spat blood from his mouth and steeled himself for the final assault. At any moment, it would come. Still, he was not ready to die, his nerve not yet spent. He imagined the sound of Eve's voice, calling to him across a great distance.

As Wolff closed in, Harry took a single backward stride, angled his hips into the mountain, planted his weight on his left leg. Patiently, painfully, he bid Wolff forward, waited until Wolff was almost upon him, the knife no more distant than the length of a man's arm.

At the last possible moment, Harry thrust out his right leg, the stiff tip of his shoe finding the soft underneath of Wolff's jaw, the supple cartilage of his windpipe. Wolff strained and gurgled, his weight bearing down on Harry's leg, the veins in his temples visible. Harry's foot was hard against Wolff's throat.

With strength greater than he believed he possessed, Harry heaved forward, his foot and leg forcing Wolff's body back from the ledge.

Later, Harry had only to close his eyes for the images to appear. Those final frantic moments, each action slowed to a stop. The strange tilt of Wolff's body, one hand to his throat, head flung upward. Left foot slipping off the muddy embankment. The loose boulder giving way. His body twisting to right itself, angling sideways in space when he could not catch his balance. The look of utter surprise as he grasped the futility of his effort. Arms extended like featherless wings, floating in air. Then, the arched pitch backward. Head dragged down, mouth open in a silent scream. His body swallowed by the endless stretch of green earth.

¡¡¡¡¡

The wind had stopped blowing. She saw him crouched on the ledge, head down, shoulders hunched, elbows on his knees. She had prayed, unfamiliar though it seemed, for someone to help the man she had met little more than a week before. The man least deserving of harm, who had no cause to risk his life for hers. Eve's legs would not move. A kind of paralysis overtook her, fearing that Thomas would reappear at any moment, believing he would come again to kill her.

She called out to Harry. His body barely stirred, but he turned to her, ever so slowly as if a great weight kept him in that spot. Red streaks lined his face, his shirt torn at the collar, the front stained with blood. She saw that he wanted to stand, but could not, that his body had begun to shake and sway; and so, forgetting her fright, she ran to him. His legs gave way, and he toppled over. He was close to unconscious, his breath ragged, his teeth chattering, the cuff of his sleeve soaked through with blood.

Whispering softly, she eased him down, laid his head on the smoothest surface she could find, elevated his feet on several large stones, and felt his wrist for a pulse. Fast, weak. Though unskilled at such things, she knew hypothermia and shock. Their effects would kill a man.

While Eve could not remove Harry's wet clothes—there was no room to maneuver on the ledge—she could conserve what little heat his body held. She shook off her jacket and skirt and wrung them dry as best she could. Lifting his head, she placed the jacket around his head and shoulders. She tucked the skirt tight around his middle, holding it in place with pebbles and small stones. Ripping her scarf, she wrapped one piece securely to stop the flow of blood from his forehead. The other piece covered the wound on his hand. She rubbed hard on his fingers until she felt them warm to her touch.

Luckily, the rain had stopped, a hint of sun shining in the west. Clad only in her blouse and light slip, Eve stretched herself beside him, her back to the sun. For what seemed a long time, she pressed against him, shielding him, channeling the sun's warmth from her body to his, one arm drawing him close, the other rubbing his arms and chest. She stroked the backs of her fingers along his cheek. This seemed to calm him so that she felt his heart beat stronger, a firmness in his body. Still, there was a coolness in the air, and his skin was cold, the blood drained from his face. The bluish tint of his lips alarmed her. With her fingertips, she massaged the space between his nose and upper lip, traced the rounded scar on his jaw, and wondered anew at its origin. She could feel his chest rise and fall. He mumbled incoherently, muddled phrases amidst names of foreign cities. She carried on the conversation, a steady stream of words that popped unexpectedly into her brain. He needed dry clothing and something warm to drink, but she could see no way, save leaving him alone, to arrange it. She could not let him go.

Beneath her hip and up along her ribs, she felt the rough stones she laid upon, cursed the narrowness of the ledge, imagined the stones leaving permanent irregular cavities in her skin. Carefully, so as not to dislodge any part of the ledge on which she lay, she inched her body upward until she rested her chin upon Harry's shoulder, her lips brushing the lobe of his ear. His breathing was rapid. Closing her eyes, she breathed in and out with him, slowing the inhalations, tasting his scent—stale sweat and fresh rain. *He's quiet now and warmer,* she thought. *If only he would wake and make some move to show me he is alive.*

The light had begun to fade, and Eve had time to wonder if anyone, besides Thomas Jasper, would know where they were. She smelled the sea in the distance and worried about the night.

Chapter Twenty-Six

There were no clear signs as to how long she had slept. Ten hours or two? Twilight had settled around them. Harry stirred fitfully beside her. She was thirsty. She wanted to be warm. She thought her own shivering had awakened her. But then, she heard the distant sound of voices, drawing closer. She twisted herself up, caught faint dots of light below. She slid off the ledge and stared down at the group of dark silhouettes. She counted four or five, each carrying a torchlight. Too many to be Thomas Jasper.

Someone called her name.

"Here!" she hollered, waving her arms, staying close to the ledge, one hand on Harry's arm, reluctant to let go, as if he would surely evaporate if she stepped away. "We're up here."

The face she recognized behind the first torch was Mick MacLeod's. "Christ Jesus. Thank the heavens. We've covered the mountain searching for you." He sounded both frantic and relieved. "Where's Harry?"

"Here, Mick." She took his hand, laid it on Harry's shoulder, felt it twitch. "Alive. Breathing, at least. But he's badly hurt. Several deep wounds. Plenty of blood lost. I think he's in shock. In and out of consciousness. I couldn't get him off this ledge. I couldn't leave him. Had to keep him warm. His pulse is finally stronger." Her voice quavered. She talked too quickly, the words catching in her throat, the reality of their rescue and her profound relief unnerving her. She fought to keep control. She made herself stop. She needed a moment to gather herself.

Realizing her need, the others moved closer until she was surrounded by four men—two constables, a cab driver, and Mick. The cab driver put his jacket and his arm around her shoulders. She heard Harry mumble.

"Go on with Dirk," said Mick. The cab driver took her elbow, pointed his torch toward the path. "We'll take care of Harry."

"How far to the hospital?" she asked.

"Not far," Dirk said. "We'll make it."

She turned back, giving instructions, her voice a register higher, "Do be careful of the gash on his right hand and the one on his forehead. I managed to stop the bleeding, but the least movement will start it again. His shoulder may be broken. The bone looks crooked, out of line. Be aware when you lift him." She was hesitant, not willing to leave part of herself behind.

Mick hauled himself up onto the small space of the ledge, his feet straddling Harry's ribs. With both hands, he grabbed the shirt and the meat of Harry's shoulders and pulled him forward to the rim of the ledge, holding him upright as he jumped down to the flat rock below it. "Up you go, pal. Didn't I warn you about green-eyed women? Here I am, hauling your arse down yet another mountain." His mind flashed back to a snowy Alpine pass north of Bergamo. At least this time, Harry didn't have a bullet in his jaw.

In the torch's harsh light, he searched Harry's face for signs of recognition, lifted Harry's eyelid, and shone the light into a pupil. No response. Mick knew he must move quickly. He stooped and hoisted his friend onto his shoulders. Flanked by constables lighting the way, he took off down the mountain.

Chapter Twenty-Seven

21 May 1949. It was all a great gap in his memory. Perhaps he was dreaming. He lay still for some time. It had been a peaceful sleep, but now he was aware of a darkened room, a strange room. Misshapen objects hovered just out of reach, an aura of watchfulness about them. He lurched in and out of wakefulness. Far away, he heard the jangle of a telephone, a door open and close, a murmur of voices. His nose detected a fusion of aromas—a rich stew, fresh breads, a familiar perfume. He was enormously hungry.

He thought hard about opening his eyes. The sedative had made him groggy, his movements a sort of exaggerated deliberation. His head ached, hundreds of tiny hammers, a relentless pounding. He tried to get up, groaned, each intake of breath a stab in his side. His arms were thick and heavy. There was a stiff bandage wrapped around his knuckles and the palms of both hands. He felt the skin tense, pulling away from itself, then a heavy throb, when he moved his fingers. He blinked slowly. His eyes focused on a blank wall, a figure slumped in a chair. *An illusion*, his first thought.

"How are you feeling?"

The voice was faint. He waited for an answer to come to mind. He was not completely in control of his mouth or his tongue.

Eve was at his side. "You've slept for days."

He breathed in shakily, formed what he thought were words. "I'm okay."

"You certainly are not," said Agnes, bursting through the door with a tray of cinnamon tea and rolls hot from the oven, the lines on her forehead deeper than usual.

He guessed she had been hovering outside the door, replenishing the tray with fresh bread and boiling water until the moment he awoke.

"You've a nasty gash in the middle of that handsome head of yours, another on your hand, ripped down to the bone. Someone's dislocated your shoulder. The doctor filled you with two new pints of blood, and that has to mix all up with the rest of you." Agnes placed the tray on the bed table, folded her arms, stood over him.

"Too true," was all he could think to say, his mouth full of cotton.

As he breathed in the aroma and the steam of the hot tea, his mind began to clear. "I am hungry," he managed, pulling himself up on his pillow.

Agnes held out a roll, placed it in his left paw and helped bring it to his lips. "Fresh bread. The finest of human expression," she said. "And we have our supper. Eve's made a scrumptious stew. Some foreign concoction with raisins and such." Agnes fussed over the bedclothes and the arrangement of the tray, assuring everything was within reach. "Drink your tea now, Harry dear."

Eve retreated to the chair, content to observe, leaving Agnes to tend to him.

He looked from one woman to the other. "Days, you say. I've been out that long?"

Agnes answered, "That would be it, dear. The ambulance chaps hauled you up the road two days ago. Straight from the hospital, you were. Doctor ordered a dark, quiet room on the ground floor. The good Lord's seen fit to provide me aplenty of those." She smoothed down the shoulder strap on her apron. "No disturbances, he said. Private nursing services for whatever length of time it might be. Eve and I volunteered."

"Not enough money in the world to beat that deal," he said, finally alert, a second roll slashed with blackberry jam reviving his taste buds. He tried to grin, but felt a broad band draw tight around his head. Agnes wiped a dribble of jam from his chin.

A faint light glowed behind the curtain on the opposite wall. "What time of day is it?" he asked. Too late to call the London office?

"Late afternoon," said Agnes. "Any minute now, Mick and Kate will be along. They look in on you before the Kenil gets busy for the night." Gathering the remains of the tray, Agnes carried it from the room, gently pulling the door closed as she departed.

He lay his head on the pillow and closed his eyes. When Mick arrived, he would need a clear head. He willed himself to breathe shallowly. The coolness of Eve's fingers distracted him from the pain in his ribs and the buzzing in his head.

"You saved my life, Harry," she began.

"Didn't I tell you it was a bad plan? Didn't I try to talk you out of it?" he interrupted. "You see what happens when things go wrong?"

"What do you want me to say? You were right?" she asked.

"That's a start," he said.

"Of course you were right," she conceded. "No need to gloat." She could not resist adding, "The plan had its merits. Less a few unforeseen problems, granted. But, don't you see, I could not have confirmed the facts of Otis's death without that private conversation with Thomas."

He turned his head on the pillow, stared into her green eyes. She was kneeling beside the bed, elbow on its edge propping up her chin.

Her expression changed. "I'm serious, Harry. You did not have to do it. You don't even know me."

"I think I do," he said. "I think I know you very well." *Not nearly well enough. I must not be in such bad shape*, he thought. He wanted to take her hand, but could not. He thought about the unshaven stubble on his chin.

At the same moment, they glanced up and noticed Mick leaning against the doorframe. "About time you rejoined the living. Seems to me you're feeling fine. What's for supper?"

"No nourishment of any kind until you tell me what's happened," said Harry looking around for another pillow to prop himself up.

"What is it you want to know?" asked Mick, plopping down in the vacant chair. "Can we at least have a whiskey?"

"The documents, the Bentley, Jasper, Gordon, Myrna Stewart," he listed them off. "Wolff's body," he added solemnly.

"And how you got off the mountain in the nick of time," said Eve. She raised her eyebrows expectantly at Mick.

"We'll save that for another day. That's a couple of trips down a mountain he owes me." Mick grabbed Harry's better hand and grasped his good shoulder. "You're going to need a new hat," he said. "Dirk found the Dobbs and confiscated it for the extra cab fare."

Harry groaned, "Took me years to find that hat. Start with the documents. What have you done with them?"

Mick eased back, expansively, into the chair and put his feet up. "Safe and sound in the Kenil's wine cellar. Day before yesterday, I contacted the London SIS office, gave them the gist of it, a few details, not many. They wanted to send someone up straightaway, take statements, review the scene. Eve wasn't too keen on it, said the documents belonged to her, and you'd want to deliver the bag in its entirety and explain the contents. We compromised on an appearance and delivery two days from today. Figured you'd be up and about by then. They wouldn't wait any longer. Day after tomorrow, you're expected at the Broadway office, early afternoon. Appointment with the Deputy Chief."

"Deputy Chief?" said Harry. "Christ, what did you say to get me an appointment with the Deputy Chief?"

"Didn't have to say much. The Edinburgh branch had apparently contacted them about Wolff's death and Jasper's apprehension. I identified myself, said you'd come across specific information related to a ratline network scheme working among London, Madrid, Edinburgh, and Buenos Aires. I was immediately patched through to the deputy. After a brief conversation, he said he wanted to discuss it in person, and set the appointment. Seemed very interested in your involvement. Wondered where you'd got to."

"What about Jasper? You nabbed him? Where is he now?"

"We'll get to Jasper. Eve knows most of that story. She talked to the locals about both Jasper and Wolff. Where's that whiskey?

This may take awhile." Mick marched into the kitchen in search of Agnes and Kate.

"That evening and the day after," Eve, now weary, paused to look at Harry.

"Go on," he said.

She frowned, the headache starting in her temples. "When you took off across the cliffs, your cab driver, Dirk, worried about where you were going and what you were about to do. Alone. First, he followed your instructions, taking both my bag—the genuine one you had with you in the taxi—and the bogus one I carried to the cathedral, to the Kenilworth. He told Mick about the chase and what happened in the park. Together, they went to the High Street Constabulary to alert the police to pick up the Bentley. They and two constables reached the vehicle in time to see Thomas arriving at the car. As I understand, Thomas—wet, disheveled and raving about being a London barrister—was then taken into custody, the Bentley impounded.

"That evening, after our rescue and your admittance to the emergency, I spent hours at the High Street station," said Eve, "explaining the most immediate circumstance—Karl Wolff's death. After the rain, when a farmer and his son went to check their fields, they found the body."

"I suppose the police authorities will want a statement from me," said Harry.

"Yes, they said as much," said Eve. "As soon as you're able."

"Where is Jasper now?" asked Harry.

"Before I got there, he'd almost convinced the Chief Constable not to hold him, said he was a victim of Wolff's, too, that he was trying to get safely away, was indeed on his way to the police headquarters to report an abduction."

Eve shivered at the length of his deception. "Imagine him free. Most likely, he would have been in some exotic resort before the day was out."

The door eased open. Kate carried a cocktail tray, Mick with the decanter. Agnes distributed the empty glasses, and Mick poured a finger of amber liquid in each. They pulled chairs close to the bed and settled, glasses in hand.

"Where's mine?" asked Harry.

"Thought you needed your rest," said Mick.

"I'm rallying," said Harry. "I've still got one semi-good hand. Let me use it."

"Rally away," said Mick. He poured another portion, larger than the others, and handed it to Harry.

"Go on, Eve," said Harry. "What did you tell the Chief Constable to convince him to charge Jasper?"

"I told him Thomas Jasper was responsible for Gordon's death and, that very afternoon, he tried to kill me as well. I told him about Wolff—at Thomas's command—holding me and poised to fling me off the cliff. That seemed sufficient for the Chief—an eyewitness and living victim able to tell of such horrifying crimes. Then I provided details of my conversation with Thomas in the car about his involvement in Otis's presumed natural death."

Harry sat up straighter. "And what did Thomas tell you about Otis's death? Were you right to question it?"

Quiet, she sipped the whiskey, wondered if any of it mattered anymore; the memories of her terror still fresh. She would relive it many times over. At least until it faded sufficiently that she might begin to believe the memory belonged to someone else. Three men dead, Harry wounded and scarred—nearly dead, were it not for his courage and Mick's determination to make him live. "He confirmed the cause of Otis's death. As the doctor noted, it was indeed a form of poison used in military operations. I don't quite know how it was accomplished that particular day on the tennis court. Given the cremation, unless Thomas admits the process to the authorities—I seriously doubt that will ever happen—the facts, the method of administering the poison, will remain a mystery. Yet, it was surely murder. Who's to be held accountable for it, I can't say." She felt Otis's ghost beside her.

"And he gave you the reason for the murder?" said Harry.

"Abundantly clear. The timing coincided with Otis's planned attempt to blackmail someone—a number of someones—over that list of names and locations we found. According to Thomas, that list identifies the new names and locations of hundreds of Nazi fugitives as well as the man who facilitated all of it, Miguel Fonde. Otis and Will Gordon were going to sell the list for a great deal of money, millions of pounds. To save his reputation and assure continuation of this relocation network, Thomas needed to stop them—one way or another."

Harry shook his head. "So he ordered Gordon's death, too?"

"Mick knows the details about that," said Eve. She folded her hands around her glass, leaned back in the chair, and waited for Mick to explain.

"The coroner determined that Gordon was set adrift in the Firth. Same type of slash—skillful, clean—as that mean thing on your forehead. It's no wonder it took more than twenty stitches to close it." Mick paused, rubbed the rim of his cocktail glass. "Eve, a young constable, and I climbed up to the place where the fight took place. With Eve's help, we reconstructed the fight and located the spot where Wolff fell. Not far away, we found the knife. German officer's dagger, ten-inch steel blade, blood groove. Beautiful weapon, and clearly designed for killing."

"You're telling me this to make me feel better," said Harry.

"I'm telling you the man was a hired killer, a professional assassin," said Mick. "I'm telling you there's no need to dwell on your part in his death."

The room was silent. No one spoke. Kate shifted in her chair, squeezed Harry's better hand.

"Right," said Harry, rearranging the pillows. "The coroner matched the blade to Gordon?"

"Still running tests, but it looks pretty certain," said Mick.

"And the last loose end—that we know, anyway—Myrna Stewart. Where is she?"

"Gone, flown, nowhere," said Eve. "The police determined she checked out of the North British Hotel at about the time Thomas picked me up at the cathedral. I can only assume he and Karl were going to wrap up this one last bit—me. Afterwards, the three of them would motor back to London and resume their game. When they didn't appear on schedule, Myrna must have known enough to flee. I talked with the Chief Constable this morning. They're no closer to finding her. As far as the authorities know, she has not appeared at her London residence or Thomas's office. Apparently, she's from a little village in Yorkshire. Her parents are to be questioned today. I doubt anyone will find her. We know, of course, she has access to all manner of clandestine travel arrangements and false identity documents." Eve could not blame Myrna Stewart for fleeing the likes of Thomas Jasper.

Their glasses empty, Agnes directed everyone—including Harry—to the kitchen for supper. Sniffing the inviting aroma, the five of them filled their bowls and settled at the kitchen table, devouring the stew.

"Tell us about your stew," said Agnes. "I've not tasted anything like it."

"Not long ago, I spent endless nights cooking such dishes," said Eve, smiling finally at the memory. "This particular dish was quite popular, thoroughly enjoyed by tens of hungry guests. By the time they were through with it, the pot was clean as a whistle."

Chapter Twenty-Eight

23 May 1949. The early express train departed Waverly Station a few minutes after seven. While Harry settled the cab fare with Dirk and bid him goodbye, Eve busied herself buying the tickets, finding a porter, and locating a compartment. The morning was light and warm, with no hint of rain. She was dressed in a flowing black skirt, gray sweater over a pale-blue blouse, and low heels. The porter took charge of the bags, handing them through the carriage window. She lifted them up onto the shelf, hung her coat, drew off her gloves, and arranged the seat. From her vantage point next to the window, she noted the relatively empty platform, so unlike the bustle and raw anticipation of her arrival.

Was it a mere eleven days since she arrived from London and naively directed the cab driver to St. Mary's Cathedral? A mere eleven days since she delivered that ominous check to the Reverend Will Gordon and foolishly mentioned her suspicions about Otis's death? A mere eleven days since she unwittingly set in motion all that had happened after?

Twelve days ago, she inhabited a different life. A different existence. So distant she barely remembered it.

Had she not lived them, she could not have imagined the events. Surely, she did not want to live them again. It was never her intent to harm anyone. She simply wanted to discover the truth. For herself. For Otis. The fright alone had almost killed her. Not fright for herself, for her own life, although there was that—the terror that her life was about to end violently. Fright for others. For Harry. Knowing her decisions were clearly responsible for his desperate struggle, his near death.

Yet, there was this odd satisfaction. Regardless of the dangers, she had finally—for the first time in her life—accomplished something of substance. She had purposely set out to achieve an end and actually done it. Done it for someone other than herself. It was important that the tasks had not been easy. That they had been difficult and sometimes painful. That she was better for it in some unfathomable way. Not that the experience of terror had made her brave. She would not claim such distinction. Indeed, she recalled her paralysis, her fear.

No, she was not completely pleased with this new version of herself, the way she had handled any number of things. But she had not quit, not run away, not avoided the truth. Eve realized she was not completely whole, that she was somewhat broken inside and would remain so for a time. It seemed exactly right, somehow, what she had done. She could not have set it right any more than she had.

She now understood she would never see things the same way, that there had been an irreversible shift in her life. She wondered if it would fade, this newly found calmness of character. Would she, eventually, slip back into her old careless self? She could not have spoken clearly of those fears to anyone. Fears for the reemergence of traits she had come to disdain. Perhaps a day would come when she could feel more confident of her own strength of character, when she could think more clearly about what she had done.

Agnes had wanted her to stay. A voice in Eve's head told her she should. Wonderfully generous Agnes. Straightforward to the point of bluntness, yet kind and strong. A person of maturity, of faith and confidence. If Eve stayed with Agnes, she reasoned she would be more likely to maintain her current self, to remain the person she wanted to be. That more valuable, decent person. Agnes would see to it. Eve knew it was her struggle to make. Not Agnes's.

She watched Harry as he walked across the platform, climbed the steps, sat down on the bench across from her. He smiled wearily. She reached across and touched him lightly. He would sleep most of the trip. She would listen to him breathe.

The train rushed forward out of the station. A sense of relief spread through her. For a few minutes they sat very still, listening to the movement of the train, the landscape gliding past, and she had a sense of the two of them enclosed in a very small world. She put her coat around his shoulders and moved to sit beside him. He held her hand. They rode like this for a time, hips touching, hands joined, no words between them.

iiiii

At three in the afternoon, when the train pulled into Victoria Station and they stepped onto the platform, a frenzied mob of early commuters rushed forward, separating them. She stood in place, anxiously searching the platform, feared he was lost, and she would not find him. In the next instant, he appeared, and an overwhelming sense of relief fell upon her. Slowly, they made their way across the terminal, walked together to the outside where the taxi line arched outward from the station, drivers waiting. The sun shone bright blue as they emerged into the light.

They shuffled along, inching forward, making small talk, remarking on the change in the weather, the bustling traffic. When they reached the front of the line, she set her bag on the pavement and held out her hand to him, a deliberate gesture—final and resolute. "Goodbye, Harry." A helpless feeling overcame her, knotting her stomach. Something valuable was falling away, and she could not bring herself, at that moment, to retrieve it.

"What are you doing?" he asked. "You're coming to Broadway." It was not a question.

She was silent for a long moment. Finally, she said, "I leave you to your secrets. Leave me to mine."

Their eyes met and held.

He frowned. "They may want to know something, a piece of information you can provide. You need to be there. You may learn more of it, too," he said.

"I know enough. It's your work, your job to do." She removed her hand from his.

"Goodbye can be something of a relative term," he said, hope clear on his face.

A confident man with a truly expressive face, she thought, recalling her earlier assessment. Her first impression when he stepped into her private world. Her resolve seemed to fly away. She turned so he could not see her hesitation.

"It can be. A relative term, that is. It will have to be." A weak smile on her lips. She spoke, looking for words that would make it easier. She would not lie to him, not pretend. "I have things to sort through."

She did not want him there when she fell apart. When she gave way to her pain, hiding it no longer. When she picked through her memories, separating truth from fiction, choosing which pieces to keep, which to throw away. When she came to decide how much of her soul had died.

We love who we love, she thought. *How foolish we are with things so inexplicable.*

She lifted her bag. "Well then," she said.

"When you finish sorting . . ." He left the rest unspoken. He caught her elbow, looked ready to bring her to him, fold her in his arms.

She backed away from him then, before it could happen, each step taking him farther from her in space and in time. She heard the taxi door open, the driver inquire as to her destination.

"Holland Park," she said purposefully, sliding into the rear seat. "Near Abbotsbury Road."

From a distance, before she disappeared into the world, she saw him lift his hand and wave.

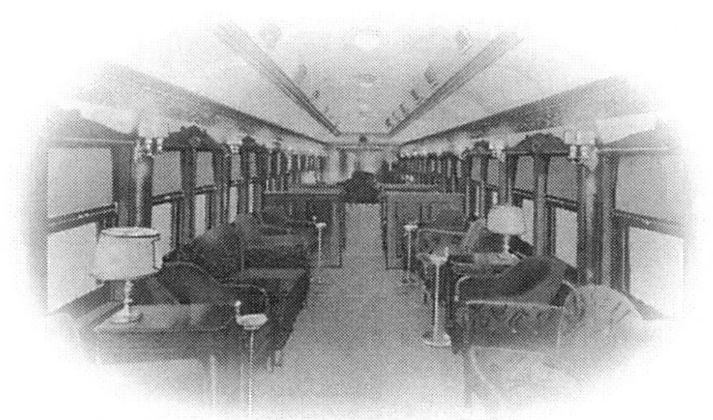

Chapter Twenty-Nine

November 1949, Monte Carlo. Alone in her room on the fourth floor of the Hotel de Paris, Eve stood at the French doors, admiring the adjacent Belle Époque building, softened by the glowing white lights. She paced, picked through the last bites on her dinner tray, chewed a thin cracker to settle her stomach, and glanced repeatedly at the clock tower above the casino. Though the clock read an hour past midnight, the Place teemed with scores of new arrivals. The brilliance of the streetlamps against the black sky, the quick movements of the uniformed valet corps, the extravagant display of vehicles and bejeweled guests at the base of the marble steps made one believe the night was just beginning instead of drawing to a close.

In the past hour, she had changed her gown twice, combed her hair from one side to the other and back again, exchanged the overstated drop earrings for the less conspicuous, though certainly noticeable, diamond studs. In the end, she stepped into the calf-length strapless gown of green silk, a thin sarsenet she had ordered from Tangier. She daubed a bit of perfume at the base of her neck, checked herself in the mirror—front, back, left profile, right profile, front again. The thick arm bracelet was necessary after all, over the elbow-length black gloves. She lingered over the style and color of her heels.

She must decide. Should she remain safely in this room or venture out, and take a chance she would meet him among the crowd? She had little notion of the timing for such things. In Edinburgh, she recalled his games commenced around nine and ended in the wee hours. Perhaps there were universal formalities. Perhaps they depended on which part of the world one played such games. Perhaps each table set a unique schedule for its players.

In truth, she did not know if he were here at all. She had simply taken a chance. More than three months ago, late one night, he called to tell her they had found and arrested Myrna Stewart. At least, that was the reason he gave. In a much too casual way, he said he was at Ramsgate terminal, waiting for the morning ferry to Ostend. From there, a couple of trains would carry him south to Monte Carlo. She told him she had never been to the extraordinarily glamorous Monte Carlo. At the time, she suspected he wanted her to come along. For her, at least, to say she would consider it. He seemed on the edge of asking. There was that tone in his voice, the words he never got around to saying. Now, she was unsure. She imagined he hardly remembered the call. Though she recalled every word. He had sounded a bit tipsy, a little unsure, had cut off the conversation before it had a chance to get started. Quite unlike the Harry she thought she knew. She had wondered, since then, if she misunderstood his meaning. If he merely intended to say goodbye. If he were off on a mission, never to return.

Since that night, they had not spoken nor, for that matter, had any contact. She found she minded his absence, his occasional call. Recently, she began to think of him every day, several times a day, in fact. Impulsively, she had taken a risk and flown to Monte Carlo. Until now, she had never thought to be anywhere near it, only read of it in travel magazines, seen it in movies—the legendary gambling casino and the famous basin, home to the most luxurious yachts in Europe.

She made her way down the stairs and across the lobby. The smooth tones of a tenor saxophone captivated her, and she stopped to listen. Earlier in the evening when she registered, she noticed the billboard advertisement at the reception desk—a stunning dark-skinned woman, the air of a sultry jazz singer in her pose. Eve stepped inside the lounge and found an empty seat at the bar. At the microphone, the exotically dressed woman, a feathered silver hat adorning her flat dark curls, crooned a French version of "Blue Skies." A medley of torch songs followed. Thoroughly enthralled, Eve waited until the woman ended her set with "You Are the Only One for Me."

The music calmed her nerves as well as her stomach. She ordered a gin and tonic. When the bartender arrived, she said, "When I heard the solo saxophone, I thought Charlie Parker was in town. The singer is marvelous. Who is she?"

"Every person in Europe knows Miss Josephine Baker," he said. "When she needs a break from the Folies in Paris, she comes here, relaxes, and entertains our small crowds." With an artisan's flourish, he set Eve's drink on the white linen napkin. "By the way, Mr. Parker stayed here at the hotel a couple of weeks ago. The boss talked him into doing a set for us. Ever hear him play?"

Eve took a small sip of her drink and smiled. "Oh, yes, the man can play a saxophone, any saxophone. Years ago, in his early days, I heard him more than once. He was in Chicago and Kansas City. There's a great jazz scene in those cities. And your Miss Baker, she's a beautiful woman."

"Miss Baker's more than beautiful. A national hero in France, immensely popular. During the war, she helped with the cause, entertained the French troops. The Belgians, too, I'm told. For the Resistance, she carried coded messages on her sheet music, in the folds of her costumes. A spy for France," he said proudly. "She helped relocate Belgian and French Jews and saved hundreds. She owns an estate in Castelnaud, not far from here."

So, Josephine Baker, this gorgeous and talented woman, was a spy. Involved in a relocation pipeline. Considered a heroic figure. For the first time, Eve wondered how many lives Otis had saved. She considered how differently he would be perceived, how different his cause.

She finished her drink, walked out into the night, refreshed by a burst of cool air that blew off the Mediterranean. A sliver of moon hung in the sky, its slender line of reflection moving in off the sea. She wrapped her cloak around her and walked the few steps across the Place to the casino. According to a sign posted at the entry, it was almost closing time.

She climbed the steps and stood for a moment, mildly astonished at the vastness of the lobby, the kaleidoscope dome overhead, the polished floor of pink granite, the towering bronze statue of the dashing medieval knight atop his horse. Inside the gaming room, glittering chandeliers hung above gilt-framed paintings and ornately carved wooden columns, an intricate pattern of carpet thick beneath her feet. The rich caramel of burled maple gave the room a somber elegance. A continuous line of sculpted relief, nude women in various poses, stared down at her.

Exiting patrons gathered at the cassier window, retrieved their evening capes as she checked her own, and queued at the exchange desk to cash their plaques. Deliberately, she made her way through the gaming room, stood alongside the kidney-shaped baccarat tables crowded with men in jet-black tuxedos milling behind the seated players. She heard the quiet murmurs of blackjack wagers, and stopped to watch the perfectly sculpted wooden ball spin along the tilted track of a roulette table. In a vacant seat next to the croupier, she sat down and placed in front of her a stack of tokens she had acquired from the exchange window. Unlike baccarat or blackjack, roulette was a game she could pretend to play without much concentration, and still keep an eye on the doors that led to the poker rooms. For half an hour, she played the colors, red or black, then switched to numbers—Annie's birthday, Annie's age. Incredibly, Eve won, or came close, on every spin of the wheel. Her stack of plaques increased threefold. Giddy with her run of good luck, she neglected her primary mission, carelessly missing the opening and closing of the doorway to her left.

From half a room away, she saw him—white dinner jacket, black tie askew, one hand in his pocket. A lovely shiver stole through her, a feeling almost forgotten. She remained seated, but followed him with her eyes as he moved toward the exit. He stopped to talk to an older man in a tuxedo that looked a size too small, a year too old. Harry shook the man's hand, nodded a greeting. Simultaneously, they scanned the room as if searching for a companion. From an arched door, two men—one plump and balding, another tall with a slight limp to his gait—joined them. For a few minutes, they talked. Harry scanned the room once more, and gestured toward the exit.

Eve dipped her head so he would not see her, suddenly hesitant, unsure why she had come. She stood, her back to him, and gathered her winnings. She tipped the croupier too much, and he smiled. She bent to scoop her purse from the empty chair she had occupied. It was then she sensed a presence behind her, felt a hand on the small of her back.

"May I?" A familiar voice.

She pretended not to hear, smothered a smile, turned to face him. "If you must," she answered.

"Are you waiting for someone?" he asked, leading her away from the table.

"You might say that," she said. "How did you find me?"

"Who could miss these silk shoes?" he asked, admiring her, his eyes full of amusement.

A sudden warmth stole over her, lighting her face. "I've missed you, Harry," the familiar smell of him filling the room.

He kissed her on the cheek, inhaled her perfume, drew her closer.

She tucked her gloved hand under his arm. Together, they walked under the glittering chandeliers, out of the casino, down the steps.

"I might be very good at spying." Eve looked at him sideways.

"A modern Mata Hari," said Harry.

"Much less public," said Eve.

"I suspect the service frowns on twelve different last names," said Harry.

"Not quite twelve," she corrected him. She laughed, a delighted laughter. "How many?"

"How many what?"

"How many last names are allowed? To be considered for spying?"

"There are no proper rules. Individual case basis, I'd wager. By the way, who is this Kicklighter chap?"

"Herbie was—still is as far as I know—a saxophone player. Tenor sax. Sweet man. Great fingers." She raised her eyebrows, a look of suggestion.

"And Pierce. You never explained that one," said Harry.

"Must I?" she asked, taking his hand in hers.

"I'll see what I can do," he said, raising her hand to his lips, slowly removing her glove, kissing the tips of her fingers.

"About what?"

"About spying, of course."

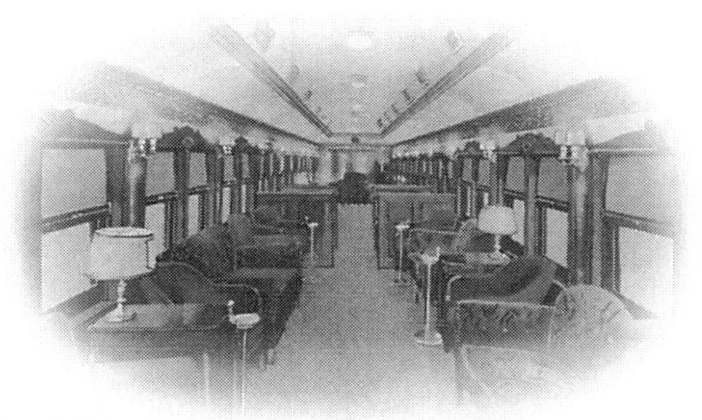

Historical Notes and Further Reading

In late 1944, when the Germans were convinced the war was lost and drawing to a close, high-ranking members of the Nazi party and collaborators in the occupied countries laid plans to ensure escape from prosecution for their war crimes. Using fascist dictators in Spain and Argentina and scores of sympathizers in Western Europe, networks were set in motion to assist thousands who were fleeing the victorious Allies. These shadowy networks operated from the closing months of the war until the mid-1950s. The escape routes they used became widely known as "ratlines."

In researching background for this novel, the author reviewed books and articles on the topic of Nazi relocation. Some of the most useful resources included:

Goñi, Uki. *The Real Odessa*. London: Granta Publications, 2002.

Perisco, Joseph E. *Nuremberg, Infamy on Trial*. New York: Penguin Books, 1994.

Steinacher, Gerald. *Nazis on the Run, How Hitler's Henchmen Fled Justice*. New York: Oxford University Press, 2011.

Walters, Guy. *Hunting Evil*. New York: Broadway Books, 2009.

Zuroff, Efraim. *Operation Last Chance*. New York: Palgrave MacMillan, 2009.

Acknowledgments

In mid-January 2011, I found myself at my first real writing institute, seated among both accomplished and aspiring authors and poets, and learning under the expert guidance of the incomparable Ann Hood. I came away from those eight rigorous days with precious tools and skills, appreciation for good writing and fine writers, and the firm assessment that my own ability to "create stories" needed plenty of improvement. The original beginning pages for this novel, raw and underdeveloped, took a beating. Rightfully so. This annual program, known as Writers in Paradise, co-founded in 2005 by Dennis Lehane and Sterling Watson and housed at Eckerd College in St. Petersburg, has been an essential ingredient in my development as a storyteller. Over the years, I have been fortunate to study with extraordinary faculty (including Les Standiford, Andre Dubus III, and my small-group instructors Laura Lippman, Stewart O'Nan, Debra Dean, Michael Koryta, Sterling Watson, John Searles, and Ann Hood) and to learn side-by-side with writers across America—many of whom are now long-distance friends.

The successful novelist rarely exists without early readers and critics. I am grateful to those—generous with time and expertise—who endured early iterations of the manuscript, including Nancy A. Teets, Barbara Scarpa, Judy Blake, Justus and Carol Doenecke, Marilyn Wittner, Betty Tribble, Grace Albritton, and Arleen Mariotti. Their comments and support generated countless and valuable improvements.

This life would not be possible but for the historical expertise and editorial and emotional support of my husband, USF Professor Emeritus of History, John Belohlavek. My love for him is immeasurable. Luckily for both of us, he stocks really good bourbon.

Finally, in this twenty-first century, some eighty years after the Holocaust, in an age of numbing national and international tragedy and chaos, we must assure that historical memory survives. I give thanks to intrepid journalists, photographers, and historians who recognize and report the evil that men do.

About the Author

Writer and illustrator Susan C. Turner's recent work concentrates in the crime/mystery arena. She prefers to set her narratives in the pre- and postwar periods of the 1930s and 1940s. *The Truth About Otis Battersby* is first in a series featuring characters Harry Douglas and Mick MacLeod. Upcoming titles in this collection include *Mission Budapest* and *Assignment in Oran*.

Born in New York, she has lived in Miami and London, and now resides in Tampa with her husband John, and precocious animal, Duffy.

Made in the USA
Las Vegas, NV
03 November 2022

58681350R00164